Praise for Tim Hemlin and his Neil Marshall novels

"Neil Marshall may be the most charming amateur sleuth in the South. His humor, sensitivity, and dumbass courage are disarming."
— MARTHA C. LAWRENCE
Author of *Murder in Scorpio* and
The Cold Heart of Capricorn

"All the ingredients—and the neat presentation—of a perfect meal."
— *Publishers Weekly*

"Hemlin has worked as a chef and knows his way around a recipe."
— *The Purloined Letter*

"A thoroughbred among mystery authors."
— DEBORAH ADAMS

By Tim Hemlin
Published by Ballantine Books:

IF WISHES WERE HORSES . . .
A WHISPER OF RAGE
PEOPLE IN GLASS HOUSES
A CATERED CHRISTMAS
DEAD MAN'S BROTH

DEAD MAN'S BROTH

Tim Hemlin

BALLANTINE BOOKS • NEW YORK

A Ballantine Book
Published by The Ballantine Publishing Group
Copyright © 1999 by Tim Hemlin

www.randomhouse.com/BB/

Library of Congress Catalog Card Number: 99-90122

ISBN 0-345-42002-0

Manufactured in the United States of America

First Edition: November 1999

10   9   8   7   6   5   4   3   2   1

To Mom and Dad,

Who need a lift
    And are always there to give one—

Thanks

ACKNOWLEDGMENTS

A special thanks to Malinda Lo, who, before her departure for academia, thoughtfully edited this manuscript. I will miss her insightful touch. As usual, kudos to Joe Blades, master editor, publisher, and gracious host. The same gratitude goes to Kimberley Cameron, my agent, for her enthusiastic support and good taste in food. Much appreciation to Lieutenant Ron Echols of the Missouri City police department for answering my questions concerning crime scenes and blood contamination. Finally, to Valerie for reading the initial—and subsequent, and final—drafts of the novel and offering her ever valuable critiques.

A good meal ought to begin with hunger.

—French Proverb

One cannot think well, love well, sleep well, if one has not dined well.

—VIRGINIA WOOLF

1

For a man who only wanted a beer and some down-time, I was getting hit on two fronts. To my left was War-ren Clay, a very talented chef but a socially inept man, clumsily attempting to woo us into business with him. On my right was my buddy and coworker, Robbie Persons, who, while totally ignoring Clay, couldn't get his mind off of Perry Stevens Catering's Fifth Annual Crawfish Boil—a tongue-twisting title that further numbed my mind. The fact that Robbie wouldn't leave the day's business back at The Kitchen was bad enough. To have Clay droning in my ear was giving me a headache. The only way the evening could get worse was if I ended up in a damn bar fight.

"You're a good enough chef," Clay proclaimed, push-ing his horn-rim glasses up his nose, "but Robbie's a great waiter and bartender, you know? We could make quite a team, like the Three Musketeers."

I groaned, turned to Robbie. "Do you hear what he's saying?" Bjork's song "Hunter" shot a bolt of energy into the early-evening atmosphere. I liked the Icelandic singer, though as the bar filled, the loud music made talking three in a row difficult. I guessed, however, Robbie caught more of the conversation than he was letting on.

"Trying not to," he said, confirming my suspicions. "I'm thinking about two hundred pounds of crawfish.

You sure that's enough?" He lifted a glass of chardonnay to his lips.

I thumped my Heineken bottle onto the bar, drawing a scowl from the bartender. Ignoring his irritation, I signaled for another round.

"Do we really have to go through this again?" I said to Robbie, and dug a fingernail into the green label.

"So what do y'all say? We a team?" Clay asked, regaining my attention.

"Just a minute," I replied. "We're conferencing." I huddled close to Robbie. "This is your fault," I told him. "If we'd gone to the Ale House instead of Sue-Ellen's I'd be savoring a Newcastle Brown Ale from the tap. I'd also have avoided—" I stopped, rolled my eyes in Clay's direction.

"Well, he sat next to you, not me." He grinned.

"But I'm only *good enough*," I whispered harshly. "He thinks you're the cherry on the whipped cream of life."

"And you call yourself a poet."

"My round, partners, wouldn't you say?" Clay announced loudly, responding to the bartender's arrival with another set of drinks.

"About time," Robbie muttered.

I glanced about. We were surrounded by neon, chrome, and mirrors, all impeccably clean. While Clay dug the money out of his snug blue jeans and conversed with the bartender, I stretched and told Robbie, "Trade places with me."

"No!"

"Why?"

"Because then he'll think I'm interested in him," Robbie replied firmly.

"Well, I'm not interested in him or—"

"I know," Robbie affirmed, "and I'm sorry. When Warren Clay called me and said something about working together, I thought he meant a joint venture between Perry

Stevens Catering and his place. Maybe even a television spot. I had no idea he had such grand visions."

Television? I wondered, but I cut to the chase. "Then help me. You know him. I don't."

The music changed to Bjork's "Bachelorette." Cool. In a different situation I might've even begun to relax.

"So what do you say, guys?" Clay prodded again, pulling himself together. Our new drinks were placed in front of us, and Clay took his gin and tonic and leaned in close. I was not a touchy-feely guy, and his drifting into my space made me extremely uncomfortable.

"Say about what?" Robbie asked.

"A partnership," Clay responded, raising his glass. "My talent and brains, y'alls talent—"

"Who has the start-up money?" Robbie inquired. "Neil and I don't."

"Well—"

"Excellent point," I jumped in, taking Robbie's lead. "Unless there's serious money behind us, there's no way we could get this operation off the ground."

"There has to be a backer," Robbie concluded. He tilted his glass in a toast and drank his wine. "Neil and I can't afford to work for free," he added.

"No, we can't," I agreed.

Clay straightened, much to my delight, and chugged on his drink. "You two wouldn't go with me even if I had money," he suddenly declared.

"That's not necessarily true," I found myself saying, not wanting to bring the man's dream down.

"It's a moot point without financing," Robbie contributed.

"Money!" Clay exclaimed, jumping up. "It's always fucking money!" He slammed his glass on the counter. Broken glass, ice, and gin shaved the air. Automatically, I stood. This strange burst of anger ran deeper than our conversation.

As quickly as the anger flared, though, Clay regained his composure and returned to his seat.

"Sorry," he apologized.

It's not okay, I thought. I wouldn't go into business with you in a million years.

But Robbie spoke. "We like working for Perry," he explained. "And there are a lot of good people out there who want to go into business for themselves. Some even have money."

The bartender eyed us angrily, but I put up a hand. "Accident," I told him. "I'll cover any charge."

Clay looked from Robbie to me and back, then glanced at the blood running down his hand. He grabbed a napkin, pressed it against his palm, then, without another word, left.

I sat down again.

"He's frustrated," Robbie informed me.

"That's an understatement." I brushed shards of glass into a small pile with a bar napkin while the bartender used a towel to sop up the gin.

"Do you know who he works for?"

"No." I tossed the napkin down.

"Sherwood Welles."

"The television chef?" I asked, and took a healthy swig of beer.

"The one and only."

"Now I understand what you meant about a TV spot. You hoped we'd get on Welles's show."

"Worth a shot," Robbie said meekly.

"Wouldn't Welles have called Perry himself if that was the case?"

"I thought we might get in through the back door with

Clay's help," he replied, and drank his wine. "I had no idea he was planning a rebellion."

"Why would he rebel?" I asked. "You think Welles is pushing him out?"

"Seems likely," Robbie agreed. "Clay's a great chef, but a bucket of dirt has more personality. Maybe Welles wants a snappier assistant."

"A Vanna White to spin the hors d'oeuvres and showcase the desserts?" I shrugged.

"You have such a way of putting things in perspective, but it's obvious you don't watch *All's Welles in the Kitchen*."

"Must have something to do with the title," I said. "There's consonance, and then there's verbal assassination of the language."

"He's got a Vanna," Robbie told me. "Even I think she's a beauty. You'd like the show. Trouble is, after watching for five minutes you realize she knows nothing about the culinary arts."

"So Welles is caught between a talented nerd and an incompetent showpiece," I commented.

"Oh, I sympathize with the man. I know how it feels."

Fortunately, before this conversation went any further or I flashed the one-finger salute, a friend of Robbie's whose name escaped me approached us. Because his hair was a mass of brown curls and his physique small and elvish, he reminded me of fitness guru Richard Simmons. And neither his flamboyant gestures nor dramatic expressions helped to dispel that image.

"Tommy, you remember Neil Marshall," Robbie said, pointing to me.

"Of course I do," he said. "So good to see you again."

"And you," I replied, glad Robbie had mentioned his name.

Tommy huddled in close to us, a hand on each of our backs. "Did you see those protesters outside?" he asked.

"No," I responded, a little surprised at the information.

"There wasn't anyone out there when we came in," Robbie added.

Tommy sighed. "Well, I guess even zealots can't wreak havoc until they finish their day jobs."

"How many of them are there?" I asked.

"Maybe a dozen, with signs calling us godless and bound for hell."

I shook my head and stood. "I may be hell-bound," I stated, and tossed a couple of dollars down for a tip, "but I'm not godless and I won't go on an empty stomach."

Tommy chuckled and slapped at my shoulder. "They aren't targeting all-American boys like you, and you know it. They want us unnatural vermin."

"You two can laugh, but I find them disturbing," Robbie said seriously.

"Don't you mean disturbed?" Tommy shot back.

"I'm going to grab a bite to eat," I said. "Either of you want to come with me?"

"I'll join you." Robbie also rose.

Tommy glanced at his wristwatch. "Charles should've been here by now. That fastidious little queen's never late."

"Does that mean you want us to wait until Charles arrives so you two can join us?" I asked.

"Sure you want to be seen—"

"I'll take my chances," I cut Tommy off.

"Charles really should be here any minute," Tommy told us. "And I'm game if he is. Let's go outside and catch him before he comes in. Then you can get a good look at the spectacle."

We walked the length of the bar, around the dance floor, and through the growing throngs of people.

"What are you in the mood to eat?" Robbie called.

"Anything but Cajun," I answered, not wanting to dwell anymore on crawfish or anything remotely related. Robbie caught my drift.

"Vietnamese?" Tommy suggested, though appeared confused at Robbie's laughter.

"Sounds good," I replied, and we pushed through the doors and into the spring evening. The air was warm but not saturated with the humidity that would claim Houston in a month or so. The sun was low and thick, its long rays the color of butter.

And then we saw the crowd on the outskirts of the parking lot, with their signs ordering repentance: GODLESS SINNERS, FREAKS, GAY USED TO MEAN HAPPY. Some people were flashing biblical quotes or making derogatory statements.

"This sickens me," I said, more to myself than anyone else.

"Ignore them," advised Robbie, then asked Tommy, "You see Charles?"

A roaring suddenly rose from the protesters. I scanned the area but at first couldn't see what caused the outburst. Then I noticed that a few of the picketers had turned their backs to the bar, and the group was slowly forming a semicircle.

"This doesn't look good, y'all," I muttered.

The shouting was growing louder.

"No, it doesn't," Robbie agreed.

"Should we?" I asked, but when I turned my attention to Robbie, he was already walking in their direction.

I followed. When his pace picked up, so did mine. By the time we hit the perimeter of the crowd we were both in a full run.

I reacted instinctively once I saw the cause of all the commotion.

Behind the zealots were four men dressed in black leather, their heads shaved to the skin. Red swastika patches were sewn to their shoulders and an animal fierceness pierced their eyes and turned their mouths into scowls. Between them a slender man was being tossed about, punched in the head, face, stomach, back—anywhere one of the crazed attackers could land a fist. By the time I pushed through the crowd and reached them, the victim was face-down, enduring vicious kicks.

Even though I was much larger than any of the four, I felt like a bull running into a pack of wild dogs as I dipped my head and drove into the two with their backs to me, knocking them off their victim and to the ground. Quickly I pushed off them and chased after a third skinhead. When he saw me coming, he backed up and raised his hands to defend himself. I took a blow on the side of my head as I grabbed his jacket, drove him back into the group of zealots, and threw him to the ground. To my dismay, my glasses flew off somewhere in the process. Robbie had tossed the fourth off and was kneeling to check the injured man. By now the first two had pulled themselves up. The shouts from the crowd faded. The skinheads and I stood, locked in a staring contest. I had no problem seeing up close. And up close the hate that emanated from their eyes was unnerving.

"It's Charles," Robbie told me, looking up from where he knelt by the victim. "He needs an ambulance."

"No goddamn queer's going to push me around," one of the skinheads finally said, pointing a finger at me. He had dark eyebrows, pockmarked skin, and blue, blue eyes.

I saw no reason to contradict his statement; he wouldn't believe me or care, anyway. "You come any closer and I won't just shove you this time," I replied, voice calm and low. My hair had come out of its ponytail and was blowing wild in the evening breeze. With a full beard that didn't quite hide the scar on my face, I knew I could appear a formidable opponent. The "Viking look" my friend, Associate Professor Keely Cohen, called it. Sometimes the image came in handy.

I felt the skinhead I'd driven into the picketers come up behind me. Robbie was watching him closely.

Then we heard the sirens. A cavalry call couldn't have been more welcome. The skinheads glanced at each other nervously.

With surprising agility, the one who'd threatened me took a couple of skip-steps in my direction. I dipped my left shoulder and raised my fists. Robbie rose to cover my back.

But the man behind me quickly picked something off the ground and then ran back to his comrades. At the last second the first skinhead backed off.

An eerie hush had descended on the crowd. The skinhead again pointed at me, but in a slow, almost ceremonial manner, as if he were casting a spell.

"I am going to kill you," he promised.

A chill the likes of which I'd never felt before ran over me. However, I managed to respond, "You'll rot in jail, first."

"I will see you dead," he repeated. Then, as the sirens grew louder, the skinheads broke into a run like the pack of dogs that they were.

The protesters, too, were beginning to disperse.

"Don't y'all go anywhere," I shouted. "Leaving the scene of a crime is against the law. You're as guilty as this man's attackers—"

"We never touched him, mister," came a call from the group.

"Never tried to help, either," I responded angrily. "In fact, you encouraged it."

"He got what was coming to him," someone called.

"God's wrath," cried another.

"Vengeance upon evil."

"Y'all are as crazy as those neo-Nazis," I yelled.

The sirens drowned us all out and suddenly the group realized it was too late for them to leave. Police cars screeched to a stop, cutting off their escape route.

"A bunch of skinheads ran off toward the west," I hollered to one of the cars that then sped off in that general direction.

Tommy came running up. "Oh, my God," he cried, and knelt down by Charles. "Oh, God, oh, God. I ran inside to call the police," he explained. "I thought you and Neil were going to get killed. Look at him, oh, God, look at him." Tears streamed down his face and his hands shook uncontrollably as he tried to gently comfort the unconscious man.

Paramedics rushed over. Robbie helped Tommy up. I heard the leader of the protesters—a stocky, balding, older man who looked vaguely familiar—tell the cops they had nothing to do with this.

My breathing slowed, as did my racing heart. I located my glasses—amazingly intact—then stepped beside Robbie and awaited questioning from the police. My friend looked at me.

"I don't know if you're a hero or fool," he said.

"I think in order to be a hero you have to have a touch of fool in you," I replied, and tried to smile.

"You know the skinhead who was behind you?" he asked. Tommy was sobbing into Robbie's side.

"What about him?"

"I saw what he picked up." Robbie paused.

I caught the worried look in his eyes.

"It was your wallet," Robbie said.

My hand sprang to my back pocket.

Empty.

I am going to kill you, the skinhead promised.

Damn, I thought.

2

The following morning I rose early and went for a long run. To say I was skittish was an understatement. Still, I refused to be a prisoner to a crazy threat. I'd reported the loss of my wallet to the police when I'd given my statement, thinking all the time about the ordeal of replacing my driver's license, Social Security card, and such. The officer had looked at me warily and advised me to watch my back. This skinhead group had been causing a lot of trouble, but now that there were witnesses to testify against them, the police figured to push hard to round them up. Would Robbie and I be able to identify them? Absolutely, we'd replied. Able and willing.

As I wound down my jog, tasting more humidity in the air today than yesterday, I noticed a familiar red Mustang parked in the driveway next to my landlord's house. And sitting on the back porch, across from the over-the-garage apartment I rented, was private investigator C. J. McDaniels. He was petting Samson, my landlord's Doberman.

"What are you doing here?" I puffed.

"Saw you on the news last night," he said. "Don't know how to keep your nose clean, do you, boy?"

"Couldn't stand around and do nothing." I pulled off my Willie Nelson bandanna and wiped my forehead and face.

"No, don't suppose you could." The large investigator rose slowly, giving Samson a final pat. "Dog's healed nicely," C.J. added.

"Yeah, he has." A few months earlier a couple of thugs had broken into my landlord's—Jerry Jacoma's—house and in the process of tearing the inside apart had knifed Samson, leaving him out on the porch. Fortunately I'd come home in time to tend to the dog before he'd bled to death.

"You picked a badass group to mess with," C.J. told me. He popped a small piece of gum in his mouth and began chewing furiously.

I locked my hands behind my head and breathed deeply and steadily. "I had no intention of picking anyone to mess with."

"You never do."

A passel of birds dominated the lush green area, creating a cacophony of chirps and calls. I looked at the old detective. The warm spring sun glistened off his balding head. His powerful arms, thick chest, and big belly were apparent even beneath the white dress shirt and blue sport jacket he wore. "You get dressed up, drive to the Heights, just to pass on that warning?" I asked.

"Business brought me out here," he explained, "but I reckoned since I was in the neighborhood I'd pay a courtesy call."

He was worried, I thought, which worried me. Normally C.J. would simply bellow into the phone, whether he was in the neighborhood or not, cajole me some, then let it go.

"Had to meet a client for breakfast at the Triple A," he added.

"You wore a jacket to the Triple A?" The Triple A Café was an old-fashioned Texas diner that was fast, inexpensive, and served good home-style food, and a sport jacket was as incongruous in there as a cotton tablecloth.

"Don't be such a college-boy snob," he chided me. "I wore it for the client who wanted to meet outside of his loop. Actually, he offered me damn good money to do this job."

"Okay, where's this conversation going?"

He chomped on his gum loudly. "I didn't accept it."

"Now I'm supposed to ask why." Again I wiped my face and forehead with the bandanna.

"Seems he wanted me to investigate Perry Stevens Catering."

"What?" The shock in my voice was evident.

"Very unhappy man. Downright nasty at times. Apparently your boss, who was referred to in a number of derogatory ways—most of them, mind you, involving his sexual orientation—is trying to steal his chef away."

My mouth opened wide enough for a bird to nest in, but only one word slid out. "Who?"

"Sherwood Welles."

I tugged at my ear. "Sherwood Welles?" I shook my head and began to laugh. Boy, Welles had that story screwed up, I thought.

C.J. walked over to his Mustang, leaned against the hood, and crossed his arms. "Welles fears his chef—a fella by the name of Warren Clay—will supply you with his 'treasure of recipes.' "

" 'Treasure of recipes'?"

"His words."

"Welles's food isn't fit to feed Samson," I retorted. "I don't care if he does have his own television show. What are you smirking at?"

"I hear this isn't the first time Perry Stevens stole an employee from him."

"Stole," I muttered, and began pacing. The situation was absurdly funny and yet enraging at the same time. "Booker Atwell worked a couple of functions for him before coming to us," I explained. "All Booker said when we hired him for his first job was that Welles was a difficult boss. Booker's too professional to spread dirt, and I didn't care, so we left it at that." I stopped. "What were you supposed to investigate?"

"Welles isn't too professional to spread dirt. In fact, he wanted me to dig some up," C.J. stated. "Tax problems, food violations, liquor license, anything to hamper your business."

"You're kidding."

"Nope."

"I don't believe this." Rage was winning over humor.

C.J. spat his gum out. "Somehow Welles knew we were friends, and he even went so far as to suggest I use our friendship to try to get information. Also, he pointed out that his chef jumping ship to Perry Stevens Catering would only spell trouble for you. As a good friend, I should be concerned you might lose your position to Clay. I countered that my friendship with you would surely suffer if I took up his offer, not to mention that it might adversely affect your employment status. So the son of a bitch tried to buy me. He thought 'my type'—his words again—would do anything for money. Pissed me off. Welles couldn't believe it when I turned over a glass of ice water in his lap and walked out."

"Why so understated?"

"I've mellowed in my old age." He unwrapped another piece of gum and popped it in his mouth.

I took a deep breath. Unbelievable. Wait until Perry heard about this. "Truth of the matter is," I told C.J., "Warren Clay, Welles's chef, approached Robbie and me about going into business with him."

"Well, he knows y'all met, so I guess he jumped to conclusions."

"Strange. And I thought Clay was being forced out."

"Don't believe so," C.J. said with a grin. "Welles was mighty hot under the collar."

"Then the man's going to explode when he discovers that Clay is breaking away on his own, not joining forces with us."

"I always heard there was a lot of pettiness and jealousies among chefs," the big investigator said, snapping his gum.

"And huge egos," I added.

I stared at C.J. There was something different about him today. Something other than the sport jacket. Then it hit me.

"You're not smoking," I observed.

"No, I'm enjoying this lovely Nicorette gum, instead."

"Linda finally wore you down." Linda was his daughter and partner in the detective business. "Just don't go through the Nicorette like it's a pack of Wrigley's. You'll give yourself nicotine poisoning."

"I start to hiccup when I've chewed too much," he barked. "But I don't want to discuss the issue, or I'll go back to Sherwood Welles and take the job."

I put my hands up, palms out. "Sorry. I don't want to discuss the issue either." But I sure sympathized, having quit smoking not so long ago myself.

"And you need a haircut," he jabbed.

"Yes, Daddy."

"Don't be a smart-ass."

"Don't get parental," I shot back.

"I'm not parental. Your hair's too long."

I laughed. C.J. was constantly riding me about the length of my hair. I'd been toying with the idea of cutting it before summer, anyway. But C.J. didn't need to know that as a plan came to mind.

"I'll strike a deal with you," I offered. "When I'm convinced you've quit smoking, I'll chop off my hair."

"I'm chewing the damn gum," he declared.

I leaned close. "I know for a fact the gum doesn't smell like smoke. And you smell like smoke."

C.J. stood straight. "I've only had one cigarette today. Maybe two."

"Fine. When you're off the cancer sticks altogether, I'll get the locks cut."

"As short as I say?"

I knew I was setting myself up, but I also knew that quitting after over thirty years of chain-smoking was a task requiring a herculean effort. A strong incentive might help.

"Deal," I assented.

A thin smile touched his lips. A twinkle glittered in his eyes. "I best be leaving," he said, and walked around to the driver's side of his car.

"Thanks for the info."

"Welles is foaming at the mouth. He'll probably try to stir up some kind of shit. Nothing I expect you can't handle." He paused and the grin vanished. "But you pay heed to what I said about the skinheads."

"Oh, I will—I have to. They've got my wallet."

C.J. hesitated at the car door. "What'd you say?"

"I lost my wallet in last night's scuffle. One of them picked it up before they took off. Had my driver's license, a few business cards, not much money, though it did have the addresses of where I live and work."

"You might want to stay someplace else until the police pick those boys up."

"I might."

C.J. squinted, started to say something, then stopped. "I should know better by now than to waste my breath trying to convince you to do anything. I'll be going. You know how to reach me."

"Much obliged, *compadre*."

He laughed, opened the Mustang's door. "Go cook something or write some poetry. *Compadre,*" he added with a mutter.

"You coming to the crawfish boil?" I called.

"Wouldn't miss it for the world."

"I'll be in touch."

C.J. fired the Mustang loud, quickly backed down the driveway, then sped away.

"Sherwood Welles," I said aloud, amazed at the misinformation. "What a trip."

Yeah, I thought, but when I told Perry, it was going to send him into orbit. Zip, bam, boom, as Jackie Gleason had said, right to the moon.

3

When I reached The Kitchen I didn't even notice the old man next door fertilizing his yard until he called out to me.

"He done parked it under my tree again." His voice was strong.

"Pardon?"

The old man drew off his John Deere cap and wiped his forehead with the back of his hand. "The little chubby guy parked his fancy car under my tree again."

I glanced to the street. Perry, who was mortified when he first heard the man's description of him, often parked his Lexus in front of the neighbor's house, beneath the shade of one of the huge pecan trees. My boss claimed it was to keep the car out of the sun and cool. Partly, I'd agree. To a large degree, however, it was payback for being referred to as "the little chubby guy."

"I'll mention it," I assured the old man.

"You tell him when he parks there it makes it hard for me to mow down by the curb. I don't want to be accused of scratching up his vehicle, but I sure ain't going to let my grass grow high as cornstalks, either."

"Yes, sir," I said, and dashed up the driveway.

Right in time to meet Conrad, our dishwasher, as he burst out the front door. Were I a smaller man, I believe the ex-con would've muscled through me. Instead he stopped short, muttered, "I'm not a dog," brushed his stringy black

19

hair from his face, and stared at me with those dark, brooding eyes. He was in bad need of a shave. Not that I had anything against facial hair, but Conrad would better serve himself if he just let it grow out instead of walking around with a perpetual five o'clock shadow all the time.

"Never said you were," I responded, offering the olive branch. Conrad and I usually avoided each other, an understanding we'd come to since Mattie Johnson's trouble. During the time Mattie was suspected of murdering her ex-boyfriend, Conrad had undermined my help by trading a private investigator some information for a carton of cigarettes. I was quick to anger, but slow to forgive.

"This is your doing," he accused me with a snarl.

"What are you talking about?"

"Think you're so fucking smart—"

"Conrad, calm down."

"I clean y'all's messes and get treated like shit." He spat on the potted begonias that guarded the entrance to the converted ranch house we called our second home.

"Back off, buddy. I've got enough to deal with." I stood straight. He was in no frame of mind to be reasoned with.

"You got to deal with a wife and an ex-wife and child support when you ain't making enough money?" he challenged. I fell silent. Conrad turned abruptly and walked past the van, down the wide driveway, and into the street.

Poor guy will be back, I thought. Ex-cons don't have a lot of choices. I didn't care much for the man, but, piecing the bits of the conversation together, I was beginning to understand his frustration. I pushed through the door and saw Robbie.

"And Conrad's problem is?" I asked.

Robbie's gray eyes showed sympathy. "Perry wouldn't give him a raise or allow him on job sites until he tidied himself up," he explained.

A small hike in salary would probably help, I thought,

but being barred from individual parties hurt. Any function we worked earned a good deal of money over our base pay. In Robbie's and my case it was between fifteen and twenty dollars an hour. For Conrad it would be at least ten or twelve. No wonder he was pissed off.

"Then he should tidy himself up," I commented. "Guess we wash our own dishes today."

"You're all heart."

"Conrad and I aren't exactly best buddies."

"I know," he replied, "and I hate to add fuel to the fire, but recently I've caught a couple of whiffs of Conrad that by no means favored cigarette smoke."

"On top of everything else you say he's toking weed?"

"Or because of everything else." Robbie was sitting on a stool at the stainless-steel table that was used for preparing pastries and tortes. The reach-in dessert refrigerator clicked on. My friend was trying to figure out a rental order, but as I tied on an apron I noticed he paused often and sighed even more.

"How's Charles?" I asked, tugging on a baseball cap with a PSC logo. Perry had grown tired of my old Astros hat and, as I resisted the traditional chef's hat for everyday work, had these special-made.

"He's in a bad way," Robbie answered. "Intensive care, critical condition at Ben Taub Hospital."

"The cops will get those guys."

"Not much comfort. And Tommy's a basket case." He tossed his pencil down and ran his hands through his short hair.

I picked up a work order for a lunch we had today. "I'm sorry," was all I could think of to say. The attack had struck close to home for Robbie, though I was as angry as he was.

"I know, Neil." He sighed. "And I'm glad we were there—you were there. I appreciate—"

"I just reacted, Robbie," I broke in.

"Not everyone would react as you did."

"You did," I pointed out. "In fact, you led. As much as anything, I went along to ensure you didn't get the shit whipped out of you."

A smile tweaked on his face, then just as quickly it disappeared. "They're going to come after us—you."

"The police will—"

"And if they don't?" he cut me off. Robbie stood and stretched. His hands were shaking.

I shrugged. "Then I hope someone's watching my back." I was scared, but I was also strong. At least for the moment, strong enough to control fear rather than have fear control me. Of course, C.J.'s warning didn't exactly boost my confidence, but there was no reason for Robbie to know that.

"I hope so, too," he said, then forced a laugh. "Trouble is, it'll probably be me."

"Knowing my luck, you're probably right." I kept a straight face.

"Okay, okay," he said, pointing at me. "I'll remember that."

A chuckle escaped me. After looking at the work order for the third time, the lunch menu finally registered in my brain. This must be old home day, I thought. First C.J. at the Triple A, and now we were serving chicken-fried steak with peppery mashed potatoes, collard greens, jalapeño-cornbread muffins, and apple cobbler. And for the classy, weight-conscious Julie Carlson, no less.

I wandered around the end of the table and noticed that the office door was closed.

Robbie straddled the stool and picked up his pencil.

"Someone in there with Perry?" I asked, nodding at the door. I was still dying to tell him about my conversation with C.J. concerning Sherwood Welles.

"Agnes Berryman," he replied, and raised his eyebrows.

"I see." Sherwood Welles would have to wait.

Robbie beckoned me closer then whispered, "Remember, I told Perry not to take the job. And it wasn't because Berryman's demanding, but I knew that after working us like dogs she'd find a million things wrong, especially when we wouldn't give her a discount because she's *Agnes Berryman*." Robbie could've been chewing glass for the way his face contorted when he mouthed Berryman's name.

Agnes Berryman owned *Texas Tastes*, a successful food-and-lifestyle magazine published in Houston. Berryman was also a showman who was constantly in the gossip columns and always rubbing shoulders with socialites at one fund-raiser or another. How we landed the dinner party for her after refusing to knock down the cost I had no idea, except perhaps we were in vogue, as Perry Stevens held his own on the social level as well.

"I'll be curious to hear what her complaints are." I'd worked the Agnes Berryman job at The Rice—renovated living quarters from the former Rice Hotel—along with Robbie, Mattie, and Booker Atwell. The food was great. Service superb. The dinner party was flawless.

"Me, too." Robbie picked up the pencil and returned to the rental order.

Another peculiarity hit me. "Why is she here to gripe? Why didn't she pick up the phone and call?"

"Likes face-to-face meetings, so she told me when I scheduled this little fête. I think that's because her *charm*"—again he grimaced—"is stronger in person."

I understood. Berryman had a surprisingly high, almost squeaky voice, and yet physically she was an elegant, handsome woman full of wit and *charm*.

Out of the corner of my eye I caught the slender image

of Mattie Johnson as she strolled up from the back of The Kitchen.

"Apple cobbler done?" I asked.

"Cooling down as we speak."

I checked it off. "Who's working the Carlson lunch with you?"

"Booker."

I nodded. "Julie's going back to her Texas roots with this meal."

"The lunch isn't Julie's but Rip's," Robbie clarified. "He has a sales managers' meeting. Guess he needs to fire up his staff before he fires them straight out for not selling enough cars."

Rip Carlson had more auto dealerships than I had shirts. But for all his money he was just a good ol' boy at heart. That explained the menu.

"I want to let you know," Mattie added, "that we're using the last of the beef."

"You went through a case for this little lunch?" I asked.

"There wasn't a case in there. Maybe half."

"Oh," I replied, and shrugged. "Guess I was thinking of the chicken."

"Yeah," Robbie piped up, "I'm sure you are. You've been going through enough bourbon for your bourbon chicken I have to pick up some more."

"We don't use that much," I objected.

"You go through more than you think. Sometimes I wonder if you're not back there slugging it down, too."

"Not the bourbon you buy, Robbie. That rotgut's fine to burn in a pan but not in your belly."

"Trisha's filling in for Claudia," Mattie informed me, and glided back to her workstation.

"Has our dear Trisha punched in, yet?" I loved the girl and her New Age attitude, but the way she allowed the cosmos to blow her around—she'd call it *guide*—like a dandelion white in the wind caused its share of frustration for everyone else around her.

"Trisha will be in after her Zen class," Robbie stated.

"But will she really be here, or will the Buddha blink and we all disappear?"

"You're weird," said Robbie.

"Been called worse," I replied, "and usually by Claudia." Thinking about it, I was glad that Claudia, the kitchen manager, was taking a rest. She was undergoing cancer treatment, and beating the big C, but often she pushed herself too hard.

The door was flung open and Agnes Berryman strode out. Her narrow face was stiff, and the way her auburn hair was pulled back added a harshness to her appearance.

"I'll not pay a dime, and that's what I came here to tell you," Berryman shrilled.

"I've already told you that if you didn't receive the service you expected, then tear up the bill," Perry responded. His voice was calm, but his back was rigid, and his red beard could've been fire on his face. "However," he added, "I don't believe the ends justify the means."

"Your waiter spilled red wine on the mayor's wife," she fumed. "Ruined a dress that cost thousands!"

Robbie pushed himself up from his seat. I turned around. This was the first we'd heard of the incident.

"I didn't—" Robbie began, but was cut off.

"Not you. The other guy."

"Booker," I stated. "You mean the waiter who's not here to defend himself."

"That'll be enough, Neil," Perry snapped.

I fell silent, though my blood boiled. Too much was happening at once, and culminating with Ms. Berryman's accusations. Perry's word, though, was company policy. If a client was that disgruntled, then he or she didn't have to pay. Period. If a client looked him in the eye and told him the food was dreadful or the service awful or any other reason he shouldn't pay, then so be it. And this wasn't the first time—oh, my boss had been taken before. But Perry placed himself above the pettiness; frauds and cheats weren't for him to judge. They'd get theirs.

"I don't appreciate your condescending tone," Agnes Berryman directed at me, and pulled at the collar of her slate-colored Gucci suit.

I knew better than to respond.

"Is there anything else?" Perry asked. He crossed his arms and balanced on the balls of his feet as if to raise his gnomish stature to the height of the tall woman he addressed.

"As a matter of fact, yes," Berryman said, and fumbled in her purse for her keys. "You should provide compensation for the ruined dress."

Robbie's mouth fell open. Perry swallowed hard. I couldn't keep silent.

"Tell the first lady of Houston I know a good cleaner she can send the dress to and then forward the bill here," I told him.

"Spare me your impertinence," she snapped. "I believe five thousand dollars will suffice. The dress was a Versace."

"Talk about impertinence," I shot back, then looked at Perry. "She wants us to pay her for the job. What a con."

"Enough, Neil," Perry said. He rocked up on his toes. "Ms. Berryman, I'll call the mayor's wife and iron this problem out."

"Abbie doesn't want to deal with you," she stated plainly, carefully dropping the woman's first name. "It'll be too embarrassing. She'll only work through me concerning restitution."

"What a crock—" I started, but a glare from Perry cut me short. I turned and wandered over to the front window.

"This is all going on the assumption Booker spilled red wine, which I don't believe," I muttered loud enough to be heard.

"Your request is unacceptable," Perry told Berryman, ignoring me. "You may leave, now."

"I know a lot of important people," Berryman warned.

"How dare you threaten me," Perry said coldly. "Get out." He pointed at the door.

Berryman hesitated. Robbie folded his arms. I walked to the door and opened it.

"You'll regret this," the magazine queen promised.

"I'm sure you believe I will." To emphasize that this was his final word, Perry wheeled around and stepped back into his office, gently closing the door behind him.

Berryman's normally fair complexion was crimson. She sighed so hard it sounded like a snort, then she marched out of The Kitchen. Unable to resist, I slammed the door shut behind her.

From the window I followed the trim woman's movements as she climbed into her BMW and sped off. She really was quite attractive, physically. Guessed she knew it, too, and was accustomed to using her appearance to get what she wanted.

"Can you believe that?" Robbie asked, and stepped beside me.

"And I didn't think anything could shock me anymore," I remarked. "That was a clear case of extortion."

"Think Berryman will raise a stink?"

I pulled at my beard. "Honestly, I don't know."

"Maybe Perry should hire your private-investigator friend," Robbie said, and laughed, though I sensed he was only half joking.

"Maybe," I replied. Robbie shook his head, turned, and went back to his rental sheet.

I drew in a deep breath and slowly released it. The reference to C.J. brought back to mind that other little situation concerning Sherwood Welles. I wondered if we were approaching a full moon that was drawing all the nuts out. Knowing I should tell Perry that we stood accused of attempting to steal Welles's chef, I nonetheless decided to keep that juicy tidbit to myself. The story would come out soon enough.

And did it ever.

4

A day later we received the first threat. Perry slit open the envelope the postman delivered and stood perfectly still by the front window. I was ridding myself of an apron, preparing to head down to the University of Houston, where I was working on my master's in creative writing, when I noticed Perry's color drain. He crushed the note and muttered, "Bigots," as he tossed the paper ball in the general direction of the trash can.

"What's the deal?" I bent over and scooped up the piece of paper.

"Go ahead, read it." Perry cupped his elbow with one hand and stroked his beard with the other.

Behind me I heard a strong rush of water and the clanging of pots and pans being washed. Trisha had the honors this time, as Conrad still wasn't back. Robbie and Mattie were out, setting up an afternoon tea. I unballed the note.

DEAD MAN'S BROTH

The heart of one arrogant caterer
The liver of one queer-loving chef
Two cups of waiter's blood

I looked up. "Someone's idea of a sick joke?"
Perry waved his hand in a circle. "Keep reading."

I stared at the computer-generated note.

> *Prepare bodies by stripping their clothes then strapping them to a butcher-block table. Cut out caterer's heart, set aside. Cut out chef's liver, set aside. Drain two cups of blood from waiter's wrist. Castration of queers mandatory. Of queer lover, optional. Burn bodies.*
> *Boil blood with bitter heart and lily liver. Strain.*
> *Serves one.*

I carefully folded the paper in half. "Perhaps we should call the police."

"No," Perry said sharply, and returned to his office.

"Why not?" I followed while I put on a denim jacket. Thick beads of rain drummed against the windows.

"First, I'll not risk this recipe of hate reaching the media," Perry stated. "Besides being bad for business, I'll not give the disturbed mind behind it one ounce of publicity. Second, what can the police do, anyway?"

"At the very least, be on the alert. Perhaps analyze the note and tell us something about the sender, something that may even allow them to track him down."

"I think we should let it lie," Perry announced. "Just plain ignore it."

The ostrich strategy, I thought. Stick your head in the sand and get shot in the ass. Brilliant. I proposed a compromise.

"What if I contact C. J. McDaniels? He's very good and very discreet."

"And very expensive."

I shook the paper in the air. "If this little love note came from the skinheads Robbie and I tangled with, then it's nothing to ignore. Those people are crazy."

"We'll wait."

"Fine." I stuffed the macabre recipe into my pocket,

not wanting Perry to throw it away and deny the threat had ever existed. "By the way, I've been meaning to tell you something. Not everyone thinks C.J.'s too expensive." I related the investigator's meeting with rival caterer Sherwood Welles.

Perry listened, face stoic, then without a word sat at his computer and opened a file that contained a proposal he was writing.

"I should've told you yesterday, but with Agnes Berryman ranting and raving I thought it could wait."

"Sherwood Welles is a blathering idiot," he said point-blank. "He doesn't concern me in the least. I'm more worried about the waves Agnes Berryman might make."

"Robbie spoke with Booker Atwell, and Booker swears he didn't spill a drop of wine on the mayor's wife. Personally, I think Agnes was the culprit. She was rather tipsy by the night's end."

"And is blaming us because she's embarrassed?"

"Or doesn't remember."

"Well, there's nothing more I can do about that situation," Perry declared. "I'm not charging her for the function."

I saw no reason to respond. He knew how I felt about that. I pulled my collar up. "I've got to go. I have a conference with one of my professors."

"Bye. Enjoy."

"Thanks."

Perry swiveled around in his chair. "Neil, let's keep this recipe thing to ourselves."

"Right. You and me." And Robbie, and C.J., I thought.

I popped over to Trisha. She ran the back of her hand over her forehead as she finished the dishes.

"Would you throw together the Black Forest cake for Dr. Clark's birthday?" I asked.

Her cherubic face brightened into a smile. "Sure, absolutely."

"And if I'm not back in time, ask Robbie to deliver it. He and Mattie should be here before you leave."

"No problem." She sighed. "But I'll be glad when Conrad returns. I keep hoping the spirit will lead him back."

"You better also hope the spirit tells me to take him back."

"Oh, She will," Trisha said, beaming. "Especially after it's your turn to do the dishes."

"You've got a point," I said, winked, and made my way out into the wet afternoon.

My faithful VW Bug waited for me like an old, wise wizard, hunchbacked and world-weary. Wizard because only by sheer magic was it still running.

With rain careening down my jacket and the PSC hat I'd left on, I unlocked my door and hopped in. My grandfather had bought me a Camry for Christmas, which I loved, but, because of finances, chose to sell. I used a chunk of the money for tuition. That still left me enough to purchase a used car, or perhaps a small pickup truck, to replace the Bug. So far, however, I hadn't had the heart to do away with my VW.

Traffic was light this early afternoon, so I reached the University of Houston relatively quickly. This semester I'd chosen to do an independent study with Associate Professor Keely Cohen, working to finish up an original collection of poems. After dashing through the rain, I found Keely in her office, talking to Professor Peter Winford.

"Neil," Winford greeted me, "nasty weather, isn't it?"

I brushed water off my coat and slapped my hat on my knees before stepping from the hall to the office. "You could say that."

"Keely and I were just talking about you," he continued.

"Yes, we were," confirmed the slender, brown-eyed lady.

"I hope some of it was good," I said, falling to an old joke.

"Peter thinks you should go all the way for a doctorate," Keely told me.

I checked to see that my ponytail was still intact. It was. "Really?"

"Would be a tremendous help to your career," Winford offered.

"I hadn't thought that far ahead," I replied. Actually, I wasn't looking past the end of the semester, when Keely was scheduled to leave for California and a position as visiting professor.

"You ought to, Neil," Keely said. She was sitting behind her desk, glancing at me but staring more at the Gauguin poster she'd hung last Christmas. The poster advertised a huge show that had occurred in Washington, D.C., in the Eighties.

"You have a lot of talent," she added. "I think now you need to fine-tune your goals."

"Exactly," Winford jumped in. He uncrossed his legs and stood from a chair in front of Keely's desk. I looked down on his bald spot. "You don't want to sling hash all your life, do you?"

Anger burned in my eyes. I forced myself to avert my gaze and study the Gauguin poster. Winford and I had never really gotten along, and though I knew now he felt sorry for having berated my early work, it was growing increasingly difficult to remain civil toward him.

"No, I reckon I don't want to be no po' cook all my days," I shot back.

"Oh, don't—don't get me wrong," he stammered. "I have the utmost respect for the culinary arts. You, however, have a higher calling."

I caught Keely's eyes. "When will you be back?"

"I don't know," she answered honestly, this time not looking away. Then repeated, "I don't know."

The move, I knew, was putting a tremendous strain on her marriage. Mark Wilson, her husband, was not only a native Texan, but a native Texan who believed Texas was still a republic. Everything outside the state was part of a foreign country, especially California. He would never leave.

"Yes, well, Keely does have a wonderful opportunity," Winford said, quickly changing the conversation. "As department head, I truly hope she doesn't fall for any California sweet talk and we can lure her back home."

Keely smiled, eyes raised, palms to the heavens, as in, *Who knows?*

"Well, well, I understand you two have an appointment," Winford continued, "so I'll leave you." He patted me on the shoulder. "Think about the Ph.D."

"Thank you, I will," I said.

Winford closed the door behind himself.

"And thank you for not hitting him," Keely said to me once we were alone.

"I don't know if I can go for a doctorate with Peter looking over my shoulder." I sat in the chair Winford had just occupied.

"You ought to consider it. I know he's not a social genius, but the man has a lot to offer."

"He's certainly not you," I found myself saying.

Keely cleared her throat, leaned forward, hands locked. "And maybe that's another reason why I need to leave."

I suddenly wanted to pull a Perry Stevens and not deal with this. But I chose not to. "Another reason?"

"I find myself thinking—" Keely began, then suddenly bit her lip and stared at the band on her finger.

The crackle of thunder billowed across the city outside.

But it was within this room that the sharp nerves of lightning struck.

What she was going to say? *Thinking of leaving? Of the effect it was having on her marriage? Of me?* I couldn't, however, bring myself to fish out her thoughts.

"You're under a lot of stress," I said, and broke the silence.

"Oh, for better or worse, the vow goes on."

"I've been there," I told her. "I understand." Susan, my former wife, and I had divorced a little over a year ago.

"Do you? I mean the vow goes on. Mark knows that, too, even though he's discovering my job is as important as his."

In other words, she needed space. And room to focus. "If you don't want to meet today it's okay," I offered.

"No, no, Neil, I want to meet. We have to go over your work." Her warm, fearful eyes touched mine.

"Then let's go over my work." Again I heard the tough old thunder outside. Or was it the pounding of my tough old heart that echoed in my ears?

"Let's," Keely agreed. She shifted in her seat, ran her hands through her short, dark hair, and reiterated, "Yes, let's begin."

Which we did. I didn't hear much of what she had to say. Or care. Keely Cohen, poet professor, was soon leaving Texas.

But in plain talk, she'd already left me.

5

The hateful recipe made a repeat performance the following day, and continued to rear its ugly head the remainder of the week. By the week's end, after a fresh copy of the same threat had arrived in the mail daily, a shaken Perry agreed to hire C. J. McDaniels to investigate. The big detective knew the situation but listened carefully to Perry's version.

"Nothing's varied?" C.J. asked, thumbing through the copies of the threat I'd saved.

"Exactly the same every day," Perry replied. Outside thunder crackled. He took a moment to shut down his computer. C.J. sat at the small round table in Perry's office. Robbie and I stood by the door.

"What about the envelopes?" C.J. set the sheets aside.

"I have them all except the first one," I said, handing them over. "Somehow I let it get thrown away."

C.J. snorted, wore a twisted frown, and examined the envelopes. Again they were all alike—business envelopes, postmarked Houston, an American-flag stamp, and a label with Perry Stevens Catering's address printed in black.

"This is going to take some good old-fashioned luck," C.J. announced.

"You mean he has to make the first move," I clarified.

"If he, she, or they intend to." He placed the envelopes on top of the papers. "Which," C.J. added, "I wager they definitely intend to." He popped a piece of gum into his mouth.

"You don't think the whole thing's a sick joke?" Perry asked hopefully. His computer hummed into silence.

"No more than I think the thunder you hear above us is God snoring or bowling or whatever you were told as a little kid," C.J. replied. "I sense cold, calculating hate. Couple that with the fact those meatball skinheads haven't made a run at these two boys—they haven't, have they, Neil?"

Both Robbie and I shook our heads. "We haven't seen them," I said.

"Not usual." C.J. stood. "Especially with them knowing your name, where you live, and who you work for. I'd have suspected they'd have come riding out for blood by now, not play mind games."

"Which is why I wonder if it's them," I stated. "They didn't strike me as intelligent enough to play mind games."

"Don't confuse hate with stupidity. Marry it to ignorance, but don't think it necessarily means a lack of intelligence. It's something worse. I recollect a short, frustrated Austrian artist who nearly destroyed a whole race of people."

"I appreciate your history lesson," Perry said, a slight tremble in a voice that tried to remain poised, and arrogant, "but what do you intend to do?"

"I strongly recommend you contact the police," C.J. responded curtly. "They have more resources than I do."

"I'd rather not." Perry straightened his bow tie.

"Why?"

"I'd rather not," he repeated. "That's why I came to you, Mr. McDaniels."

"I hope to hell it's not an image thing." C.J. stood. "You might want to consider camping away from your apartment," he told me. "The mind games will last only so long before boredom sets in and the need to act becomes an uncontrollable urge."

"I'm crashing with him this weekend." I nodded at Robbie.

"Now, that's a great plan," C.J. commented dryly. "Bunk with the guy who's also on the hit list, that way they can nail you both at the same time."

"What if you have someone who works for you stay with us?" Robbie asked innocently. "I have plenty of room, and that way if anyone shows up, you have someone on hand to nail them."

I felt my face redden. His employee was his daughter, Linda, a sultry woman I'd had a tempestuous affair with when we'd first met.

"She'd probably like that," C.J. quipped, and looked me up and down. "But who'd pay for such an extravagance?"

"Oh," Robbie said, barely audible but mouthing the sound clearly.

"Speaking of pay," C.J. directed at Perry. "I require a retainer."

Perry looked at me as if it was my responsibility. *What do you mean money? He's your friend who's supposed to help us.* I was trapped, but C.J. sensed this and took the initiative.

"Or you can always go to the police," the investigator added.

Perry pulled out his checkbook, winced at the amount C.J. demanded, but followed through with payment.

"One last thing," he said as he folded the check and stuck it in his top pocket. "Satisfy my curiosity and tell me why Sherwood Welles would want you investigated."

"I have no earthly idea," Perry declared.

"Figured as much. You're not trying to entice his chef into your business, are you?"

"I certainly don't need Sherwood Welles's chef. Anything my staff can't do, I can."

"And you're not into anything illegal?"

"Absolutely not," Perry said, chest out, indignation up. For a second I worried he was about to snatch his check back and rip it into confetti.

"Oddest request I've had in a while," C.J. said absently. "From Sherwood Welles, I mean." He took the gum out of his mouth and, with the lump pinched between finger and thumb, searched for a can to toss it out in.

Perry pointed beneath his desk. C.J. dropped the gum in. I watched the interaction, understanding that C.J. wasn't going to let any path go untrodden.

"Do you know Welles personally?" he asked.

"Yes."

"I realize you're rivals—"

"No, we don't get along." Perry jumped ahead. "I would think you'd deduced that judging from the job he tried to hire you for."

"Why don't you get along?" C.J. asked.

"Welles is jealous of me," Perry declared.

C.J. froze. "Do you have your own television show?"

"No."

"He does. But you say he's jealous of you? It doesn't figure."

"Though Welles is great at selling himself, he's very insecure, which is why he can also be downright mean," Perry explained.

C.J. leaned his thick body toward Perry. "How do you know all this?"

"I've dealt with the man enough."

"Enough that he'd want to hurt you?"

Robbie and I continued to watch the verbal volleys in silence.

"I hardly think so. There's nothing I have that he wants,

and nothing he has that I want, including his chef. I'm sure once he discovers the true intentions of his employee, Welles won't give me a second thought." Perry turned to his desk and pulled out a notepad. "I have work to do," he said. "If you don't mind."

"Right. Call me if you see anything unusual," he told everyone, and dropped some business cards on the table. I walked him out through the front door.

"I've got a funny feeling your boss isn't laying all his cards on the table," C.J. pronounced.

We stood beneath the porch awning, torrents of rain thickly dripping to the pavement. In front of The Kitchen the large leaves of the young magnolia tree looked like primeval shields as they took a beating from the heavens. Across the street a row of blackbirds clung to the telephone line, and in the distance, up on the freeway, clouds of water kicked up by tire after tire created a perpetual mist not unlike clouds of smoke lingering after a series of explosions. C.J. cleared his throat.

"Perry's rather peculiar about his privacy," I began.

"Peculiar, huh?" He waited for me to explain.

"Perry's gay," I said plainly, "but he doesn't figure his sexual orientation should matter one way or another in his business life. So he fiercely protects his personal life and lets his work stand for itself."

C.J. grunted and reached into his pocket like he was searching for a cigarette, then grunted again and fingered another square of the Nicorette gum. God, did I sympathize.

"Something's missing," he said almost to himself, turned, and ambled through the heavy rain like it was a sunny day, the pellets of water not fazing him in the least.

I wondered if he'd always had an umbrella of determination over him.

And decided yes.

6

Robbie had a horde of chores planned for Saturday, none of which I could be of any help with, nor did I have any desire to tag along. So he quietly slipped out early and left me dozing on the couch, the gentle bubbling of the air filter in the fifty-gallon aquarium the only sound in the town house. I must have fallen into a deep sleep because I didn't hear the phone ring until it was too late. Robbie had Southwestern Bell Call Notes, and I didn't know his code. He'd have to retrieve the message himself later.

Not wanting to sit alone all day and watch the fish swim around the gigantic tank, I made a quick call to Candace Littlefield to see if I could spend the afternoon with her down at the stables. Candace had become my adopted little sister shortly after her granddaddy had died, basically leaving the girl to fend for herself near the end of her high-school days. I'd found Candace a place to stay, then helped her make the transition to college where she was doing quite well.

A few miles off Highway 288, in the direction of Pearland and Brazoria County, and a couple of miles down a small farm road, a black mailbox marked the entrance to the stables. Keys's Stables. Candace, who I made sure inherited the modest spread, had kept the name in honor of our slain friend, Jason Keys. Jason had been a good man and, though by no means perfect, certainly hadn't deserved to be murdered. His killer was convinced Jason had been corrupting Candace.

Thinking of Jason's death brought to mind my recent confrontation with the pious protesters and hate-driven white supremacists. Over the phone Candace had summarized things rather succinctly, if perhaps a touch naively, when she'd declared, "Mean people suck."

True. And it was even worse when the mean thought they'd inherit the earth.

Candace was an energetic, green-eyed, freckle-faced young woman soon to be leaving her teens. A rodeo barrel racer with aspirations of being a large animal vet, she already had the horses saddled when I coasted to a stop on a grassy stretch in front of the trailer house. I climbed out of the Bug and waited for her, taking in a series of deep breaths. The weather had broken and the sun sparkled through the swaying pines and live oaks. Not too hot, not too cool, one of the precious few beautiful days of a Texas spring. Should've had the crawfish boil this weekend, I thought.

Of course, it was good that we hadn't. Wonderful weather, but the threat of nasty company.

Riding her favorite horse, Granger, a beauty as dark as crude oil, Candace led Flying Dutchman, the sorrel, over toward me. I ran a bag of groceries into the trailer, setting a package of skinless, boneless chicken breasts and some chorizo into the refrigerator, then stepped outside in time to meet her.

"Thought you might want to ride a bit, clear your mind," she offered, and inched the brim of her Stetson up. The short-crowned hat had a string tie that dangled just below her chin. "Helps me when my thoughts get all jumbled."

"Mighty thoughtful of you," I mocked her thick twang.

"Don't you start in on me, Neil Marshall."

I swung into the saddle. "Wouldn't think of it."

We set out at a walk to warm up the horses and allow for easier conversation.

"You doing okay, living here alone?" I asked. A few months ago she'd moved here from Sondra Anderson's house. Sondra was a transplanted Virginian and a writer friend of mine who had graciously opened her house to Candace when the girl was at her lowest.

"You ask me that every time we talk," she responded. "For the last time, *yes*, Papa Neil."

I laughed. Hadn't I reacted to C.J.'s badgering much the same way not a short time ago?

"What about you?" she prompted.

"Another day in paradise."

"Didn't sound like that over the phone." I couldn't tell if Candace was ignoring the sarcasm or if it flew over her head.

I pretty much recapped what was going on, filling in more details than I'd related over the phone.

When I finished she was silent a moment, then asked, "You got your gun with you?"

"At my apartment."

"Why the hell didn't you bring the .38 with you to Robbie's?"

"Slipped my mind."

"Living in the city's dulling your senses," Candace commented. "Anyone trying to get into my place faces both barrels of a side-by-side shotgun, not to mention the Winchester or the .357."

"You sure you feel comfortable out here?" I asked.

"I'm not paranoid. I'm simply prepared."

"Yeah, for an Iraqi invasion."

Wind rustled the hard branches of a pecan tree, tickled its narrow, bright green leaves.

"Well, those Neanderthals sound more powerful than the Iraqi army. You know, you and Robbie are welcome to sack at my place for a while."

"Thanks, kid. We'll be okay."

She wrinkled her nose, her eyes gazing at me like, *Are you sure?*

"Come on, let's ride," I said, and nudged Flying Dutchman into a trot, then an easy lope.

We rode a few miles up the dirt road before we brought the horses down to a walk and headed back. My mind had been massaged, the rhythm of the ride a physical mantra. Calming. Yet, breathing steadily and deeply, the workout was not unlike a long, easy run. And the gravy was I'd been able to share the experience with Candace. There was no doubt a good deal of the benefit derived from the company.

I dismounted at the stables, behind Candace, who had beaten me back. "Thanks."

"You're welcome." She took Flying Dutchman's rein from me. "I'll tend to them. You go wash up."

"I won't argue because I brought dinner," I announced. "You did for me, now I'll cook for you."

Candace grinned. "I got the better end of that deal. I was beginning to get can opener's wrist, for all I care about cooking."

I hiked across the grass and the mud, yanked off my boots on the trailer steps, and cleaned up. I flicked on the small television to catch the evening news, mostly waiting for *Sports Saturday*.

The sun leaned low and mellow through the blinds. I unpacked the pico de gallo and tortilla soup I'd made at The Kitchen, a six-pack of Tecate, fixings for the rice and guacamole, and then pulled the chicken breasts and chorizo from the refrigerator. We were dining first on the soup followed by beer-battered chicken with the pico, chorizo Spanish rice, and guacamole. A menu my Taco Bell aficionada would appreciate.

I soaked the chicken breasts in Tecate with a little lime while I prepared the egg mixture and flour coating. On the news they were talking about the president's latest escapades. I sliced into the avocado, hitting the pit, and wondered what was going on in the emerald city. I'd voted for the man. With a sharp twist I separated the avocado into halves. An interview with Lady Bird Johnson came to mind. Something about her saying that what would upset LBJ the most about these times was the lack of respect people have come to have for the office of the presidency. I rammed my knife into the pit of the avocado, twisted again, and pulled it out. Lyndon Johnson was a son of a bitch who did some good things, and some bad. But he revered the office and its responsibilities. I took a spoon and scooped out the vegetable's meat into a bowl of lemon water, then proceeded to work on the next one. This political scene was more than lost respect for your country's leader. When the position he holds has dropped down to bait for a frenzied media, how could society as we know it survive? How low could the office fall before it became ineffective? Loss of respect eventually results in loss of power and ability to lead. And like so many people I was ready to toss my hands up in the air in exasperation.

Fortunately, Candace clomped in and broke my internal diatribe.

"You didn't have to take your boots off outside," she said. "I never do."

"Being respectful." I finished the second avocado and left it in the lemon water.

"What are you fixing?" Candace loosened the drawstring and hung her black Stetson on a hat rack, then kicked off her boots next to it.

I diced onion, tomato, and a touch of jalapeño, then

minced a couple of large cloves of garlic while I ran down the menu for her.

"Sounds acceptable."

"I'm so glad you approve," I quipped.

She grinned and trotted off to the bathroom to wash up.

The news had faded so far into the background I almost missed the headline story when the program switched from national to local events.

"And leading off tonight's news, police say there are no new leads in the murder of chef and local celebrity Sherwood Welles. Welles was found stabbed to death after placing a 911 call to report that someone had broken into his office, where he was working last night."

I slowly set my chef's knife down on the counter and moved closer to the television, turning up the volume once I was within reach. The screen flashed to the crime scene. Yellow police ribbon separated the front of Welles's kitchen, where emergency personnel worked, from the curious onlookers. A barrage of lights strobed. A glimpse of the victim, covered by a white cloth, was shown being carried on a gurney away from the house.

"Welles's body was discovered by police responding to the emergency call," the reporter explained over the footage.

I squinted and caught the image of Lieutenant Paul Gardner momentarily in the background.

"Really, Neil," Candace called as she reappeared, "I do appreciate—"

I raised a hand. "Hush a minute and listen to this."

"What?" she asked, noting the concern on my face.

I let the anchorman explain.

"Police say Welles was upstairs in his office when a group of unknown assailants broke into his downstairs commercial kitchen. Welles immediately phoned 911 to report the break-in."

Next they broke to a subtitled account of the conversation between Welles and the dispatcher while we heard the scratchy original over more images of the police at Welles's place.

"Someone has broken into my kitchen."

"Be calm, sir," said the dispatcher. *"I'm alerting the police."*

"I hear voices." Terror sprang from Welles's voice down the back of my spine.

"How many?"

"I don't know."

"Can you see them?"

"No, I'm upstairs in my office."

"Stay where you are, sir," the dispatcher ordered. *"The police are on their way."*

There were the sounds of heavy crashing, metals rattling, and shattering glass.

"They're destroying my place. Let me get into my desk." His voice was shrill. *"Damn their hides."*

And then the line went dead; the only sound was the dispatcher calling, *"Sir? Sir?"* in short breaths like she was trying to revive an unconscious patient.

"By the time police arrived, some seven minutes later," the anchorman continued, "the assailants were gone and Sherwood Welles lay dead amid the debris of his ramshackle kitchen."

The scene cut to a police spokesperson. "This doesn't appear to be a case of burglary but of intent to vandalize. Apparently he was either discovered by the assailants or surprised them by making his presence known."

"Is there evidence he was forced out of his office?" a reporter asked.

"We don't know yet. A complete investigation is under way."

"Why would he voluntarily leave his office when told

to stay where he was by the dispatcher?" a second reporter asked.

"We don't know."

"Was he carrying a weapon?" another reporter called. "Maybe a gun to ward off the intruders."

"No weapon was found on Mr. Welles's body," the spokesperson replied. He rocked from foot to foot, obviously ready to end the interview. But the reporters kept firing questions.

"Did Welles hang up, or were the phone lines cut?" the first reporter wanted to know.

"The phone lines were not cut."

"Do you have any leads?"

"We have a couple of leads we're looking into. I have no further comment pending the investigation." And he turned from the press, ignoring all final questions shouted at him.

"This is spooky," commented Candace.

I glanced at her and agreed.

Again the picture changed, this time to a shot of Welles working in his studio kitchen.

"Best known for his local cooking show, *All's Welles in the Kitchen,* the robust chef entertained thousands the past five years with his flamboyant personality and culinary expertise," the anchorman reported over the muted segment of Welles's show. "Chef Sherwood Welles was forty-three."

When they changed stories, I clicked off the television, not caring to see the sports any longer.

"What do you make of that?" Candace asked.

"Looks like Perry Stevens isn't the only one targeted by those fascists." I picked up the phone and tried Robbie first. He still wasn't home, so I left a message asking him if he'd heard the news, summarized the information in the improbable case he didn't know, and told him where I was. Next I phoned C.J.'s office. Linda answered.

"I just found out about Welles," I responded to her greeting.

"Where are you?" Linda asked. "C.J.'s been scouring the countryside for you."

"I've secluded myself at the stables with Candace."

"I think he even tried phoning you there."

I glanced at Candace's answering machine. The light was flashing red. Oh, well.

"He also left messages with your friends," Linda continued, "at your apartment, your work, even your boss's house, who he's also been wanting to talk to but been unable to track down."

"What does he want with Perry?"

"The police discovered C.J.'s card on Welles and called him in to find out why," Linda answered. "Now the police want to talk to Perry Stevens, Robbie Persons, and you. So, of course, does C.J."

"Fine. But all I can do is corroborate what C.J. told me, and repeat what I've heard from Perry and Robbie. I never met the man."

"Seems kind of funny no one can find any of you immediately after Welles's death."

"What is that supposed to mean?" I demanded, irritated.

"Don't get bent out of shape, Neil."

"You figure the three of us got together, busted into Welles's place, and did him in?"

She laughed. "I hardly think so."

"Thank you," I snapped.

"But the cops won't rule anything out, so we need to convince them, too."

"Good God," I muttered. "Tell the cops to find the skinheads."

"Believe me, C.J.'s already gone down that road."

I sighed. Candace opened a Tecate, gently poured the beer into a mug garnished with a lime slice, and handed it to me. "Thanks," I whispered.

"Where are the two other Mouseketeers?" Linda asked.

"Cute. Robbie's been running errands all day. I don't know where Perry is."

"C.J.'s not in now, either. Stay put and I'll have him call you when he returns."

"Yes, ma'am."

"You're learning." And she hung up.

I clicked the cordless phone off and took a swig of beer. "Yet another strange day in the life of Neil Marshall," I toasted.

"How strange?" inquired Candace. "Like, are you a suspect?"

"If I really am, I don't take it seriously."

I set my beer on the counter, mashed the avocados, and resumed making the guacamole. Candace leaned back against the small sink and crossed her arms. She listened without comment while I related the half of the conversation she hadn't heard.

"So the cops want Perry to fess up," Candace observed when I'd finished.

"What do you mean?"

"They want the real reason Welles would hire a detective to dig into Perry's affairs."

"Suppose you're right," I said, and added chopped cilantro to the mix.

"You know I'm right. The whole thing's weird as a three-legged heifer. There has to be more." She uncrossed her arms and dragged a finger through the guacamole after I stirred in the onions, tomatoes, garlic, and sour cream.

"Needs salt," she commented.

"Would you let me finish?" I objected.

"Damn, chefs are so temperamental."

I grumbled and proceeded to complete the dinner, using a light batter on the chicken breasts flavored with the beer, lime, lemon pepper, coriander, and salt. In the meantime I browned uncooked rice with the chorizo, garlic, cilantro, and onion before adding chicken stock. The phone remained surprisingly silent—until we were sipping coffee, sitting on lawn chairs outside, listening to the horses talk to each other down in their stalls, and enjoying the fading sun and gentle breeze.

It was C.J. He'd tracked Perry down.

"But there's a problem," the detective added. "He won't talk to me, or anyone, he says, without his lawyer."

"Did I hear you right?" I asked.

"You best have a crack at him," C.J. suggested, "find out what he's scared of. Better we do before the cops."

"Where is he?"

"His house."

"It'll take me about forty-five minutes."

"I'll meet you outside." C.J. hung up.

I glanced at Candace. "You want a to-go cup for your coffee?" she asked, and brushed a strand of auburn hair from her eyes.

"Or two," I replied, and held out my mug. "Something tells me this is going to be a long night."

7

I met C.J. outside Perry's place. Streetlights blinked on as the sun slowly descended, branding rich streaks of russet and crimson into an ever-darkening sky.

C.J. kicked at the ground then fanned himself as I approached. It took a minute for me to catch on, but I did.

I pulled my hair. "Still long."

"Obviously." He walked past me toward Perry's door.

"And you still smell like smoke," I added. Not that I was actually close enough to tell, but the wisps that had dissipated into the air, not to mention his gestures, were telltale clues.

"We have more important things to worry about," he grumbled.

"Perhaps I'll braid a long strand of my hair," I said as though thinking aloud. "A narrow, tight braid that could hang by my left ear. Be rather Native American. Hey, that gives me an idea. Maybe I should get my ears pierced and pick up a pair of Dream Catcher earrings, too."

C.J. scowled at me and leaned against the doorbell. "Do whatever you want," he barked, then added, "while you still can."

I tried to spy into the town house but the blinds were drawn tight on the glass door and the hall light was out. All appeared still. Strangely, I didn't even hear Aspen, Perry's little white Pekingese, yap.

Again C.J. pressed the doorbell.

"You sure he's here?" I asked.

"Positive."

Finally Perry's voice came over the outside intercom. "Who is it?"

I raised a finger to silence C.J. and answered, "Neil."

"Neil? What are you doing here?"

"Can I come in and talk?"

"I'm not up for conversation right now," he replied.

"It's important, Perry. It has to do with Sherwood Welles's death."

He didn't respond. I heard a dove call from a chinaberry tree across the street. Farther down the neighborhood a Harley suddenly roared.

"Perry?" I spoke into the intercom.

"Can't it wait, Neil?"

C.J.'s lips tightened and his eyebrows furrowed, but he remained quiet.

"You're going to have to talk to the police sooner or later, so why not cover the ground with us first?" I stared at a bed of azaleas that bordered the walkway. Dusk's gentle breeze tousled the bright flowers.

"Us?"

"C.J.'s with me."

Again silence. "Very well." He finally relented. "I'll be right down."

A moment later Perry appeared, cradling Aspen in his arms. Once the dog realized our presence, the yapping began. The shrill barking did nothing to curb C.J.'s growing impatience. Perry unlocked the door and let us in.

We followed him into the living room that rose from the parquet floor three stories high. A state-of-the-art stereo system surrounded by shelves of compact discs, mostly classical, and leather-bound books dominated one wall. A de Kooning sketch hung on the opposite wall, and a Giacometti sculpture rested in the far corner. C.J. and I each took a posh white chair. Perry sat on the cane rocker.

"Hush, Aspen," Perry scolded, though he scratched the Pekingese behind the ear.

"The police wanted to know why my card was in Sherwood Welles's billfold," C.J. began.

"And?" Perry prompted.

"And I told the cops he wanted me to investigate you."

The yapping became sporadic as the small dog squirmed out of Perry's arms and scurried over to me. He licked my hand after I stroked his head a few times. Aspen, however, was hesitant about approaching C.J., which was probably wise. The big detective eyed the dog the same way he'd eye a roach right before stepping on it.

"They found this very curious," C.J. added.

"Coincidence." Perry crossed his arms and leaned back.

"There's no such thing as coincidence," C.J. said, "only connections that have yet to be uncovered. And your hesitancy to let us in here confirms the gut feeling I've had that you're holding something back."

Perry sighed and leaned forward. I noticed a slight tremble in his hand as he reached down to pat Aspen. "Sherwood Welles was my stepbrother," he told us, voice low. He lifted his gaze from the Pekingese to C.J. then me.

"Your what?" I asked.

"My stepmother's son."

"After all the years I've worked for you, I never knew that," I stated incredulously. Stunned didn't begin to describe how I felt.

"It wasn't any of your business. Besides, Sherwood and I didn't get along."

C.J. groaned. "It *was* my business. The cops will never believe I didn't hold that juicy tidbit of information back.

What else do you have to say? Start with how badly you two didn't get along."

Perry stiffened. "I assure you I didn't kill the man."

"Did you hire someone to?" C.J. questioned.

"You impertinent—"

"Cut the indignation crap," C.J. interrupted. "I've had enough of it. And believe me, the police are going to be rougher on you than I am."

"I've put a call in to Alice Tarkenton." Perry pinched his beard and held his head stiffly. This facade of strength, though, fooled neither one of us. Perry was shaken and scared.

"You'll have to come clean with Alice, too, if you expect her to help you," C.J. added.

Alice Tarkenton was a crusty old chain-smoking lawyer who'd gotten me out of a couple of scrapes in the past. If there was ever a female Rooster Cogburn, she was it. Difficult to deal with, but when the charges started flying, she didn't hide under any wagon.

Perry picked Aspen back up and set the dog in his lap. He opened the button closest to his throat, smoothed the lapels of his red polo shirt, and began talking.

"I was thirteen when Dad remarried. Sherwood was ten. I'd always gotten along fine with Shirley, my stepmother. In fact, she'd helped smooth things over between Dad and me more than once."

"*Had* gotten along?" C.J. asked.

"Shirley died two years ago."

"I'm sorry."

"Me, too. At any rate, Sherwood was another story. We couldn't stand each other at first, which I suppose was not exactly abnormal for stepchildren. But Shirley worked at it, especially when she discovered that Sherwood and I both had an interest in cooking. Shirley's father had been a chef and had owned a restaurant in Dallas, so she knew the business and told a million stories about her experiences." Perry paused, laughed to himself, lost for a moment in another world. C.J. and I waited.

"Funny thing," Perry continued, "was I didn't learn until later that Shirley hated cooking. Her father had put her to work at his restaurant at an early age and she truly came to hate the business. Tells me how hard she tried, working with us the way she did. Eventually the situation calmed. In fact, it even reached a point where Sherwood and I were planning to go into business together." He stopped.

"When did the falling-out occur?" C.J. asked. He shifted his bulky weight in the chair, crossed his legs, and interlocked his fingers over his big belly.

"Well, it was a gradual thing," Perry replied. "Sherwood had the interest, but he really was an inferior chef."

"He had his own television show," C.J. pointed out.

"His personality was his strength. I'll give him credit for that. He could turn on the charm like nobody you'd ever seen."

"And you resented him for that."

"I resented the deceit," Perry stated. "He wasn't honest with people."

C.J. nodded like he'd expected that answer. "And, of course, you are—honest with people—including him."

"I called him the culinary Liberace. Marginal talent hidden behind showmanship. What Sherwood accomplished he did so through dumb luck. He was a sloppy, undisciplined showman with good people behind him."

"Like Warren Clay," I offered.

Perry turned to me.

"Clay's a nerd but he has a good reputation," I explained.

"Let's get back to the culinary Liberace," C.J. said.

"I had nothing to do to with his death," Perry repeated.

"I believe you," the big detective replied, and edged forward. "The police won't. Why exactly did you and your stepbrother go separate ways? What did you say to—"

"It was what Sherwood said," Perry interrupted. "He had the nerve to tell me he wouldn't carry useless baggage. He had the flair, the talent. According to him, I had nothing." Perry set Aspen down and then stood. "I was blindsided. And he laughed. I swore then I'd never have another thing to do with him. And I didn't."

C.J. sighed a huge puff.

Perry started to add something when Aspen went into a terrific barking fit. Almost made me wish C.J. had stepped on the dog.

The doorbell rang.

"If it's who I think it is, you might as well let them in," C.J. informed Perry. "My car's parked directly out front, as is Neil's."

Perry's eyes darted from him to me and back.

C.J. rose and caught Perry by the arm. "Is there anything else? The man came to me to investigate you."

"Paranoia was part of his personality, too. He was on top and wanted to stay there."

"That's it?"

"I don't know what else it would be."

C.J. hesitated. I knew he was trying to figure how far to push Perry with the doorbell gonging.

"The funny thing is," Perry continued, "I find myself grieving for Sherwood. He was a jerk to me, as I suppose I also was to him. But there were good times. And Shirley didn't deserve this happening to her only child."

"Sounds to me like she had more than one child," C.J. told him. Then he escorted Perry to the door, where, waiting behind the blinds, was none other than Lieutenant Paul Gardner of the Houston Police Department.

8

I stood at the end of the hall and watched. Wearing a gray Brooks Brothers suit complete with vest, Gardner looked more like a man who'd just attended a Saturday-matinee production of *Madame Butterfly* than a detective investigating a brutal murder. Tall and lean, he bowed slightly and nodded as Perry opened the door. The easy smile that pressed his lips dipped for just an instant when he spotted C.J. Perry, not noticing this, ushered the lieutenant inside.

Gardner and C.J. had crossed paths many times over the years, sometimes on friendly terms, more often not. Having seen them interact a few times myself, now, I had the impression that Gardner viewed C.J. as a nuisance he'd rather not deal with. I also had the sense that was the way the lieutenant looked at me. Could've had something to do with the time I took the rap for a murder in self-defense I hadn't committed. Or perhaps the time I disregarded Gardner's orders and showed up anyway at Chip Gunn's political rally looking for a friend of mine. And all hell broke loose. I shook the memories from my head and moved forward to meet the lieutenant's outstretched hand.

"Mr. Marshall, the culinary poet in residence," he greeted me.

"Lieutenant."

"How's your grandfather?"

Gardner had met Grandpa last Christmas when the old man had come down from Colorado to visit me. And brought a whole pack of trouble—in the form of a few thugs out to do serious injury for some mineral rights he owned—with him.

"In heaven," I replied. "He's fly-fishing in Wyoming. I plan to join him in a month or so."

"A well-deserved vacation, I'm sure," Gardner said.

"You didn't come here to jabber about his fishing trip," C.J. spoke up.

"No, I didn't." Gardner's voice was deceptively soft and easy. A ploy to instill trust, his tone could turn hard and cold without warning. The lieutenant glanced at an officer in blues who stood at the hall's entrance. The uniformed cop pulled out a small notepad and pen and waited to take notes.

Aspen leaped from Perry's arms to the floor, sprawling out like the head of a dust mop before collecting himself and investigating the lieutenant. The Pekingese sniffed Gardner's shoes.

"Shall we sit?" Perry suggested. We did, though Gardner took my chair, so I went to the plush couch.

"Why would Sherwood Welles want to hire McDaniels to pry into your affairs?" Gardner asked Perry casually. The lieutenant folded his arms, crossed his legs, and leaned back. For all the interest he showed, Gardner came across like a non–sports enthusiast preparing himself to endure someone's rambling account of last night's Astros game.

"I must begin by telling you something almost no one knows," Perry began. "Even Neil and McDaniels weren't privy to this until a few minutes ago."

Upon hearing that Welles had been Perry's stepbrother, Gardner's eyes darted to C.J. Just as C.J. had suspected, I could tell by Gardner's glare he didn't believe the private investigator hadn't known. Perry, though, continued and repeated almost verbatim what he'd told us. The uniformed cop quietly took notes.

When Perry finished, Gardner pursed his lips and waited a moment as if to allow the echo of the nervous man's words to fade into the high reaches of the vaulted ceiling. Gardner finally cleared his throat and leaned forward.

"Perhaps you can answer one more question," he said.

Perry tensed. C.J. and I glanced at each other. There was something else.

"Where were you Friday night, say, between nine P.M. and midnight?"

"Here," Perry replied.

"The whole time?"

"Of course."

"Anyone with you?"

"Only Aspen."

Gardner again smiled, reached down, and scratched the dog behind the ears. "I'm sure he's as honest as the day is long, but I'm afraid he's hardly the type of witness who'll hold up in a court of law."

"Court of law?" Perry choked.

"What kind of car do you drive?" Gardner asked.

"A Lexus."

"Maroon?" the lieutenant continued.

"Black."

"Close enough."

"Get to the point," C.J. ordered.

"A dark-colored Lexus was spotted leaving the scene of the crime shortly before the police arrived," Gardner stated.

Perry's face paled. He stared straight ahead. Why hadn't he told us? I wondered.

"Got a license-plate number?" C.J. asked.

"No."

"With all the Lexuses in the city, you can't prove that one belonged to Stevens," C.J. said.

"Perhaps, perhaps not." Gardner refocused on Perry. "You maintain you weren't at Sherwood Welles's house at all Friday night?"

"Are you charging him?" C.J. broke in.

"Mr. Stevens?" Gardner pushed, ignoring C.J.

"You might want to wait to say anything more until you talk to Alice," I volunteered.

Gardner's eyes, however, continued to bore into Perry.

"That is correct, Lieutenant," Perry answered, disregarding our help.

Gardner rose, nodded at the officer with him. The cop closed his notebook. "I suppose you also knew nothing about Mr. Stevens's proximity to the crime scene?" the lieutenant addressed McDaniels.

"I knew nothing of it because he wasn't there," C.J. fired back. "You ask me, you need to look for the same group of skinheads who jumped Neil and his friends. Welles's death shows a strong resemblance to a hate crime."

Gardner tipped his head back. "Ah, yes, I heard about that. But no one matching that description was seen anywhere near Welles's place."

"Funny how a dark Lexus was spotted but not a loud group tearing the place apart," C.J. said dryly.

"I see no humor in the situation at all," Gardner replied, a coldness honing the edge in his voice.

"Neither do I," C.J. shot back, stood, and leaned toward Gardner.

Gardner then caught us all off guard. He pulled a folded sheet of paper from an inside pocket of his jacket and placed it in Perry's hand. "I have a warrant to search your car," Gardner said. "The boys from the crime lab should be out front by now."

C.J. snatched the paper from Perry. "Search it for what?" He studied the court order then released a long sigh.

"Evidence, of course." Gardner retrieved the warrant from C.J. "Is your vehicle in the garage?" he asked Perry.

"Yes."

"Would you mind opening the garage door?"

Perry hesitated.

"Do I have to define obstruction of justice for you, Mr. Stevens? This is a court order that should, in fact, matter little to you, as you were nowhere near the vicinity of Mr. Welles's place of employment the night he was murdered."

"Laying it on a bit thick," I commented.

Gardner didn't smile. He ran his fingers through his salt-and-pepper hair.

"Open the door," C.J. told Perry.

Perry rose, a little wobbly, and complied. Sure enough, on the other side of the garage door was parked an HPD crime-lab van. It attracted the attention of the neighborhood as a small crowd gathered across the street in the waning light. C.J. picked up the phone. Perry returned to his seat, holding Aspen, who was yapping hysterically at the commotion. Gardner went out the door to the one-car garage followed by the uniformed officer. Silently the lieutenant watched while the blue stood in the driveway to intercept any curious onlooker who dared to approach. I closed the door.

C.J. muttered something into the phone and hung up. "Alice Tarkenton got your message. She's on her way," he announced, then approached Perry. "Tell me the truth," he directed. "Were you anywhere near Welles last night?"

Perry took a deep breath. "Yes."

"Oh, no," I muttered.

"Can't you tell a straight story?" C.J. shook his head,

paced, and popped his huge right fist into the meaty palm of his left hand. "For someone who can't stand deceit, you sure have your fill of it."

"I was scared after I found out what had happened."

"Did you see Welles?" I asked.

"Yes."

C.J. stopped, stared up with his hands out as if asking God, *Why me?*

"But he was very much alive when I left him," Perry said.

"And I'm supposed to believe that? You implied you hadn't had anything to do with him in a dog's year."

"I went there to discover why he'd hired you to investigate me." Perry petted Aspen, who was still growling periodically. "We had words. He accused me of trying to steal away his chef. I said that was preposterous and called him a paranoid culinary actor. He ordered me out, and I left."

"You say anything else?" C.J. put a foot up on one chair's arms and stretched forward, arms crossed on his leg.

"Do you mind?" Perry stared at the detective's foot on his furniture.

"Did you say anything else?" he repeated.

"Only for him to stay out of my business."

"Or else?"

"No or else." Perry continued to stare at C.J.'s raised foot.

C.J. pushed off the chair. "I wish I could believe you."

"I do," I said, drawing the attention of the both of them. And I did. I couldn't picture this dwarfish man in his bow tie and jacket doing any more than acting indignant, or at worst rapping someone over the head with the end of his umbrella. Hardly the image of a maniacal killer thrusting a knife into a man's heart. "The way Perry talked about his late stepmother I can't imagine he'd do anything that she would've disapproved of," I explained.

C.J. grunted. A hint of a smile touched Perry's lips. We all then fell silent for a long time.

After about an hour and a half the police left. They had taken pictures from every angle, checked a couple of scratches on the car, took some kind of prints of the tire treads, then searched the inside and trunk, it seemed, with tweezers, apparently looking for signs of blood or, better yet, a crimson-stained knife. They found no knife. But I didn't know what they discovered. Gardner said nothing but, "Good evening."

Alice Tarkenton, the grizzled lawyer, had arrived by then. Dressed in a gray sweat suit, she'd come directly from her club, where she was having a drink with Dark-horse Knowles after playing racquetball with the famous criminal lawyer. She advised the police not to harass her client unless they had a damn good reason.

Lieutenant Gardner assured her he'd be certain to have a very damn good reason.

With the cops gone, C.J. and I hung around only long enough for Perry to go through the scenario one more time to update Alice. I figure we stayed to be sure he told the same version again. The whole version. He did.

Much to Perry's dismay—and C.J.'s—Alice chain-smoked the whole time. Finally, the private investigator couldn't take it. After pacing the room, he said little and headed out the front door. I followed, proud he hadn't broken down and bummed a smoke from Alice.

Once outside I asked, "Why didn't you say anything about the threats we've been getting?"

"Don't know who they're from." C.J. popped a piece of Nicorette gum in his mouth and took a series of deep breaths. "What if Welles had been sending them? Then we'd have handed the cops more evidence against your boss. Your boss," he repeated. "He's a piece of work."

"You're just figuring that out?"

The sun was gone and a warm breeze rustled through the live oaks that lined the street.

"Feel like tossing down a cold brew?" I asked.

"Why not?"

"The Black Lab's not too far." I paused. "You did well not begging for a cigarette off of Alice."

Suddenly he grinned. "That's only because I want to see you scalped."

"You may yet." When we reached the cars I asked, "Think the cops found anything?"

"Why ask me? You're the one who believes him."

I shrugged. "Thought you might have an opinion."

"I feel like I've been bit in the ass, that's my opinion."

"Well, I think Perry's let it all out," I said. "What else can happen?"

"Don't ask." C.J. spat out his gum.

He was right.

I shouldn't have.

9

A few days later I was toweling off after a shower when the phone rang. I jumped, instinctively reached for the .38, then chided myself for being so skittish. My apartment had remained untouched while I'd stayed at Robbie's, but the stillness I'd entered into had me on edge. Initially I'd come by for a couple of dress shirts, khakis, and a pair of brown loafers, but I'd felt so wound up I'd decided to go for a run to sweat off the anxiety. Obviously, even a good stretch of the legs hadn't quite done the trick.

I caught the phone right before the answering machine did. Since the incident at Perry's town house, the police had been strangely quiet. Any minute now I expected to hear how the cops had cracked Welles's murder and somehow implicated Perry, leaving the skinheads on the street to continue their war party. The call I received, however, was far from what I was expecting.

"Neil, this is Keely."

"A much more pleasant voice than I'd bargained for."

"But I fear not a bearer of good news," she admitted.

I draped the towel across my shoulders and brushed a clump of matted hair from my eyes. "What's wrong?"

"Have you seen the latest issue of *Texas Tastes*?"

"What?"

"The magazine."

"I know what *Texas Tastes* is," I replied. "What about it?"

"Go out and pick up a copy. There's a review that makes some rather unflattering comments about Perry Stevens Catering."

"Agnes Berryman," I muttered.

"Who?"

"The owner of the publication. She's in the midst of a row with Perry. This is all he needs."

"I see. Well, the article's written by a food critic named Nathaniel York."

"Nathaniel York," I echoed, then asked more to myself than Keely, "Why does that name sound familiar?"

"York's a fairly well-known food writer and critic."

"Yeah, but there's something else." I groaned and rubbed my temple. Given time I'd remember.

"Want me to read any of the notorious highlights?"

"No thanks. I'll catch it later."

"Good," she said with relief. "I didn't really want to breathe life into these words by speaking them aloud, anyway."

I wiped the ends of my wet hair. "That bad?"

"Not a pretty sight."

"Okay. Appreciate the warning." I paced with the cordless phone to the front window and peeked out the blinds. All was well. Even Samson lay sprawled on Jerry's back porch, snoozing away under an overcast sky.

"If I don't run into you the next couple of days, I guess I'll see you after I get back from house-hunting in California," Keely said.

"Guess so. Good luck finding a place to stay." My voice sounded odd with its forced perkiness. Not my voice at all.

"Why, thank you, Neil. Y'all still having that crawfish boil?"

"I don't think Perry will cancel it even if he's in jail."

Keely forced a laugh, said she was sorry to be missing the party, bade me goodbye, and we hung up.

After slipping on some khakis and a cream-colored L. L. Bean dress shirt, I ran a comb through my hair and headed off. The morning was quickly disappearing. Not that I was overly concerned, as today there was a lull in our schedule. In fact, a rarity—no jobs at all. The only item on my agenda was a meeting with Robbie and Perry concerning the crawfish boil. First thing, though, I stopped on the way to The Kitchen and purchased a copy of *Texas Tastes*.

I sat in my Bug in the newsstand parking lot and thumbed open the magazine. There the review was, under the inauspicious headline: LOST IN THE SHADOW OF A GIANT.

Sensing the gist of the review before I read it, I began to feel ill.

Nathaniel York wrote:

> *Recently I had the opportunity to sample the fare of Perry Stevens Catering at a party in Houston. Though not as well known as the bayou city's television chef Sherwood Welles, Mr. Stevens has enjoyed a fine reputation and respect throughout the culinary community. Hence with high expectations and great anticipation I eagerly looked forward to meeting Mr. Stevens and his art.*
>
> *I could not have been more disappointed.*

A groan escaped me, and I slapped my thigh with the magazine. A shark attack in Galveston bay would've been more subtle. Still, I continued.

> *Beginning with the rubbery calamari and limp, fried ravioli served as hors d'oeuvres, to a very uninteresting*

gazpacho—*a soup used with the proper adjective*
Texas *in its title, which meant, I suppose, Mr. Stevens
added a handful of cilantro to this usually refreshing
recipe—and through a main course of dreadfully over-
cooked red snapper, I was left shaking my head. Or
rather, holding my nose.*

Okay, I thought, a good Texan takes care of irksome
situations one of two ways—the first barrel or the second
from his shotgun. In this particular position, I was of that
attitude. Or perhaps C.J. could put me in touch with an
affordable hit man. Then something hit me.

This wasn't Agnes Berryman's menu. But the food did
sound familiar. I recognized the cuisine from an event we
had catered a couple of months ago.

I'd naturally assumed the review was in response to
Berryman's feud with Perry. However, it couldn't have
been. I flipped the magazine over to the cover. May issue.
Here we were at the end of April, and this issue would've
been at press about the time of Berryman's party. Now,
Agnes owned the publication, but she certainly wouldn't
have stopped production over her tiff with Perry. So there
was only one conclusion.

Agnes Berryman's magazine was out to pan Perry
Stevens before she'd hired us to do her party. So why did
she hire us, then? Didn't she read her own layout? Or was
she adding fuel to the fire?

I skimmed the remainder of the article, noting the comments on the bland crawfish tequila sauce that dressed the
red snapper and the overdone angel-hair pasta the entrée
rested on. Nothing was really said of the Italian cream
cake I now remembered we served for dessert. The son of
a bitch must have liked it but couldn't bring himself to say
so. The piece wound up:

For someone who feels he deserves to be ranked in the same category as Sherwood Welles, Perry Stevens matches up as well as a hot dog against a crown roast. Few in the state of Texas, never mind Houston, can escape the tall culinary shadow of Sherwood Welles. Perry Stevens is not one of the few.

I glanced back at the beginning of the article and caught the black-and-white glossy of the author. I expected a rotund face, and was not disappointed. Something faintly recognizable about the photograph set the little voice in the back of my mind to whispering. Trouble was, it was like a bad itch I couldn't scratch—I couldn't make out a word. Again, I had faith it would come to me.

I cranked up the Bug and headed off into the humid April day. So much for a relaxing day at The Kitchen. No doubt Perry had seen York's interpretation of yellow journalism by now.

He had.

The man was hot enough to steam crawfish with his bare hands. When I came through the door he was pacing around The Kitchen, occasionally slamming the magazine against whatever stainless-steel table he passed by. I'd never seen him worked to such a fury. With all he'd gone through, this was the ballbuster. Gently, I closed the door and caught Robbie's eye as he stood up front, leaning tensely against the butcher-block table. His eyes widened when he saw me and he released a sigh, apparently grateful he wasn't alone with Perry any longer. Mattie had the day off.

I tossed my copy of the magazine on the table.

"I'll sue," Perry barked. He stopped pacing when he saw me. "What the hell's up with Agnes Berryman? She find it necessary to have her pound of flesh as well as not pay?"

"Good morning to you, too, Perry," I replied.

"They're out to ruin me." Veins bulged from his neck.

"York's not referring to Berryman's function."

"What?" Perry gave me a double take.

"That wasn't the menu we served."

"Neil's right," Robbie said, and set the old work order down on top of my magazine. "I looked up the job. It was a dinner party for Amy Day."

"Robbie, Mattie, and I worked that one," I said. "Everything was perfect. Ms. Day loved it."

"Yes, she did," Robbie agreed.

"Do you remember seeing Nathaniel York there?" I opened the magazine and showed Robbie the photograph.

He shook his head, his cool gray eyes showing disappointment at the answer to a question he'd obviously already asked himself.

"You know him?" I asked Perry.

"I've met him once or twice, enough to know who he is. That's all."

"Why does he look familiar?" I asked in general.

"He looks like his father," Robbie stated.

"You know his father?" I asked.

"His picture's on billboards all over town. The Reverend Gideon York of the United Church of Christian Soldiers and Moral Activists."

"Of course," said Perry. He stroked his beard. "The gay basher."

There was a click and a tumble and the vault of my mind opened. "Now I remember," I said, and studied Nathaniel York's picture. Outside Sue-Ellen's. The zealots watching the skinheads beat Charles. The leader disclaiming responsibility for the crime. Stocky, balding, late fifties, early sixties. The Reverend Gideon York. I was simply staring at a younger version in the magazine.

"I hadn't noticed," Robbie said after I related my revelation, "but now that I think of it, you're right."

"So what does that mean?" Perry tossed the magazine down with a thud on the table and threw up his hands.

"I don't know," I replied feebly. "But the connection's too coincidental to ignore."

Perry raised a hand to his forehead and rubbed his temples with a forefinger and thumb. "I think I'm going to be sick," he muttered, and walked off into his office.

"Me, too," I agreed.

"If it's any consolation, there was nothing unusual in the mail." Robbie picked up Amy Day's work order and set it on his small desk.

"Two days in a row, now, no recipe of hate."

"Not since Monday," Robbie confirmed.

"Which means the last threat was probably mailed late Friday," I stated, and sat on a stool.

"Before Welles's death. Seems rather obvious he sent them."

"Perhaps too obvious."

"Who else, then?"

"I have no idea," I stated, and rose.

I followed Robbie's gaze out the front window. A dog had torn into a bag of trash down the street. Kentucky Fried Chicken cartons, pizza boxes, and beer cans were among the debris littering the pavement and small plot of grass in front of the house.

"I'm sorry for Welles, and I'm sorry for Perry," Robbie said, "but if that macabre message stops, that's fine with me."

"Don't you find it odd we haven't heard anything from the skinheads?" I asked him.

"Maybe they're more talk than action."

"I don't think Charles would agree."

Robbie shot me a *go to hell* look, then softened. "Suppose you have a point. I don't get it, either."

I stepped over to the phone and punched in C.J.'s number. The ringing sequence kicked the line over to the investigator's answering service. I left a simple message for C.J. to call me ASAP.

I was glad I did. About five minutes later the police arrived and arrested Perry Stevens for the murder of his stepbrother, Sherwood Welles.

10

"The cops claim they have a witness who can place Perry at the crime scene," Alice Tarkenton told C.J. and me. We stood outside the Mykawa station. A balmy wind tossed the American and Texas flags at irregular intervals. As calm as the area was, it felt like we were standing in front of an Art Deco mini-mall that failed to attract customers. Of course, I knew there were plenty of customers inside the complex. An innocent man being one.

C.J. chewed his Nicorette gum while Alice pulled hard on a cigarette.

"What witness?" I asked.

"The fella who washes dishes for y'all."

"Conrad?" My feet came to an abrupt halt as if they'd shut down on their own accord. We'd met Alice as she was leaving the building and were following the tough old lawyer to her car.

Alice shot me an irritated glance over her shoulder. "I don't have time to stop and gab."

"How'd the dishwasher become a witness?" C.J. questioned, staying in step with Alice.

"Swears he was looking to change employers," she elaborated. "Says Welles told him to drop by Friday night because he would be working late and there'd be no interruptions."

"Isn't Conrad the ex-con?" C.J. directed to me when I caught up.

"Sure enough."

"Exemplary witness," the investigator quipped.

"Ed Krieger appears to believe so," Alice stated.

I winced at the mention of the assistant district attorney's name. From prior experience, I knew the man was as mean as a pit bull and had about the same size brain.

We reached Alice's Cadillac. "Let's hear Conrad's story," C.J. said.

Alice swung her briefcase onto the hood and dug in her purse for keys. "I tell you, boys, it's a doozy of a tale. Old Conrad paints Perry as the meanest and most unfair boss on earth. So he was poking his nose around, attempting to sniff out another job when he crossed paths with Welles. Conrad says Welles was very anxious to talk to him. But it seems when Conrad arrived, Perry was already there and arguing something fierce with Welles." She tugged out her keys, complete with a lipstick-size tube of red pepper spray attached. I wondered if the spray was for protection or to freshen her breath and invigorate her cantankerous attitude. She unlocked the car door.

"Did he see the murder?" I asked.

With a quick flick, Alice rid herself of the dying cigarette. "No."

A wave of relief filtered through me.

"Which is too damn bad," she added. C.J. nodded in agreement. So much for relief. At my confused look, Alice explained, "Honey, if Conrad had claimed to have witnessed the murder, I could've ripped him apart. His story is consistent, and works alongside the 911 call. Had he let out more information, provided more opportunities to find holes in his statement, my job would be a hell of a lot easier."

"Can't you still rip him apart?" I asked.

"Of course, but it's going to take more work." She tossed her briefcase in and paused. "Best start digging everywhere you can," the crusty old lawyer told C.J. "The DA's office is building their case."

"What did Conrad say when he walked in on them?" I asked before she climbed in her car.

"He watched through the window, became nervous Stevens was there, and left. Might not sound like much, but it's a very believable story that places Perry within the premises the night Welles was murdered. Considering the troubled relationship between Stevens and Welles, even Ed Krieger can present a strong argument to a jury. Not to mention we're not sure what else the police will come up with."

"Find anything on Stevens's car?" C.J. asked.

Alice swung down in her seat. "Nothing, so far. Certainly not the murder weapon. I suspect, however, they're still processing the lab work." She pulled her door closed, lowered her window.

"I didn't realize the murder weapon was missing," I put in.

"That's a piece of information the police withheld from the public." She smiled slyly as if to say, *but nothing gets by me*.

"Do you know specifics about the weapon?" C.J. asked.

"Twelve-inch blade. Probably a chef's knife."

"That's what I figured," he acknowledged.

"Now, don't go wasting your time by running in there to console him," Alice stated curtly.

"Wasn't intending to," C.J. shot back as he headed for his Mustang.

"I wasn't talking to you, you blockhead," she called after him, then returned her focus to me. "Perry doesn't need moral support from y'all. Let someone else handle that. Talk to him when you can ask him something you ain't already asked."

"Yes, ma'am," I responded, and wondered if she also used improper English in court to emphasize her points.

"I have to be downtown, in court, in less than an hour," she added, and glanced up from her wristwatch. "Keep in touch."

After a short wave, Alice drove off. I followed C.J. over to his car. He was on the phone to Linda, his daughter and business partner.

"No," I heard C.J. say, "you check out the deal with this magazine—" The big detective looked at me to prompt him.

"Texas Tastes," I said.

"Texas Tastes," he repeated, and paused. "Great, I'm glad you like the magazine, but I want you to find out why that reviewer—" he shot me another inquiring look, and I provided York's name — "was so antagonistic, and see if you can reach"—I was right in step and threw out Agnes Berryman's name—"the woman who owns the rag."

Another pause.

"Well, maybe it's not a rag, but it's all froufrou to me." C.J. punched the phone off.

"What do you want me to do?" I asked.

"Go home and let us handle it."

"I can't just—"

"Don't argue, Neil." He slipped down into his Mustang.

"What are you going to do?" I asked, then realized I stood over him with my fists planted on my hips.

"Got an address on that Conrad character?"

"At The Kitchen."

"Then go there now and phone it in to me," he ordered.

"And then what?"

"Then wait."

I kicked at the ground. "Give me something to do even if it's just gofer work."

"When I think of something, I will." He fired up the Mustang. "Reckon I'll go over to the television station while I wait for you to get that address. Might not be a bad idea to poke around over there, see what I can discover about Welles and his program."

"I'll call you with the address," I said through a sigh.

"Good boy. Watch your back. The skinheads are still roaming wild, and I strongly suspect they had something to do with tearing up Sherwood Welles's place."

"Unless someone's trying to direct attention away from himself and toward them," I suggested.

"A definite possibility. Nonetheless, keep your eyes open." And he tore off, squealing his wheels across the police station's parking lot. Alice had pegged him perfectly— C.J. could be a blockhead. And in more ways than one.

A grin spread across my face. I anticipated C.J. would give me the brush-off. And though it was true Conrad's address was on the computer at The Kitchen, I didn't have to go there to get it.

I knew where Conrad lived.

11

Conrad lived in the Heights in a small bungalow only a few miles from my apartment. A mass of peeling white paint, the house overlooked Interstate 10. By the dog days of summer the hot smell of oil, exhaust, and rubber would dominate the area, not simply be a minor undertone in the air. Add to that the discordant grumble of traffic around the clock and the result wasn't one of the choicest pieces of real estate in the city.

But the Heights was like that all over. Some spots nice, others not so nice. They seemed to match the personalities of the people who lived there. I had barely turned off the VW's engine when Conrad edged partially out onto the front porch, shielding himself with the screen door.

The clouds had broken without any rain to speak of and a strong late-afternoon sun took over. As I approached I noticed the house had wall-unit air conditioners, not a central system. Not unusual, but I failed to see any water condensing off them or hear the drone of their motors.

The grass was long and partially overran the broken concrete walkway that led to the house. A stump of what had probably been a live oak or pecan tree stuck out like a blister on the small front lawn. Judging from its diameter, the tree had been large and most likely had produced a canopy of shade for the bungalow. Its absence, even in an

April sun, was missed. I could only imagine what August would be like.

"That's far enough," Conrad announced. "State your business."

How John Wayne. I stopped at the base of the two stone steps that led to the tiny porch. Sweat dampened my shirt.

"Why did you lie?" I blurted, not fully convinced he had lied and vaguely wondering if my animosity toward him was getting the best of me.

He fully emerged from the house and released the screen door so it swung closed. "I didn't tell no lie." He tossed a smoldering cigarette at my feet. Funny thing, I didn't watch the ember as it almost hit me. My eyes were transfixed on the face of Jesus, complete with thorny crown, tattooed on his arm.

"You were at the crime scene Friday night?" I said, and forced myself to look away from the body art.

Conrad's white T-shirt was soiled and his faded jeans frayed near his bare feet. He stood stiffly, one arm behind his back, the other at his side. I hoped he wasn't concealing a hunting knife—or any kind of knife for that matter—behind him.

"I talked to Perry's lawyer. She gave me a rundown of your statement," I explained.

"I was at Welles's kitchen. I saw Stevens and Welles hollering at each other. And then I saw on TV what happened to Welles. Even a genius like you should be able to figure out what went down."

"And you're saying you simply left."

"I didn't want Stevens to see me. A bad job's better than no job and I didn't want to go and lose it before I had something else lined up."

"What's to say you didn't hang around until Perry was gone and kill Welles yourself? Maybe you became angry at him because he wouldn't hire you," I theorized. "And with your temper . . ."

I let my voice trail off and watched for his reaction. He was tense, eyes smoldering, but when he drew his hand from behind his back, I saw that it was empty. He crossed his arms, Christ stretching across Conrad's modest biceps.

"If I was to knife anyone, it wouldn't have been Welles," he said, voice low. "Besides, the cops believe me."

"Don't be so sure."

"Oh, I am. I've had enough dealings with them bastards to know they'll suspect everyone—I bet even you're on their list—but I've played it so I'm low down."

No doubt you're low-down, I thought, but since he was talking openly, refrained from vocalizing my opinion. Conrad took my silence as a signal for him to continue.

"I went to the cops on my own free will," he said. " 'Course, I weren't sure someone didn't see me there at Welles's and, me being an ex-con, read the wrong thing into my visit, so I figured it best for me to come clean up front."

"And screw Perry in the process," I shot out.

"I didn't encourage him to kill the man."

"You didn't witness the act, either."

"I didn't tell the cops I did," he announced with a sense of righteous indignation ringing in his tone. "I told them exactly what I saw. What they do with the information is their business."

"You're a piece of work."

"How the mighty done fall," he replied bitterly. "Y'all think you're so much better. But you don't know me. You don't even know what my last name is, do you?"

In fact, I didn't.

"Well," he went on, "I may have spent time in the pen, but I never murdered no one."

"Perry didn't murder Welles, and you know it."

"I don't know nothing of the sorts. Killing happens on your side of the tracks the same as mine. Trouble is, you don't like to see it. You hide the blood under your cotton tablecloths and lace napkins. Maybe under your demitasse cups or spit-polished Paul Revere bowls—see, I ain't as ignorant as you think. Now get your ass off my property." He pointed at my Bug. "Get in your raggedy car and go."

"You must really hate us," I observed.

He grinned, and simply repeated, "Get."

"Bad job or not, you're out of one," I pointed out.

"No, I'm out of yours. I got a lead on another."

I looked at him skeptically, but he didn't take the bait and explain any more. With nothing further I could think of to say, I turned and walked back down the hot, depressing path, then drove away without looking back.

The Kitchen was eerily silent. Not often had I shown up in the middle of the afternoon to find everything locked up, lights out, and no one around. I cracked the blinds to let in some sun and turned on the front-room lights only. A message scribbled by Robbie said he was at the hospital, as Charles had shown his best improvement yet. I made a mental note to touch base with Robbie to find out if that meant Charles was finally out of intensive care.

A growling stomach reminded me I'd missed lunch. In one of the back refrigerators there was some leftover mesquite-grilled beef tenderloin. The thought of warming some thin slices in butter, melting strips of provolone cheese over the meat, topping it with fried onions and bell peppers, and finally tucking it all between a couple of slices of sourdough bread had me salivating. Stomach growling, mouth drooling, the image of gourmet sophistication. But the hot sandwich would have to wait. The few duties I had came first.

Before checking the answering machine in the office, I

made sure the front door was locked. With my luck there'd be a skinhead invasion with only me holding down the fort.

I flicked the office light on, saw that the message machine was full, and decided not to spend the rest of the afternoon checking it. Most likely there were three hundred messages wondering if we were still having the crawfish boil, which I didn't want to ponder at the moment, and which, I was certain, Perry wanted to go on. Crazy.

Actually, there was no one I needed to talk to besides Robbie, Mattie, Claudia, and, of course, C.J. Hesitantly, I punched in his number. I hoped he didn't yell too loudly for me going to Conrad first.

I caught C.J. on his mobile. "Took you long enough," he barked.

"I knew you were at the television studio," I said, trying to sound confident and not sheepish. "What'd you find out?"

"You first."

"What do you mean?"

"Don't bullshit me. I knew you were heading over to see the dishwasher. What'd he say?"

I sat in Perry's desk chair. "Basically the same story Alice gave us, with a few snipes in."

"Snipes? Like what?"

"How the high and mighty have fallen. Class snipes, mostly."

"I guess you saved me a trip," C.J. said.

I thought a minute. "You set me up."

"Damn straight. I knew if I told you to go home, you'd find something to run headlong into. That's why I staked the television station out for myself."

"You could've just asked."

"You're always more alert when you hang out on a limb, and that's how I want you right now. Alert."

You asshole, I thought. But he was right. "So what'd you find out about the TV station?"

"I'll tell you over dinner. This call is costing me money."

I recalled the hot beef sandwich I was going to make and decided C.J. best have someplace good in mind. "What do you have—"

"Carrabba's," he interrupted. "Seven o'clock. I'll put it on the expense account."

Even now you won't give Perry a break, I thought. Carrabba's was a wonderful Italian grill, though by the time we'd be finished, it wouldn't be inexpensive.

But I said, "We'll have to wait two hours at seven."

"Probably not in Sugar Land."

"Sugar Land?" That beef sandwich was starting to sound really good. "I don't want to drive all the way out to Sugar Land. I doubt the food even tastes the same."

"Great." He ignored me. "Meet you in a few hours."

"C.J.—"

And he disconnected us.

"Sugar Land," I muttered aloud, and returned the receiver to its base. "Why in the world couldn't we just go over to the Carrabba's on Kirby Drive, wait or not?" My stomach growled. Oh, shut up, I told it.

I pinched open the blinds and peeked out each of the windows in Perry's office. Only a couple of ladies of the evening getting an early start caught my attention. Judging from their rather hard-bitten appearance, they hadn't started early enough. Next time, girls, get up with the breakfast crowd.

"Sugar Land," I again muttered. What was C.J. up to?

Then I recalled I hadn't told him about Conrad alluding to a new job. Perhaps important, perhaps not. It was, though, the kind of information C.J. wanted to know.

Instead of the grilled tenderloin, I grabbed an apple to tide me over. Then I turned off the lights and let myself out, locking up behind me. At dinner I'd mention Conrad's job.

I bit into the apple, failed to convince myself that since it was better for me than the beef it tasted better, and drove over to my apartment for a change of clothes that would help me blend into the rich suburban Sugar Land crowd.

12

I fought commuter traffic down the Southwest Freeway and exited with the masses at Highway 6. Sugar Land was named appropriately, as the Imperial Sugar factory still operated in the old part of town, down by the railroad tracks. Not so long ago this area was considered countryside to big sister Houston, downtown being some twenty or so miles away. But as Houston expanded like a high yeast dough, the big city closed in on the once-small town on the southwest side. To a large degree, Sugar Land was a set of Houston 'burbs. Corporate America and planned communities, with more popping up every day.

When I finally inched through the green light, I turned left onto Highway 6. The construction of First Colony Mall, the Barnes & Noble, and all the restaurants, many like Carrabba's—which had branched out from Houston— had occurred in just the last few years. In fact, I didn't recognize the area from the breadth of fields and limited clusters of houses it used to be.

Carrabba's was on my left. The parking lot was surprisingly full, though I found a space not too far back. From the groups of people sitting outside having a drink, it appeared there would be a bit of a wait here, too. The tantalizing scent of grilled meat in the air kicked my already complaining stomach into high gear. The apple had long ago been forgotten. I hoped the wait wasn't too long.

I spotted C.J. sitting alone at a small table on the side of the restaurant. He was enjoying a mug of beer and smoking a cigarette. A beer sounded good at this point. But he was smoking a cigarette, I heard myself thinking again. Damn.

C.J. read my mind. "Don't give me any shit about smoking," he grumbled when I got close enough.

In a short, brisk motion, I chopped the air with my hands. "Fine."

He eyed my outfit. I'd worn a dark blue sport coat with matching pants, a light blue dress shirt, and thrown on a red Oscar de la Renta tie for good measure.

"You'd fit right in out here if it wasn't for your hippie hair," C.J. observed. He was more casual in a navy polo shirt and khaki pants.

"And maybe the boots," I added, and flashed my black Tony Lama's.

"Maybe."

"How long's the wait?"

"Half hour, forty-five minutes," he replied.

I could live with that and pulled up a chair. "So why are we eating in candy land?"

"Sherwood Welles did a lot of work in this area," he said.

"So has Perry Stevens."

"You know who has a house in Sugar Creek?"

"Hakeem Olajuwon."

"Besides The Dream."

"Who?" I humored him. A waitress turned the corner. I caught her attention and ordered a Peroni, a decent Italian beer.

"Agnes Berryman." C.J. snubbed the remains of his cigarette out in the ashtray. It was the only butt there.

What he'd said finally hit me. "No, she doesn't. Berryman has taken up residence at the old Rice Hotel, downtown. At least that's where we did our party for her."

"Two possibilities," C.J. pondered aloud. "One, she's in the process of moving since the Rice didn't open that long ago. Or, two, it wasn't her place."

"Or, three, she has two places."

C.J. finished his beer and ordered another when the waitress brought mine. "Put his on my tab, too." The waitress smiled automatically, though when she did I realized how pretty it made her look. Funny, but I hadn't been noticing other woman since Keely and I had become close friends. I wondered what this meant.

"If she had a house in New Braunfels I'd agree she'd keep a place in Houston, too," C.J. was saying. "But this seems a little close. I'll stick with either option one, she's moving, or option two, she borrowed the flat."

"So what's the big deal if magazine queen Agnes Berryman lives in Sugar Land?" I asked, and took a sip of beer. "A lot of celebs and sports figures have houses in the area." I picked up a napkin and wiped foam off my mustache.

"She was one of Welles's major clients. From what I discovered at the television station, too, she was often on the set, as was Nathaniel York."

"What does all this mean?" I asked.

"I don't know yet." C.J. felt his pocket for a cigarette, then caught himself, popped out a piece of gum, and chewed instead. "Linda came across York's review of Welles. It was a very good review."

"Naturally. From the references York made in Perry's article, it's obvious the critic thought Welles was the Chef God."

"Right." The waitress set C.J.'s beer down and informed us our table would be ready soon. I thanked her and received the smile again. Cute, though I laughed at myself for being so easily entertained.

"And the folks there at the television station weren't exactly teary-eyed at Welles's passing," C.J. continued.

"From what I got out of them, he was an *enfant terrible*. Fits, yelling at whoever was handy, the works. One camera-man said it was York who'd often intervene and calm Welles. What's that say to you?" He gulped about a third of his beer down. I nursed mine.

"Welles and York were apparently close," I responded. "Perhaps real close."

"Lovers?"

"Possibly."

"You're guessing."

"But it's possible," I repeated. "If he wanted to use York and his position on the magazine staff, think of the publicity. The jobs with Berryman. I wonder how influen-tial York could've been in landing Welles the television show, too?"

"Berryman is a large advertiser during that slot." C.J. folded his arms.

"What's to become of the show?" I asked.

"The station manager said it'll go into reruns until they decide what to do."

"You mean until Agnes decides to find someone else or back out."

C.J. shrugged.

"I don't imagine Welles's assistant will take over," I commented.

"A downright shame if you ask me."

"You watch that program?"

"Here and there," he told me. "Didn't you ever watch the show?"

"Maybe twice," I defended myself, "but Welles came across to me as just another ego in the kitchen, so I didn't waste my time."

"Hell, I didn't watch it for him. And if you didn't notice his assistant, then you must've been comatose."

"So I understand."

"Beautiful young woman. A knockout blonde, but her hair wasn't her major attribute."

"Dirty old man."

"No, just alive. Her name is Wanda Sims," he added.

"Never heard of her. Where does she work?"

"Lonestar Model Agency."

"I'll be damned," I said to myself. "No wonder Warren Clay wanted to start his own business. Upstaged by a model."

"Wanda told the show's director she couldn't boil water, but that didn't matter to Welles."

"I'm sure he liked it," I told the detective. "Unlikely to show him up, then. She get along with Welles?"

"Apparently, but I haven't talked to her."

"Do you want me—"

"I think I'll send Linda," C.J. cut me off. "Beautiful women don't impress her. Speak of the devil."

I turned and noticed Linda Garcia stroll over to us. She went by her mother's maiden name as a safety precaution, a way to distance herself from C.J. As independent as she was, too, I'd also come to believe she chose to go by Garcia in order to establish her own identity away from her father.

"I miss the cocktail hour?" she asked, glanced at her dad, then stared at me, her head cocked slightly to the left.

"Table's about ready," I said. Linda had an exotic, light-complexioned look that favored her Hispanic mother. Dark hair, dark eyes, and trim. That was what lured me right into our short—but passionate—romance. Lovely, until she opened her mouth.

"Another Neil Marshall mess," she remarked, and sat with us. "Got to bail you out again, huh, kid?"

"Kid, yourself, missy. And I don't need you to bail me out of anything."

Linda patted my arm. "Now don't get all bent out of

shape. The problem with you, Neil, is you can't take a little kidding."

"And the problem with you is you try to run a guy's life," I retorted.

Hands up, Linda said, "Oh, don't worry, buddy. There's no chance of that with you."

"Good." I chugged down the beer I'd been nursing.

"Children," C.J. stepped in. "Have your spat some other time when I'm not a witness to it."

Linda's eyes ran up and down me as in, *fat chance*.

"Cool down," C.J. reiterated to his daughter. "Every time you break up with a man you're hell on wheels for a month."

"You and hotshot Sergeant Hernandez split?" I blurted.

"Never you mind," her father barked.

"Sorry," I muttered to C.J.

"Now, did you find anything out?" he asked Linda.

"York wouldn't see me, and Agnes Berryman wasn't at home or in the office."

C.J.'s eyes narrowed. "York wouldn't see you? Where'd you find him?"

"His apartment in town. Has a maid running interference. I couldn't get him on the phone, and short of forcing myself past the maid, he wouldn't see me when I went to the Rice Hotel."

"The Rice—" C.J. began.

"Hotel?" I finished.

"Yeah, what's the big deal. They've done a nice job of renovating the place."

"I guess that answers that question," I told C.J.

"Most likely," he replied, "Berryman was using his apartment for the party. But why? You sure it was her party, not York's?"

"Positive," I affirmed. "At least that was the way it was

presented to us. Agnes's dinner party. The mayor and his wife were invited, and came."

"So what's the big deal Berryman uses someone else's place instead of her own?" Linda asked.

"Could be nothing," C.J. said. "But I see a picture forming of some very intertwined people."

"So we start asking if intertwined was beginning to mean tangled," I offered.

"Or hog-tied then strung up," C.J. said.

"There's one more thing." Linda dug into a purse that was large enough to hide a small nation. She pulled out a stack of copies. "After striking out for the second time with York, and since I was already downtown, I decided to cruise by the library to check out some back issues of *Texas Tastes*. A tough job, but you said to dig, C.J.

"Anyway, after going through about two and a half years' worth, I noticed something about Nathaniel York's columns. After every two or three mostly positive reviews there tends to be a negative one. Fiercely negative. I copied all the bad reviews, then as many of the others as I had time for." She tossed the pack in front of me. "I figured the places picked out—and on—would mean more to you than me. This is your ballpark, Neil. Might be something there, might not."

"I'll look them over," I said.

"Well, that's better than nothing," C.J. grouched.

"Relax, I'll try Berryman and York again tomorrow," she said. "God, everyone's so uptight."

"Not every day your boss is arrested for suspicion of murder," I said. "Been a long one."

"Doesn't sound that unusual," Linda told me, but obviously the comment was directed toward C.J.'s unpredictable lifestyle.

"I imagine little would."

C.J. cleared his throat. Before he could reply, the waitress called his name to indicate our table was ready. I dropped a couple of bucks down on the table for a tip, and with a sudden quietness, we wandered inside for the long-awaited meal.

13

In my dream I'm jogging in the Heights. I round a corner and suddenly I'm twenty miles away in Sugar Land. I'm unsure how I know it's Sugar Land. I just know. Then an attractive woman, fortyish, pounces from the front door of a large house with a brick facade. She wears a black leather sweat suit and runs along beside me. But not with me. She stares straight ahead, her face a mannequin's expression. I realize she doesn't even know I exist. We turn another corner, almost in sync, and the woman transforms into Agnes Berryman. But I don't say anything because we come upon Perry as he's setting up for the crawfish boil. I stop. Berryman doesn't break stride. She turns a stiff head as she passes and gives Perry a hateful, icy gaze. It turns the sky black. I shiver. My shirt's damp with chilly sweat. Perry glances up in disappointment. A gust of wind ripples through the red-checked tablecloth he's holding.

"I thought you were in jail," I say.

"They found me guilty," Perry replies. "I should have told you everything. Then maybe I wouldn't have had to die."

I awoke with a start and found myself sitting in bed. My heart was off to the races. I often had vivid dreams, but their meaning wasn't always so clear. At least this time one meaning seemed clear. *I wouldn't have had to die,* I thought. I kicked the sweaty sheets aside. There was a slight tremble to my hand as I put on my glasses.

I went into the kitchen and drank a tall glass of cold water. It was shortly after five, with the embers of a new day smoldering over the horizon. I was tired, having slept poorly, and when slept, perchanced to dream. That last dream, though, won the blue ribbon. Or better yet, black.

Arguing with myself that I wasn't going to run today, I dressed in a pair of gray sweatshorts and an Aspen Food Festival T-shirt. Continuing the argument that I was too tired, I could use a break, it might not be safe, I rolled my Willie Nelson bandanna into a headband and tied it on. I grabbed my Nikes, checked that I'd locked the door on the way out, then trotted down the narrow staircase in my stocking feet. End of discussion.

The morning was pleasant, probably in the sixties. I sat on the steps of Jerry's back porch and pulled on my running shoes. Samson the Doberman rustled awake from his sleep. He growled and snapped a couple of barks until he realized it was only me. Then he ambled over and slurped the back of my neck while I finished tying my sneakers. I scratched behind his ear before I rose and stretched my tight muscles.

I took it easy the first half mile, allowing myself to loosen up. In my dream, Perry was dead. And it was because he hadn't told us something. There were times when I wondered if I read too much into my dreams. Or listened too closely. Keely would say no, it was impossible to listen too closely. Of course, she took meticulous notes on her dreams and used them as a guiding force.

My rhythm was off, and I drew in a chestful of air, released it in a rush, and concentrated on getting into that meditative mode. Steady breathing, smooth strides, the soft touch of Nike on pavement.

It struck me that the dream concerning Perry could be

anxiety as much as anything else. On parting last night, C.J. suggested I pay a visit to Perry this morning, run the things we'd learned by him, and see if he had anything to offer. Perhaps I was afraid I'd miss a crucial offering. I might overlook a clue or piece of evidence.

Running the current events by Perry also presented a problem, partially because I wasn't sure I understood them myself. Why did it matter that Agnes Berryman lived in Sugar Land as opposed to the renovated Rice Hotel? And what was she doing in my dream? And then, why did it matter that Nathaniel York lived at the Rice Hotel and loaned his apartment to Berryman for her party? More important, why wouldn't York see Linda? Was he hiding something? If so, what?

And precisely what was Welles's relationship to York? Were they involved? Had Welles used York to reach Berryman and, in turn, land the television spot? In that scenario, how were Welles and York getting along? If they weren't getting along, where did that leave York? The spurned lover? Feeling used and full of rage?

Having gotten ahead of myself, I let that line of thought go. This was a case where a little information could be dangerous.

The neighborhood was quiet with the exception of an occasional barking dog or the appearance of an early riser walking out in his or her bathrobe to collect the morning paper. I kept myself aware of my surroundings, not that I really feared an ambush from the skinheads at this hour. Though, logically, that made little sense, as a skinhead could get up as early as anyone else. But the question was, what were they trying to do, lull me into a state of complacency? Didn't exactly seem their style. So why, as they knew where I lived and worked, had they not made their presence known in nearly a week?

From what I was aware of, the police hadn't rounded

the skinheads up. So maybe they hadn't been around because they were simply not around. In hiding, out of town, until the situation cooled.

Though it sure sounded like their handiwork at Welles's kitchen.

After about a mile and a half I began winding my way back home. An easy three-mile lope was about my speed this morning. My physical speed, at any rate.

Then there was Conrad, I thought. Why was the DA so quick to use his testimony against Perry? How could they dismiss the ex-convict as a suspect so easily? Unless they had more evidence against Perry.

Instead of clearing my head, this run was cramming it full of dirty laundry and hitting the spin cycle. I'd have to make a chart later. Visual people need charts, and at the moment I needed a big one.

I coasted to a stop in front of Jerry's house, then paced from the street to my garage apartment in back to walk off the run. Last night Linda had gotten the assignment to talk to Wanda Sims, Welles's television assistant. I had tried to appeal, but C.J.'d overruled and told me to see Perry. He also suggested I use my friendship with chef Warren Clay to see if he could shed any more light on the relationship between Welles, York, and Berryman. I told him that Clay wasn't really a friend, at best an acquaintance, and he wasn't too socially observant, but I'd suck it up and parley with the man. C.J. had decided to pick up where Linda had left off and badger York himself.

Unwinding, I took a few minutes and browsed through the magazines Linda had given me. Nathaniel York's reviews were as Linda had described. Two or three good, then a bad one. In chronological order. Like a full moon, every fourth issue was when the werewolf in him came out.

Separating the bad reviews, I noticed a further pattern. Two were known gay establishments. One other I was acquainted with the owner, who was also gay. The last I wasn't familiar with, but I'd bet a year's salary it followed suit.

I tucked it all away for future use.

After showering, I pulled on a pair of blue jeans, a denim shirt, and my worn brown leather boots. If I wore preppie attire for too many days in a row, I broke out in a rash.

I picked up the phone and punched in Robbie's number. He answered on the first ring.

"I won't be in today, so if there's anything going on at The Kitchen—"

"You kidding me?" Robbie cut in. "We've had mega cancellations."

"I saw the machine was stuffed with messages."

"And you left them for me," he complained.

"Hey, if it can't be grilled, baked, or boiled, I don't deal with it," I replied.

"Asshole."

"Speaking of, any sign of our evil friends?" I asked.

"Not one."

"Strange."

"I can deal with that kind of strange," he said.

"You deal with many types of strange, I don't want to go there."

"I repeat my earlier comment—"

"How's Charles?" I interrupted, and deflected the conversation away from his new pet name for me.

"Out of ICU, but he's still in pretty bad shape."

"No longer in ICU. That's a start." I paused.

"Are you okay?" Robbie asked.

"Fine. I'm going to see Perry." I thought of my dream and again felt a chill, though I kept it to myself. "Considering C.J.'s not all that fond of the man, he's working hard to prove him innocent."

"McDaniels knows Perry has money and can afford to pay for his services," he explained.

"Cynic."

"Caught it from you. Look, what should I do about the crawfish for the boil?"

"Cancel." The words had the possibility of sounding strong. They were practical, no nonsense, definitive. However, they were also defeatist, admitting the event wouldn't fly, and they brought me down.

"Perry's going to be mad."

"Then don't cancel the order. At least not yet."

"I guess I should go ahead and cancel. After all, so what if Perry gets mad?" Robbie pondered. "What's he going to do about it?"

"Fire us?"

He forced a laugh. "Okay, well, if there's anything I can do—"

"As a matter of fact, there is," I said. "C.J. told me to talk to Warren Clay—"

"And you want me to." He spoke with such pain it sounded as if those were the last words he'd ever say.

"No, not that. Call him up, invite him to lunch, and we'll see him together. Clay knows and likes you. You might be better at getting him to open up than me."

"I don't want him opening up too much. The man's chasing me."

Okay, he could still talk.

"Relax, I'll hold your hand," I assured him.

"Sometimes you're a real—"

"I know, asshole. Well, what do you say? I'll drop by your place after I see Perry, then we'll meet Clay together."

"So really it's you who needs me to hold your hand?" he asked, a lilt of victory entering his voice.

"Absolutely. He won't open up to me."

"You've never signaled you wanted a chance."

"Robbie?"

He chuckled. "Okay, I'll hold your hand. But not his."

14

Perry's arraignment was in the afternoon, but as of nine in the morning he still hadn't been moved downtown. Not knowing what kind of reception I'd get if I blindly entered the station and announced I wanted to see Perry, I put a call in to Lieutenant Gardner first. Gardner politely assured me I'd have no trouble visiting Perry. I didn't.

I sat in the visitors' room opposite Perry. He was still dressed in his civilian clothes, minus his bow tie, belt, and shoelaces. The prison jumpsuit would come once he took up residence in the downtown jail.

Perry appeared haggard. Large dark circles tugged at his dull eyes, and he carried himself stoop-shouldered. The strength was gone. If he were a fighter I wouldn't allow him to answer the next round's bell. Unfortunately, I didn't have that option, and the beating he was taking from the trauma of it all would continue.

"Hang in there. Everyone's working to find out who really murdered Welles," I began.

"Everyone but the police," he replied.

"So who needs their help?" I forced a smile, received nothing back. Beneath the harsh lighting and surrounded by a hollow, gray feeling, this place could depress God. So cut the levity and just get on with it, Neil, I told myself.

"I've got to ask you some questions, Perry—"

"I didn't do it." For the first time his eyes bored into mine. Good, the tenacity hadn't totally disappeared.

"I know," I replied patiently. "What do you know about your stepbrother's relationship to Nathaniel York?"

"What do you mean?"

"Besides the good reviews, York was apparently on the television set quite often while Welles was filming his show," I said.

Perry clenched his jaw, dipped his head back. "I told you I'd met York enough to know who he is."

"Elaborate."

"Why not? I'll tell you who he is, or rather what he is."

I waited. A guard stood motionless in the background. Perry closed his eyes a moment, apparently wanting to choose his words with deliberation.

"Nathaniel York is a hypocrite, a liar, and a whore."

So much for deliberation.

"Let's take those one at a time," I said slowly. "Give me an example of why he's a hypocrite."

"Publicly he's homophobic," he stated. "If you look at his reviews, he often rips apart gay establishments."

Backed up what I'd earlier discovered.

"And the flip side obviously is . . . " I led him to continue.

"Privately, he's as gay as Divine was."

Then that backed up my theory that he and Welles could've been an item. "That flamboyant?" I asked.

"He has his moments." Perry cocked his head and smirked.

"Why the contradiction?"

"Insecurity. Fear of society's reaction."

"In this day and age?" I asked. "In this business, no less."

"I think York likes the don't-ask, don't-tell mentality," Perry concluded. "His insecurity and fear must also stretch to his father."

"The gay-bashing Reverend Gideon York." I shook my head. "Talk of what has to be a hell of a dysfunctional family." A visit to the good reverend appeared in order.

It seemed Perry had nothing more to add, so I moved on.

"The liar part?" I asked.

"Reviews like mine," he replied.

"Whore?"

"Short of a bike dyke, he'll jump anything in pants."

"Prison's hardened you," I quipped.

Perry almost smiled. "York made a pass at me," he explained. "That was how I discovered as much about him as I desired."

"You rejected him," I confirmed.

"Without hesitation."

"Do you think that spurred the bad review?"

Perry gazed at me like I'd just shot myself in the foot, then he leaned back and crossed his legs. "Yes."

"So why did York treat your stepbrother so well?" I leaned forward against the counter that separated us.

"I think that's rather obvious."

"You mean they had a little tryst going on, so Welles was protected," I stated.

Perry started to speak, then stopped, a flash of confusion on his face. "Who had the tryst?" he finally asked.

"York and Welles."

"I think not," he disagreed firmly. "Sherwood was as straight as a sharpening steel. I thought you figured that out when I informed you about him and me parting ways."

I felt a touch foolish, but I understood now. "When Sherwood Welles found out you're gay—"

"He didn't want anything to do with me," Perry finished.

"I see."

"The affair I'm talking about was between Sherwood and Agnes Berryman. At least that's the rumor I heard."

"Then why did you agree to do that job for Berryman?" I asked incredulously.

"Agnes Berryman came to me," he explained. "Up front she said she usually used Sherwood but he was tied up out of town with another job and couldn't do this dinner party. I asked her why me, of all the other caterers around. Agnes indicated she knew who I was and if I was interested perhaps she could serve as the mediator and open the lines of communication between Sherwood and me. I took that as a sign from him, that he was ready to make amends. I believed Agnes Berryman."

"Meaning you think she deceived you."

"I think she used me to get back at him for some reason," Perry speculated. "She knew how paranoid Sherwood was when it came to me. And that review was already planned. The final eye-opener was seeing how furious Sherwood was with me on the night he died."

"Why'd you take the job? You said you no longer cared about Welles," I continued, and ran a hand through my hair then clutched the back of my neck. I squeezed at the tension settling into those muscles.

"Haven't you ever said something that you didn't really mean in order to protect yourself?" Perry inched forward, apparently waiting for an answer.

"Of course."

"Then there's always the risk of letting things go on too long, as I did. Now he's gone, and I'm left with the guilt of not having forgiven him."

And the threat of a guilty verdict for having murdered him hanging over your head, I thought. I redirected the conversation knowing these were feelings Perry would have to work out for himself. Later.

"So York wrote only good reviews for Welles—"

"Because of pressure from Berryman, I'm sure," he broke in.

"I can't argue with that," I consoled. York's latest review still stung Perry even in the midst of this other chaos.

"When she whistles, York comes running, tail wagging," he added.

I scratched my beard. So we'd been looking from the wrong angle, I thought. It wasn't Welles using York to get to the boss. It was a direct connection to the boss. "I guess I'd figured Welles was gay partly because of the way his kitchen was trashed. It resembled a hate crime."

"I can't explain that, but Sherwood wasn't gay. If he was, he wouldn't have had that buxom blonde for an assistant. He'd have had some cute boy."

"Nathaniel York puts up a public persona. Guess I used that logic with Welles."

"No, Sherwood liked the ladies."

"Know anything about his relationship with his assistant?" I questioned.

He shook his head.

I thought a moment to make sure I'd covered all relevant points. "Before I leave," I said, "did you see Conrad at Welles's kitchen the night your stepbrother died?"

"No."

"He says he saw you arguing with Welles."

"I know."

"Were you?" I asked.

"Yes. He accused me of trying to steal his chef and clients, and I called him paranoid, pompous, and ignorant."

I forced myself to sound upbeat. "Alice will get you off."

"I know," he repeated without confidence.

I paused. "Did you notice anyone hanging around when you left?"

"No," he snapped, and I realized he'd answered that question a hundred times already. "And Alice knows what time I left, which was shortly before Sherwood made the 911 call."

The DA would probably allege that Perry left Welles's place as he claimed, but then immediately came back.

"As if I'd tear into Sherwood's place like a gorilla," he muttered. "But Krieger's convinced that's what I did."

"Ed Krieger is depriving some village of an idiot."

Again, almost a smile. However, when I stood and the guard came forward to lead Perry off, that hollowed look returned to his face. "Hang in there," I called.

Perry only turned away.

Not being privileged enough to own a car phone, I had to wait until I reached Robbie's place to call C.J. There was the possibility he wouldn't be as surprised as I was to learn that Sherwood Welles wasn't gay, but I doubted it. At the very least, he'd be interested in the rumor of a liaison between Welles and Berryman.

Robbie let me in and offered me a beer, but before lunch was a bit early even for me. I joined him in a glass of iced tea, then rang C.J.'s answering service and left him the word on Welles.

"I wondered about him," Robbie said after over-hearing my phone conversation. "I thought he was gay, but then I had my doubts, too."

"You don't advertise your sexuality," I pointed out. We sat at his glass-topped breakfast table.

"I can act butch with the best of them," he said, lowering his voice.

I rolled my eyes. "Where we going to lunch, Mary?"

"I take you to a gay bar and you think you can get personal," he said.

I laughed and squeezed a wedge of lemon into the tea. "Lunch?"

"Getting Warren Clay to meet us wasn't easy," Robbie said. "Even for me."

"Then I'd have struck out."

"We're buying."

"Figures. What was the problem?"

"Thinks we're crawling back to him for jobs now that Perry's in jail. Not to mention there's a little friction between us since our boss is accused of killing his."

"I understand his assumption concerning the jobs, but he seemed disenchanted with Welles, to the point where he was leaving."

"Because Clay was leaving doesn't mean he wanted his boss dead," Robbie scolded me. "I think he'd have preferred Welles stick around. Clay was going to show him."

"Clay wanted his due and for Welles to regret having driven him off," I rephrased.

"That's what I think. And don't forget," Robbie added, "that Welles tried to hire C.J. to investigate us because he was afraid we were luring Clay away. Who knows, if Welles hadn't died, maybe he'd have offered Clay more money and recognition to stay."

"Or not. Remember we're not talking about the most personable man in the world. Welles might've gotten a kick out of watching Clay flounder."

"I think he'll make it," Robbie said.

I drank some tea. "I don't. Clay's another village idiot."

"Another?"

"Never mind. I was thinking of something I said to Perry."

"How is he?"

"Taking it hard." I recapped my meeting with our boss.

Robbie finished his tea and stood. He was also jean-clad but instead of a denim shirt wore a maroon polo.

"He will get out of this mess, won't he?" Robbie asked tentatively.

"Of course. Let's go." I handed him my empty glass. God, I wished Keely was around to talk to.

Suddenly I felt like I'd been slugged in the gut. I'd done fairly well so far keeping my feelings in check, basically shut off in that area. Then, when I least suspected it, they jumped me like emotional skinheads, which they had no right to do.

Keely was never mine to lose.

So why was I humming "Send in the Clowns" instead of whistling "The Best Is Yet to Come"?

15

Robbie drove with the windows down and the balmy spring air rolled in on us. A tune by the Wallflowers sprang from the radio. I liked their sound. Jakob Dylan was very reminiscent of his father, Bob, mixed with a heavy dose of Dire Straits. Robbie wasn't paying much attention, nor had he told me where we were going to eat, which dimmed my hopes that it was someplace interesting. Or else it was barbecue. If it was a sin in Texas to dislike barbecue, then I was plain going to hell. Rarely did I eat it, and that was only when I'd cooked the ribs, chicken, catfish, or sausage myself. Never brisket.

Finally I couldn't take it any longer, especially as we cruised down Kirby, where there was a choice of either real or plastic food.

"Where are we going, Robbie?"

He grinned. "Luther's."

My heart sank. Fast-food brisket.

But he turned east onto Westheimer and then swung into the parking lot for the Avalon Drug Store, formerly an old-style drugstore with diner that had gone upscale with the times.

"Funny," I commented.

"You get so hyped up on what you eat and where you eat sometimes you need to chill."

"There's too much good food and precious little time in

109

this world to waste it on places where the container has as much taste as the entrée." We closed our doors and Robbie punched on his car alarm.

"Take something as simple as a french fry," I continued. "When's the last time you had a real french fry? A tasty french fry, not one that's been processed and frozen? When's the last time you took, say, a golden potato, cut it into wedges, and deep-fried it until the potato was perfectly browned on the outside and fluffy and rich on the inside? A little salt, a little pepper, and dip the wedge in balsamic vinegar. Simple, wonderful, and real."

"You're a fanatic."

"Damn right I am," I said, then, not missing a beat as we approached the entrance to the Avalon Drug Store, added, "Or have you ever done oven fries? Wedge that potato, drizzle a little olive oil across them, add salt and pepper, maybe some red pepper and garlic powder, too. Occasionally I add a little basil or oregano. Then bake the wedges at a high temperature, sprinkle some Parmesan cheese on just before they come out, and God, they're good.

"That's how you make a real fry, and there aren't many places that prepare them that way. When I find one, though, that's where I'll go to eat," I concluded.

"I take it back," Robbie told me, "you're not a fanatic, you sound like Perry."

Then he laughed at my scowl.

"In spite of your arrogance, you're still making me hungry," Robbie admitted.

"Is it arrogance to desire the best?"

Robbie raised his eyebrows.

"Well, okay, my dad always told me I had champagne taste on a beer budget," I conceded.

"A wise man."

We took a table near the back, close to the glass window.

The place had started as a hash-slinging diner and drug-store over at the Avalon Center. Even though a number of years had now passed since they'd moved, the name still conjured up that small place that filled every morning with the high-and-mighty power brokers of River Oaks. Perhaps it remained so, but the Fifties atmosphere had given way to Art Deco lighting, an all-window facade facing Westheimer, and lots of colors and shine.

"You think Clay chose this place on purpose?" I asked as the waitress set glasses of water in front of us.

"We're waiting for one more person," he told her. She nodded, took our order for iced tea, then strode off to get another water glass.

"I'm sure you're right," he answered me. "He thinks we're out to make a big deal, so you go where the big boys play."

"Or played."

"True."

I glanced at the menu. Everything was slick and Nineties. So sad. "I know I'm going to have a burger, so why am I scanning the menu?"

"Professional curiosity."

"I suppose."

"But you know their fries won't match up to your standards," Robbie stated casually while staring at his menu.

"When plan A fails, one must fall to plan B."

"Which is?" He glanced over the top of the menu.

"The Julia Child approach."

"I should've guessed."

"Satisfaction's all in the taste," we said in unison, though Robbie's tone was slightly mocking.

"Nothing wrong with that attitude," I told him. "If the flavor's there, the texture, the temperature, then whatever you're eating will probably taste good. And what more do you want?"

Robbie laid his menu down. "I've learned not to argue with you over Julia Child."

"You said she's arrogant."

"I said you were as arrogant as she is." He bit his lip. "I don't want to argue over Julia Child."

"How can you?"

"Exactly. According to you, she's Saint Julia, patron of the culinary arts."

"She is," I agreed, "and always will be."

Robbie sipped his water, glanced out the window. "Here he comes."

I watched as Warren Clay entered through the front door, peered around with his eyes squinted behind his horn-rim glasses and a hand, for some reason, shading his eyes. He caught sight of the hand that I held up and waved back as he scurried in our direction. Observing him move made me think of a dog—a mangy, hungry dog. He was lean and a little gaunt, but there was something about him that vivified my concerns. One such imaginary fear was that if I'd already had my hamburger, he'd take it off my plate and start eating it. Again, he sat next to me.

"How's your hand?" I asked, noticing it was still bandaged from the broken-bottle incident.

"Fine," he answered a little loudly. "Cuts like this take time to heal, don't they? And I'm being cautious so I don't contaminate any food while I work, if you know what I mean?"

Of course I know what you mean, I thought.

"You still have work to do?" Robbie asked.

Clay sighed. "I'm meeting some obligations that Sherwood committed to before he—"

Suddenly his voice choked.

I held Clay's eyes. "I'm sorry about Sherwood Welles, but I don't believe Perry Stevens murdered him."

An instant anger gleamed. The junkyard dog. "Maybe we'd better not talk about this, huh?" he said.

"No, this is one subject we need to discuss," I insisted.

His eyes narrowed.

The waitress asked if we were ready. Robbie and I each ordered burgers. Clay, not looking at the menu, did the same.

"When this place was over in the Avalon Center," I said, "you'd get your hamburger complete with the cook's finger imprints on the top bun from where she pressed it down."

"How appetizing," Clay groused.

"I thought it was funny, something that might happen in your own home," I said.

"You didn't mind because the burger tasted good," Robbie taunted, "and, after all, that's what matters."

"Very good, Robbie." I turned to Clay. "What do you think of Julia Child?"

"She's almost as good as me," he responded. Seriously.

"And I thought you were arrogant," Robbie told me.

"There's always a bigger fish," I said.

Clay acted indifferent to our observations and tucked a napkin in his lap. "So you guys changed your mind, huh?" he began. "Need jobs now, don't you?"

"You always turn your declarative sentences into interrogatives?" I asked.

He gave me a blank look.

"No, we haven't changed our minds," I told him. "And we still have jobs."

"Perry Stevens going to run his operation from the state pen in Huntsville?" Clay snickered.

"I've already addressed that issue," I said.

"You two guys don't want to throw in with me, right?" Clay clarified. He turned from me to Robbie and back. "Then I'm wasting my time."

"Did you see Welles the night he died?" I asked.

"Not after six when I left to go home."

"Was he alone?"

"Yes."

"What did you do that night?" I pressed.

"Hey, what is this? The police have already asked these questions. I don't have to answer you, especially if you don't want to be partners." Clay started to tug his napkin from his lap. Robbie put a hand out to stop him.

"Neil gets excited," he reasoned. "We're only trying to help Perry by finding out what was going on. And I'm sure you know everything about everything, child."

It was hard to tell if Robbie was being sarcastic or shoveling on the bull. Probably a bit of both, though Clay didn't read it either way.

"Of course I do," Clay replied, and left his napkin alone.

"So why weren't you on the television show?" he asked. "I mean, you were the main talent."

"That's right, and then he gets some bimbo as an assistant."

"Why?"

"Obvious reasons, moron," Clay snapped. "And he was also having an affair with her."

I leaned forward, elbows on the table, and interlocked my fingers. "I thought Welles and Berryman were an item."

Clay grinned perversely. "They were. And when she suspected something was going on, she sent Nathaniel York to the set to spy on them. When York confirmed it, Berryman went berserk."

The waitress brought us our hamburgers. No handprints on the buns. How disappointing.

When she'd refilled our iced teas and left, I asked Clay, "How did York confirm the affair?"

"I don't know," he responded, and took a huge bite of

his burger. "But I heard Welles and Berryman upstairs in his office yelling at each other one day," he added through a mouthful of food.

I focused on Robbie so I wouldn't lose my appetite at Clay's table manners.

"Berryman told him he'd better fire the bimbo or she'd see to it his show was canceled," Clay told us.

"Could she have canceled the show?" Robbie asked.

"In a heartbeat."

"But he didn't fire his assistant," I said.

"He ran out of time," Clay stated rather condescendingly.

We fell silent. I had eaten about half of my burger and picked at my fries before striking up the conversation again.

"You know anything more about York?" I asked Clay.

"He's kind of a sleaze, has a reputation, you know?"

"He hit on you, too, didn't he?" Robbie broke in.

"Yeah, and I was desperate," he remarked casually. "All of us go slumming once in a while, don't we?" He chewed on a fry, glanced around.

"That's high rent for slumming," I commented.

Clay laughed at me. "You don't know anything about that family, do you? They aren't much above white trash, and now York's embarrassed by his daddy's ranting and ravings from that high religious horse. And scared."

"Scared?" Robbie prompted.

"That's what I think. I believe Nathaniel York's worried his father would kill him if he found out."

"If the old man learned he had a gay son," Robbie restated.

Clay nodded. "He beat Nathaniel when he was a kid."

"Then the younger York has done well to pull himself up as far as he has," I said.

The waitress came by and refilled our drinks.

"He's Berryman's pet," Clay said, disgust basting his words. "And probably more."

I turned to him. "What does that mean?"

"The man has no pride."

"No," I said, and set my food down, "you meant something else."

"Like what?" he challenged.

"The implication was sexual," I pointed out.

"Maybe he likes to keep up appearances for Daddy."

I stared a minute. Perception was at times as good as reality. Could explain why Berryman used York's place. The presence of a woman would help to curb rumors on a certain level—his father's level. Any more, though, was strictly conjecture on Clay's part. It also occurred to me that his attitude stemmed from something else.

"York broke it off with you," I stated.

He eyed me like *I* was the scum of the earth, then he shook his head at my ignorance and continued eating.

I finished my burger, as did Robbie. Clay worked a while longer on his then dug into the fries. He obviously hadn't heard my treatise on the matter.

I wanted to thank him for the information he'd given us, but I just couldn't. Perhaps because he expected me to.

Instead I asked, "What did you do the night Welles died?"

Again he tensed. I hoped he wouldn't bite me.

"I went to see *Titanic*," he answered. "Alone. And I think the movie's overrated."

"I liked the flick," Robbie chimed in innocently.

"I haven't seen it," I put in.

"You'll probably like the movie, too," Clay told me, the edge not leaving his gaze, "because you're a romantic, not a realist."

Interesting comment, I thought to myself.

"Now that you've soaked all the dirt out of me that you

can," Clay declared, and tossed his crumpled napkin onto his plate, "I'm leaving. This is your last chance to throw in with me, you know? When Perry Stevens gets convicted, don't come crawling back on your bellies."

"We won't," I replied.

He stood.

"So you're fixing to step into Welles's shoes and keep the company going?" Robbie asked.

"I'm fixing to keep the company running, all right," Clay told us, "but I'm going to show it was Sherwood Welles wearing my shoes all these years."

And without a thank you or a have a nice day, Warren Clay turned and left.

16

"I'm going to run up to The Kitchen and check on things," Robbie announced as he pulled to a stop in front of his place.

"All right." I pushed open the door but remained seated. "Do you think Nathaniel York's bisexual?"

"Does it matter?"

"I don't know."

Robie chewed on his lower lip. I couldn't see his eyes, as they were hidden by a pair of Oakley sunglasses. "If he is, it's not because he wants to be."

"You think he leans more toward homosexual?"

"Oh, yes. I know the type," Robbie informed me. "For whatever reason, he's afraid to come completely out of the closet."

"Once again, 'don't ask, don't tell, besides, look at this woman who is here with me.' "

"That pretty much covers the situation as we know it," Robbie agreed.

"What if York's relationship with Berryman caused tension between her and Welles?" I speculated. "What if that's the reason he had a tumble in the hay with his assistant?"

"Assuming the rumored affair between Welles and his assistant is true."

"Yes. Assuming it's true."

"What if?" Robbie reciprocated.

"Right. We have 'what ifs' blowing by us like tumble-weed." I rubbed the back of my neck. "Though I do figure Clay may be right that York's using Agnes Berryman in a game of misdirection."

"Is he using her or is she assisting him? Big difference."

I still didn't move. Thoughts streaked through my mind like flashes of a strobe light. "Do you think what went on between Clay and York was more than a one-night stand?"

"He sure gave you a dirty look when you suggested it was," Robbie stated, and chuckled. "You hit a nerve that convinced me York somehow slighted Clay. Clay didn't mince his words one bit."

I agreed, and unclear what to say further, climbed out of his car. "Later, Butch."

"So long, Sundance," he replied without missing a beat.

I grinned, swung the door closed, and he shot off into the west.

The day was absolutely beautiful. A little warm, but not too humid. I noticed the top of a magnolia tree catch a gust of wind as if an invisible baseball had been tossed into its leafy glove. The tree swayed back slightly then straightened and held on for the first out of the afternoon.

Without hesitation, I hopped into the Bug and drove down to C.J.'s office. Located above a new-and-used record store, it wasn't far from where I'd just lunched. Had I made Robbie aware of my business this afternoon, he would've encouraged me to follow him over to the diner in my car to avoid doubling back. So much for forethought and communication on my part. That was one small symptom of what appeared to be an overall problem at the moment—I was overlooking details, failing to plan ahead, or having trouble staying focused. And I knew why. The busier I kept, the less I thought of Keely moving. Sounded like a physics theorem. *If I were more active than she was, would she be out of my orbit?*

There was also another theorem, whispered the back of my mind—*Damn it, Neil, slow down and think*.

C.J.'s fire-red Mustang as well as Linda's four-wheel-drive, three-quarter-ton pickup truck, also known as a Texas Cadillac, were both parked out front. I added my classic VW to complete the collection. The outside door was unlocked, and I climbed the narrow stairwell to his office.

Sinatra emanated from down the hall, something about flying to the moon. I half expected to see C.J. smoking. He wasn't. Instead he was sitting at Linda's desk in the front room, feet up, and chewing like a cow.

"You still in mourning?" I asked, and pointed to the radio. Usually it was tuned to a country-and-western station.

"Yes."

"He certainly did it his way," was all I said.

Linda stepped in from C.J.'s messy office in back. She flipped open a yellow legal pad. "My mother called Sinatra a male chauvinist and an egotist, among other things," she said, "but she listened to him all the time and watched all his movies. Go figure."

I took one of the chairs in front of the desk. C.J.'s wife, Linda's mother, had died a few years back. The mourning question had been a casual one in reference to The Voice. But C.J.'s pensive attitude and laconic response was a glimpse into his usually closed heart. The roots of loss ran too deep not to produce a blossom of pain.

Sinatra finished his song, and C.J. turned the radio down. Linda was in the seat beside me, notepad open and cradled in her lap, her legs crossed. A healthy cross breeze from the open windows worked on years of stale cigarette smoke that still clung to the air. Traffic noise drifted in and out at irregular intervals.

C.J. got right to business. "What do we have?"

"For starters," I spoke up, "did you get my message about Sherwood Welles?"

He touched the tips of his fingers together and stared at them as he responded. "Not gay, rumored to have been bedding down Agnes Berryman."

"And Wanda Sims," Linda put in. "But this is no rumor. According to Sims, Welles was crazy about her."

Clay nailed that one, I thought, let's try another. "She know Welles was fixing to fire her?"

"You're kidding?" Linda tapped the pad with her pen. "If she knows, then she's sure hiding it well. Sims is pretty busted up inside, boo-hooing through box after box of Kleenex."

"Warren Clay overheard an argument between Berryman and Welles where Agnes said, in effect, get rid of Wanda Sims or the show's history," I informed them.

C.J. locked his fingers together and rested his hands on his belly. "Was he murdered before he could sack Sims, or was he locked in a war of wills with Berryman?"

"The impression I get is that he intended to give Sims her walking papers but met his fate before he could follow through," I said.

"You're positive Wanda Sims knew nothing of her impending dismissal?" the brawny investigator asked Linda.

"She liked the job, seemed to trust everything was fine and dandy."

"Ask her point-blank," C.J. ordered.

Linda sighed, glared in my direction.

"Pardon me, lady," I said, "I wasn't the one handing out the pink slip."

"That girl's bawling her eyes red for a man who was going to fire her, and I have to tell her that." The pen tapping became more intense.

"Sounds to me like she shouldn't be crying for him," I told her.

Linda snarled. "Men," she cursed.

"I know, the bane of all existence," I shot back, "but are you telling me Sims didn't know Welles was sleeping with Berryman?"

"I believe that girl thinks she was his one and only."

I was mystified, and it must have shown.

"Then she's stupid, huh?" Linda asked, and leaned toward me. "Is that what you're thinking?"

"How could she not know? Berryman was often on the set. And the flip side, how could Berryman not know about Sims and Welles?"

"Perhaps Berryman and Welles kept their relationship low-key," Linda offered, "I don't know. I do know that Welles told Sims that there was a no-fraternization rule and they had to keep their relationship hushed."

"She bought that?" I asked even though I had the sense that Linda wanted to hit me.

"Wanda ain't too bright, Neil," Linda said, falling into slang as her father did when stressing a point.

"Good points and good questions, children," C.J. broke in. He swung his feet from the desk and tossed the gum he was chewing into the trash can. "Something I'll ask Agnes Berryman myself." He turned to his daughter. "You'll have to follow up on Wanda Sims, Linda. I don't want to learn later that this young, beautiful, distraught woman plunged a knife into Welles's heart after she found out he was two-timing."

"Same thing can be said of Agnes Berryman," Linda pointed out.

"That didn't escape my attention," he replied.

"Did you talk to her?" I asked.

"Couldn't reach either her or Nathaniel York."

"Maybe that's not so bad. Let me tell you about Nathaniel York." I stood and paced to the window and back while letting them in on York's poison pen, his struggle with his sexuality, and supposed fear of his father. I finished by adding that he was Berryman's spy in uncovering Welles's relationship with Sims and that he and Warren Clay had a fling that left Clay bitter.

"Of course," I added, "Clay's also bitter about playing second fiddle to Welles the past few years. He's looking to get his due now."

C.J. stood and stretched. Unconsciously he slapped his shirt pocket, then frowned.

"Keep on chewing," I said.

His eyes ran the length of my hair. "I am."

Linda tossed the pen on the notepad. "I might as well get it over with." She grabbed her keys from her desk. I was going to suggest she call, but I reasoned that would be considered insensitive. Perhaps to the point where she'd pull the gun from her purse and blow a hole in my head.

"I'll let you know how many trees it costs in Kleenex," she added, and marched down the stairs.

"I want you to come with me," C.J. suddenly said.

I eyed him warily. Usually I had to beg, steal, or lie my way into one of his investigations. "Why?"

"I want someone to see you."

"Someone to see me? Not the other way around?" I clarified.

"Right. If I've got people ducking Linda, then ducking me, it's time to start a fire and smoke them out."

"I don't follow."

He clicked off the radio. "You don't have to. Just get in the car."

"With an offer like that, how can I refuse?"

"You can't," he said, and locked the office door behind us.

17

Gideon York's Church of Christian Soldiers and Moral Activists was located on the south side near downtown Houston in an area where it was not a bad idea to rent a soldier for a bodyguard. At all times. The church—and I use the term loosely—was housed in a large warehouse. A Cyclone fence topped with barbed wire enclosed the building and a surrounding parking lot. Bolted on the inside of the fence was a white sign with the church's name in red-and-blue letters. There were black burglar bars across the two front windows of the warehouse and a thick gate shielding the main door. Three huge garage doors lined the remainder of the facade, all closed.

The gates on the fence were propped open. C.J. turned in and parked next to an army Jeep.

"That his pulpit?" I asked, pointing to the vehicle.

"As a matter of fact, it is."

"I was kidding."

"I've read about this guy," C.J. explained, "and from what I understand, he opens that center garage door, pulls the Jeep in, and stands like he's the reincarnation of George Patton the whole time he preaches."

I studied his face.

"I ain't pulling your leg," he drawled, and climbed out of the car. I followed. On a pair of flagpoles waved the American and Texas flags. Topping the poles were white crosses. Another white cross was bolted at a forty-five-degree angle above the front door. Written in red letters between the cross and the door were the words: VENGEANCE SHALL BE MINE.

"I hope they don't have an arsenal in there," I muttered.

"The cops say they don't."

"I was kidding, again." I couldn't even force a smile.

"I'm not. The police have been monitoring this place pretty hard."

"Great. Is Gideon York crazy, or are we for being here?"

"I reckon you could toss a coin on that one." C.J. pulled on the black iron gate. It was open.

"Why did you want me along?" I asked.

"I want you to be sure that it was Gideon York leading the protesters the evening your friend was beaten."

"I'm sure."

"More important, I want to see his reaction when he sees you, and you tell him his son's gay," C.J. said in a hushed voice.

"You want me to tell him his son's gay?"

"Yep. Since he spotted you outside a gay club, whether he'll admit it to himself or not, your words will carry some weight."

"My words will carry weight just because I was at a gay club?"

"In his mind, you're gay."

"Suppose so. I guess this is one way to stir things up."

"We'll see." C.J. didn't knock. He turned the knob and we walked in.

To the right was a small office with windows that looked out on the warehouse area. There was no one inside. Blinds covered the windows but they were only half-closed. I noticed a desk with a multiline phone system, another desk with a Compaq computer, and a couple of filing cabinets. On one wall was a large laminated map depicting in detail the streets of Houston. Opposite it was a framed picture of Oliver North.

C.J. had wandered a few steps ahead of me. Lighting was spotty. When I fully faced the cavernous warehouse area, I about jumped high enough to see God Himself.

Hanging in the center of the building was a life-size carving of the crucifix. I walked closer. A spotlight shone on the image of Jesus as it dangled down on a steel cord attached to the crown of the cross. Slowly, it rotated at will one way, and then another, presumably so everyone seated in the semicircle of folding chairs arranged around the visage would, sooner or later, catch the full image.

Another American flag stood in the back in one corner, and a Texas flag occupied another. Lining the walls were framed photographs or paintings of almost every military leader since Washington. Eisenhower, MacArthur, Andrew Jackson, Norman Schwarzkopf, Patton. Robert E. Lee. No U. S. Grant, though.

There was supposed to be a sense of comfort to a church. I didn't think even Rambo would feel comfortable here.

"This guy has the gall to advertise on billboards all over town?" I asked.

"And they have proven themselves worth the expense," a voice boomed from behind us. "I have come to learn that there are many lost souls in this city looking for guidance from someone who's not a bleeding-heart liberal."

"That's scary," I told C.J. I stood beneath the crucifix. He motioned for me to turn around.

"I'm Gideon York, reverend-general of the operation," the man stated. "What do you want?" I noticed he was wearing fatigues.

"Do you picket gay bars often?" C.J. inquired.

"Not as often as I'd like to, the godless sinners."

C.J. grinned like they were in cahoots. "You ever get rough?"

York didn't buy it. "Who are you?"

"Are a group of skinheads part of your congregation?"

"You a cop?"

"Private." He gave his name.

"Well, I told you I'm a general, Private McDaniels, so why don't you and your partner make like a couple of whores and hit the street."

I bet he made that up all by himself, I thought.

"Mighty Christian attitude," C.J. said dryly.

Gideon York was staring at me. Finally I saw the recognition spark in his eyes.

"You saved that faggot," he accused, extending his arm and pointing a finger at me. He drew closer. Gideon was shorter than C.J., who I was a head taller than, but stockier than I recalled. If York were a side of beef, there would be enough bulk to feed a small town.

"I suppose I'm going to hell for that."

"How dare you enter my sanctuary!" he bellowed. "You filthy sinner, get out!"

Two huge men entered behind him, also wearing fatigues. At the commotion, they unceremoniously dropped the boxes they were carrying. Together they were the width of Texas.

"How can you hold that attitude considering your own son's gay?" I demanded. There, I hoped C.J. was happy. And I hoped he had a plan to handle the gorillas if this turned ugly. Or uglier.

"That's a dirty lie made up by the godless like you who want to discredit him," Gideon fired back.

"Is that Nathaniel's story?" I asked.

"The unrighteous cannot combat the virtuous without the help of Satan. Nathaniel writes honestly—"

"You mean he's honestly prejudiced. He bashes gay

restaurants and bars and caterers as a way to hide his sexuality."

"Lies!" He started to approach me, then suddenly did a one-eighty and faced his men.

"Why does it matter if your son's homosexual?" I called. My voice scratched the interior like a pepper mill grinding above a platter of hot meat.

"Lies," he repeated, and threw up his arms while walking away.

"What are you afraid of?" I decided to see how far I could push him. "Or are you like your son? Homophobic by day and, and, and," I stammered.

"And a real cocksucker at night," C.J. completed.

My mouth dropped open. "That's rather politically incorrect," I whispered to C.J.

"You didn't have the guts to finish it," he responded.

"A what?" Gideon bellowed. He stopped, fists clenched at his sides, and slowly turned.

"Isn't that what were you going to say?" C.J. asked me.

"Something to that effect, but not so crude."

"The Lord says, 'Do not enter the path of the wicked and do not walk in the way of evil men,'" Gideon proclaimed, his clenched fists rising.

Perhaps he did know his Bible as well as an AK-47. "Proverbs," I informed C.J. "In his own unique way, York's letting us know he's not homosexual. Oh, and homosexual's the politically correct term."

"I haven't been politically correct since the Sixties," C.J. stated loud enough for York to hear. "Not since those commie-hippie-fags ruined this country."

Gideon eyed C.J. warily. "Yes, sir, ruined a damn good country with their flag burning and long hair"—he glared at me—"and deviant sex."

"I didn't have deviant sex in the Sixties," I declared defensively. "I didn't have any kind of sex."

"You're a product of it," Gideon attacked.

"You got me into this," I accused C.J.

"No, your attitude did, kid," he replied. "Yours and all the people like you. Country was great before I went to Vietnam to fulfill my duty. Came back and all of a sudden I was a killer. Southeast Asia was hell, but so was coming home."

"You were in 'Nam?" Gideon asked.

"Yes. I volunteered early on. Were you?"

York's eyes darted, and I knew he was deciding whether to tell the truth or not. Finally his gaze rested on the image of Christ, and he came clean. "No. No, I wasn't. I tried, but I have a—no, I wasn't."

A what? I wondered.

"So I wage my battles here," Gideon explained. "Against queers like him." He nodded in my direction. "For God will scatter the bones of the ungodly."

"Sure, after you break them," I accused.

"I fight using the word of God."

"And the brawn of oxen," I added, implying his thugs.

"Be careful," C.J. warned under his breath, "he's a man of cloth—a dangerous one—don't sound unrighteous."

"Me unrighteous?" I said loudly. But that set Gideon off again.

" *'Do you not know that the unrighteous will not inherit the kingdom of God?'* " he thundered.

"He's digging into First Corinthians for the knockout punch," I whispered to C.J.

" *'Do not be deceived,'* " Gideon continued in an affected, bass, preacher's tone, " *'neither the immoral, nor the idolaters, nor adulterers, nor homosexuals will inherit the kingdom of God.'* "

"You left out the thieves, the greedy, the drunkards, the revelers, and the robbers," I said.

"He was stressing a point," C.J. announced.

"Precisely," York agreed. This tentative bond that was forming from C.J.'s game was making me ill.

"Try this," I countered. " '*You hypocrite, first take the log out of your own eye, and then you will see clearly to take the speck out of your brother's eye.*' Matthew. I'm a New Testament kind of guy."

Gideon, appearing unimpressed, partially quoted the verse that followed mine. " '*Do not give dogs what is holy; and do not throw your pearls before swine.*' "

"What is this?" C.J. muttered. "Dueling Bibles?"

"I don't reckon that's all he duels with," I followed through clearly. "I don't wonder if he has an underground army to tear up, say, a defenseless man's kitchen?"

Gideon stiffened. "That hippie fag's been a bad influence on you," he told C.J.

"I don't pay no mind to that kind of crap," the big detective said lazily. "I mean, why would you have an underground army when you have the Big Guy looking over your shoulder?"

"What do you make of Heckle and Jeckle over there?" I asked. "Those two could take over any Central American country they had a hankering to."

C.J. waited for Gideon to respond.

"There are a lot of crazy people in this city," York explained, straight-faced. "A person in my position needs a couple of good men to watch his back."

Crazy people in this city. A person in my position. The man was serious. The words in my mouth stuck like caramel to my teeth. I couldn't get a syllable out.

C.J. stepped up to the plate. "What does a person in your position fear?"

"Retribution for spreading the Word. For spreading truth," he replied, then pulled from Isaiah. " '*Truth is lacking, and he who departs from evil makes himself a prey.*' "

"Is that like a good offense is a good defense?" I asked.

"You ought to learn a little tolerance, especially considering your son. *'If anyone says, I love God, and hates his brother, he is a liar.'* The First Letter of John."

"Enough," he cried, and drew from John himself. " *'He who commits sins is of the devil.'* "

"And you," I adapted to Isaiah, " *'put on garments of vengeance for clothing, and wrap yourself in fury.'* "

"Heretic!"

"You call him a cocksucker," I told C.J. softly, "and he's still attacking me."

"Because you're a bad person," C.J. whispered back. "And you're also keeping up with him, hitting him where it hurts."

"I'm bad? This guy sounds like your classic frustrated artist," I announced, referring back to C.J.'s example of what happens when hate and intelligence tie the knot. "Remember the little altercation the last frustrated artist caused in the world?"

Gideon paced back and forth then whipped around. "You're calling me a Nazi," he said. "I'm no Hitler. You see these American flags around here? I'm for God and America, love it or leave it."

"How democratic—agree or get out."

"The kid doesn't understand patriotism," C.J. explained.

"Patriotism, my ass," I shot back.

Gideon pointed toward the high ceiling. " *'Then I looked, and I heard an eagle crying with a loud voice, as it flew in midheaven, "Woe, woe, woe to those who dwell on the earth—"'* " On cue with the *woes* his trembling finger angled in my direction.

"I know," I responded, "Revelation, somewhere between the fourth and fifth angels blowing their trumpets."

"I must say I'm impressed," said C.J. "You do know the Good Book, but this could go on forever."

"Like Satan, he knows the words but twists their meaning to suit his needs," Gideon expounded.

"A more suitable self-description I couldn't have said myself," I told him.

Suddenly York grabbed his ears. "Get the hell out of here, the both of you! This is private property, get out!"

Neither of us said anything. I'd never been kicked out of a church before.

"You're not part of my parish, and I don't want anyone in here who went to 'Nam and then sold out." He faced me. "And I never wanted the likes of you."

"Does your son belong?" I asked calmly.

He tensed, trembled, then turned surprisingly calm. "These are my deacons," he said, and extended an arm toward them. "They'll show you out."

"We know the way," C.J. said. I followed his lead.

The two Brahma bulls blocked the exit. C.J. didn't stop until he was a couple of feet from them.

"The Lord will have his vengeance for your lies and blasphemy," Gideon told me.

"The Lord?" I questioned. "Will He arrive in the form of four skinhead angels of death?"

"I don't associate with them. I don't have to."

I glanced at the breadth of fatigues before us. "I guess you don't when you have your own national park on legs."

C.J. cracked a smile.

"And I don't allow violence inside my church," Gideon declared.

"But outside is a different war game," I said, and verbalized the unspoken threat. "So what you're telling me is that we're walking out of here without getting our legs broken because we're, well, inside. But next time?"

"God be with you, boy." His eyes glazed over and a grin crept to his face as if he were suddenly lost in a world wild with fantasy. A world, I was sure, where I didn't fare too well.

C.J. pushed by the wall of muscle with me in tow. Once outside neither one of us loitered.

"He doesn't allow violence inside his church," I repeated, disliking the taste of the words. "Is he a walking oxymoron or what?"

"No, just a moron." C.J. fired up the car and we sped away from the center for dysfunctional militant evangelists.

"Now, what was the point of that visit?" I asked.

"I reckon Nathaniel will be calling on us."

"We going to play hard to get, too?"

"Only with Gideon's goons." He clicked on the radio, combing for more Sinatra, I suspected. Then he asked, uncharacteristically, as if he couldn't stand it, "How'd you come to be so biblical?"

"My mother," I replied without explanation.

He grunted. "Came in handy." Brief but with admiration.

Inside I smiled, but I stated, "And sure, you set me up as the bad cop while you pry and sympathize as the good cop."

"Whatever works."

"They could be after me more than ever."

"They could," said C.J. "Except he got pretty pissed off when you made the Nazi crack. And those skinheads are walking swastikas. Might not be his style."

"Is that your gut reaction?"

"Hard to tell. A strong sense of violence covers York."

"No kidding," I told him. "Next time I want to be the good cop."

He only laughed.

And, surprisingly, I felt good.

18

C.J. and I both decided that even though Gideon York had a Houston address, it didn't follow that his mind resided there, too. Bullets and Bibles mixed as well as alcohol and automobiles. Gideon York was a man ignorance had blessed repeatedly until he was so frightened of the world that, as was true with many fanatics, only two constants remained—religion and violence. Or rather, violence in the name of religion. Changing attitudes, tolerance of other people's views, and free will were threats to York's order. What men like York didn't see was that any attempt to maintain their order only begot chaos. And out of this chaos, the new social order simply became stronger, more determined to shake the Yorks from its hide like a dog scratching at fleas.

C.J. responded to my social diatribe by grunting.

"A grunt," I said. "I talk about social change—global change, for that matter—at the close of the millennium and you can only grunt? What are you thinking?"

"There's an outside possibility they ripped apart Welles's kitchen," he reasoned, "but the way he was murdered wasn't their style. A group of skinheads or radicals like beating people, not finishing them off cleanly, almost mercifully."

"Almost," I agreed. "But something with that scenario

bothers me now that we've met Reverend-General Gideon York."

"I'm waiting," he said after a moment. C.J. was traveling with the flow, or at times nonflow, of the late-afternoon traffic.

"The good reverend-general strikes me as a man who'd tag along and watch his ruffians smash up a place. Say they're interrupted, unexpectedly so. I could picture York crying something biblical, drawing a handy chef's knife, and plunging it into Welles's heart."

"You're saying Welles got whacked because he was in the wrong place at the wrong time?"

"Why not? A victim of fate, of Gideon York's self-created chaos. It could as easily have happened to Perry," I ventured. Something occurred to me. "Gideon's clever enough to send a threat dressed up as a sick recipe. It didn't have to come from Welles."

"I'm not assuming the threats did."

"They stopped when he died."

"Could be to throw suspicion," C.J. suggested.

"Gideon York—"

"He made quite an impression on you. But if he sent threats, don't you think they'd reflect his holy-roller attitude?"

"I suppose they would," I acquiesced.

"And Welles doesn't fit the profile," C.J. continued. "He wasn't gay."

I thought a minute. "You're right. Damn."

Again he grunted.

"But what if he *thought* Welles was gay," I offered.

C.J. slowly chewed a piece of gum. "I suppose it's possible. Trouble is, we have no evidence they were there."

"If you go strictly on that criterion, then the situation doesn't bode well for Perry," I noted.

"Somewhere there's a clue, a shred of information, that's going to inject a touch of sanity into this situation."

"What do you call this, buckshot detective work? Blast everything and find out what remains."

"Not as eloquent as your social commentary, but close enough."

"So you *were* listening to me," I exclaimed.

"What haven't we blasted?" He ignored my comment.

"You mean who. Agnes Berryman and Nathaniel York. And since York will come to us—"

"Off to see Berryman," he finished, and headed for her office.

We cruised downtown as much of the workforce began to head out for the day. *Texas Tastes* was located in the Republic Bank Building, which, actually, no longer went by that name. I'd lost track of what it was now called. Not that it mattered. For me the building would always be tagged as the Republic Bank, and with its sculpted, tiered facade—classic as opposed to slick modern glass—it was, next to the Esperson Building, the most handsome structure in the city.

People spilled out of the elevators while a handful of us got on to take the ride up. *Texas Tastes* occupied an entire floor some twenty-plus stories above the city streets. After gliding to a stop and stepping out, we immediately faced a receptionist.

"Can I help you?" she inquired.

C.J. began to speak when the phone rang.

"One moment, please," the young woman said to C.J., pushed the active line on the phone, and spoke into the delicate microphone of the discreet headset she wore.

I glanced around. Not being well educated in interior design, I had no clue whose flavor had decorated the office. There was a feel of modern-classic, if such a thing were possible, with an array of highly polished furniture and Texana objects—I noticed a letter from Sam Houston displayed under glass—starkly arranged in a well-lit, whitewashed room.

The young woman ended the phone conversation and looked at C.J.

"I'm here to see Agnes Berryman," he told her.

"Your name?"

"C. J. McDaniels and I don't have an appointment."

"Well, I'm afraid, then—"

"Is she here?" C.J. interrupted.

"I'm not at liberty to say."

C.J. leaned down. "Push whatever button on the phone that connects you with her office and tell her this: I want to talk about the murder of Sherwood Welles."

The receptionist stiffened, color drained from her face.

"Go ahead."

"She's already talked to the police."

"I'm a private investigator. Push the button."

The woman did. Hesitantly she identified C.J. and stated his purpose.

"Also tell her," C.J. added, moving even closer, "that I know about her affair with Welles. Would she like to finish the conversation in private?"

"I can't repeat that," the woman said, suddenly appearing very young in her girlish embarrassment.

C.J. slowly nodded.

"Ah, yes, ma'am," she suddenly said into the phone. "Yes, he did—" The woman returned her attention to C.J. "She hung up. She heard what you said."

"Good." He stood straight and folded his arms. I could see him counting in his head, waiting for a door to open. One right behind the receptionist did, and out steamed Agnes Berryman.

"How dare you?" she started in on C.J., but stopped upon seeing me.

"Mr. Marshall, what sort of low trick is this?"

"I need to ask you a few questions," C.J. spoke up. "Is there someplace private we could go?"

"I could call security," she replied.

"Then I'd be forced to go to the police with my information, and you would have no choice but to deal with them," C.J. stated quietly.

Agnes Berryman really could be a beautiful woman, I thought, if her face wasn't always contorted in anger and there wasn't a chip the size of the Astrodome on her shoulder.

With a huff, she stormed back through the door she'd emerged from.

"Was that a sign she wants us to follow her?" I asked.

Berryman poked her head out. "Well?" she snapped.

"No," C.J. said, "*that's* the sign."

We entered a conference room where the wall behind the head of the table was one large window looking out onto the city. A number of tall buildings surrounded us. In a strange way it gave me a rather secure feeling, kind of like hanging on to your father's pant leg when you were little and looking up at a benevolent protector.

Berryman half sat on the head of the table and crossed her arms.

C.J. didn't bother to wait for a prompt. "You were having an affair with Sherwood Welles," he stated.

"So?"

"He was having an affair with Wanda Sims," he added.

"Did that little bimbo tell you that?" Berryman's auburn hair, wound up in a bun, accented skin that was smooth as granite and a pair of deep-set seething eyes. Dressed in a black pantsuit, she bordered on frightening. However, she appeared to have no effect on C.J.

"Yes," C.J. answered her question.

"That's her little fantasy," Berryman said. "I heard she

told everyone who'd listen she was dating Sherwood, when, in fact, he hardly noticed her existence."

"He must have noticed more than that," C.J. objected. "I've got a witness who overheard an argument between you and Welles in which you demanded he break it off and fire Wanda Sims or you'd pull the plug on the show."

Berryman winced. She opened her mouth a couple of times to speak, and I knew she wanted to deny it. But she just couldn't bring herself to do it.

"That little tart chased him until finally, one time when I wasn't there to protect him, he broke down."

"Why didn't you fire her earlier?"

"She was good for the show." Berryman smirked, then added, "Until cost outweighed gain." Her eyes rested on the tabletop.

"That made you pretty angry," C.J. said. "You still are."

Slowly, his implication dawned on her. "You bastard." Berryman stood straight and swung to slap him.

C.J. blocked her blow with the back of his hand. He maintained his poker face, though from the sharpness of the pop, I knew that had to sting.

"I loved him." She was fighting hard to hold in the tears.

"There are acres of gravestones loved ones helped erect."

"Damn you." She turned her back to us and stepped to the window.

We waited in a silence thick as cast iron.

C.J. eventually shuffled from foot to foot, but I spoke first. "Perry Stevens didn't murder Welles," I affirmed.

"No?" she said to the window.

"No."

Berryman dabbed at the corners of her eyes, drew a deep breath and released it, then turned around.

"Then who did?" she asked.

"We don't know," C.J. answered.

"Perry, I'm sure, wanted to, as there were times when I could have . . ." Berryman allowed her voice to trail off without completing the thought.

C.J. pulled a chair out for her. She accepted it and we all sat.

"Did you know he was threatening Perry Stevens?" he asked.

Her eyes narrowed. "How so?"

C.J. cued me and I informed her of Dead Man's Broth.

"There were many sides to Sherwood, but I don't think terrorism was one of them." She sighed.

"If he did send the threats, you knew nothing of it," C.J. translated.

"Had he been acting so roguish, I'd have—" She stopped, then said, "Correct, I knew nothing of it."

Instead of focusing on what she was about to say, or pushing her further on what she had, C.J. waited. It worked.

"You see, Sherwood was charming, a delight to be with," Berryman began. "I'd laugh for hours on end. At the same time he would overreact to problems. He'd get mean, act paranoid—for instance, one time an employee of mine and I flew to Austin to do a story on Laura Bush. We stayed overnight, in separate rooms, of course. Sherwood went raving mad. He had the audacity to accuse me of having an affair, threw the poor guy through part of the staging on the television set, and swore he no longer trusted anyone.

"Later I found out," she added, "that was the weekend he and the bimbo got together. He was projecting himself onto me."

"Would that friend be Nathaniel York?" C.J. asked.

Suspicion cloaked her face but she eventually nodded.

"And turn off your dirty little mind," she told C.J. "I'm not exactly Nathaniel's type."

"I bet that's not what his father thinks," I said.

"Really? I don't know anything about that."

"The man's a lunatic," I told her.

"Yeah, well, we all have family members we don't want to own up to."

"Who's yours?" asked C.J.

A smile slithered onto her face. "That's really not important, is it? Do you have any other questions?"

"Where were you the night of Welles's death?" C.J. took out his gum and stuck it in the plastic casing it had come in. He set the refuse on the table. Agnes Berryman looked disgusted.

"I've already answered those questions for the police," she replied. "Anything else?" Her guard that had briefly dropped was up and firm again.

"Would you have canceled the show?" he went on.

"If he hadn't agreed to fire the bimbo? Absolutely. And we were right in the middle of a big project, too."

"Which was?"

"A joint venture between my magazine and his show. We were calling it *Together in Texas: A Collection of Contemporary Culinary Artists*. He was going to host a chef from around the state, feature the guest's operation, and I was to follow up with an article and recipes. And if this had proven a success, we were going to take it national, then maybe even international." Berryman shook her head.

Grand dreams, I thought. "What's the fate of the show?"

"I don't know." A short laugh escaped her. "Sherwood's chef with the droll personality approached me about taking over."

"Warren Clay?" I asked.

"That poor little fool actually thought he could fill Sherwood's shoes."

"You don't," I stated.

"Indeed not." She paused. "Ironically, the only person I can think of who even comes close is in jail."

My mouth fell open. "After the disagreement you two had?"

"I'm not saying he'd get the job, only that he'd have been a prime candidate. He stood up to me. I respect that. And the bottom line is business is business."

I caught C.J.'s eye. We stood together.

Berryman remained seated, an elbow on the table, and her chin resting in her hand.

"Thank you," I said, but received no response.

"One last thing," C.J. asked.

Her eyes lifted to his direction.

"How bad was the blood between Welles and Nathaniel York?"

"Oh, there was a little animosity," she admitted, "but I wouldn't really consider Nathaniel a serious suspect."

"Why not? You said Welles slapped the man around."

"And he probably enjoyed it," she replied dryly. "Besides, if it's not with a pen, Nathaniel doesn't have the guts to confront anyone."

"He's been avoiding us." C.J. drew attention to that fact.

"Like I said, he's not big on confrontation."

"Why did he write a nasty review about Perry?" I spoke up.

She shrugged. "That's the way he saw it. When it comes to his column, Nathaniel has a free rein," she explained. "I don't suggest, nor do I edit."

Yeah, right, I thought.

"Believe what you like, but that's the truth," she added.

"I want to talk to him," C.J. declared.

"He's not in the office today," she replied.

He tried to gauge her response. I couldn't read whether or not she was telling the truth.

"York at home?" he finally asked.

"Perhaps."

"That'd be the Rice, wouldn't it?"

"Yes."

C.J. thanked Agnes Berryman, and we left her sitting alone, at the large conference table, the silence of the evening closing in around her. I felt drained and a last glimpse of Berryman only added a touch of melancholy. Whether she was mourning the loss, regretting the deed, or both, I was unsure.

Out on the street, I told C.J., "I feel like someone's given me a whip and told me to stave off the wind."

"Call it a day, Neil."

"You want to grab dinner and try to make sense of this?"

"I have to meet a client in Galveston," C.J. said. "Something about a missing wife."

We paused at a crosswalk and waited for an ambulance siren to scream by before we continued.

"If she's missing it's probably on purpose," I observed.

"Usually is, but I'll hear him out. Don't worry, I'll be back tonight. And ready to tangle with Nathaniel York tomorrow."

After a minute I asked, "What do you think Berryman was going to say about the threats to us?"

"Something to the effect of wringing his neck had she known." He glanced at his hand. There was still a red mark from her slap. "She packs a wallop," he commented. "Might've been able to do it, too. Under the circumstances, she must have decided it was a politically incorrect thing to say."

"Politically incorrect?"

"I was trying to sound like a smart college boy."

"A man's got to know his limitations," I shot out.

C.J. looked back at the Republic Bank Building. "So has a woman," he said soberly, and we reached the car without another word.

19

I tried reaching Candace, thinking a good horseback ride might be relaxing, but she wasn't at the stables. Keely tugged at my mind. I knew, though, she was fixing to leave for California and having enough trouble with Mark that she didn't need me pestering her. A quiet evening at my apartment appeared to be the schedule when Robbie phoned.

"I talked to Alice. Perry's being held without bail," he told me.

"I imagine that pretty much sums up how things went at the courthouse." I poked through my kitchen cabinets, looking to see what I had to eat.

"Pretty much," he agreed.

"She offer an assessment?" Behind a nearly empty bottle of olive oil there was a can of enchilada sauce, some chicken soup from when I had the flu last winter, a bag of dried red beans, and maybe a quarter cup of rice. I wondered why I'd save such a small amount of rice.

"Actually, Alice is fit to be tied," Robbie continued. "She says the Oilers have a better chance of moving back to Houston than the DA does of winning the case."

"Why the hell's it going to trial then?" The question was directed more toward the cosmic forces that be than toward Robbie. I pulled open my refrigerator, the inside

145

of which was more stark than my cabinet. Somebody needed to do some shopping around here.

"I guess the flecks of blood and towel fibers they found in Perry's car was the clincher," he stated.

I let the refrigerator door swing wide open, took the cordless phone from my ear, banged it a couple of times on the countertop, then asked Robbie to repeat what he'd just said.

"Damn, Neil, my ear's on the other end, here."

"Sorry, but there's something wrong with my cordless," I added. "I thought I heard you say there was blood in Perry's car."

"There wasn't anything wrong with your phone."

"Not good. Next you'll say they matched the blood to Sherwood Welles."

"I guess I don't have to."

"And Perry has no idea how the blood got in his car," I concluded.

"Actually, he fessed up to Alice that he found a bloody chef's knife wrapped in a kitchen towel in his trunk."

I groaned.

Robbie took that as a sign to continue. "Now, he has no idea how that stuff got in his car."

"Naturally."

"Perry freaked out and dumped the knife and towel, then barricaded himself at his home."

That explained the lock-in. "Where'd he dispose of the evidence?" I asked.

"He doesn't remember. Some trash can between The Kitchen and his town house," Robbie replied.

"Did he even attempt to clean his trunk?"

"Does it matter now?"

"No," I responded. "But not only did he panic, he tried to keep it from us. Damn."

"And Perry's on the verge of a nervous breakdown," he added.

"So when are the Oilers moving back?" Besides a half gallon of milk, a couple of eggs, a stick of butter, there were two bottles of Shiner Bock. Having determined I had nothing to fix for dinner, I closed the door and opened one of the brews as a consolation prize.

"Alice smells a setup," he said.

"No kidding?" I quipped.

"All right, smart-ass, who done it?"

"Swing and miss," I told him. "About everyone I've come in contact with could've done it."

"But only one positive ID."

A mouthful of the cold, rich beer slid down the back of my throat. "And your point is?"

"I don't believe Perry was the only person at Welles's kitchen the night he died," Robbie said.

"He wasn't."

"Besides Conrad," he said. "And Conrad's lying."

"Or selectively telling the truth." I thought it was time C.J. took a crack at Conrad.

After a short stretch of dusty static, I asked Robbie if he'd eaten.

"I suppose I ought to have something," he droned.

"What if I meet you at Kim Son for Vietnamese?"

"I don't want to drive downtown."

"We don't have to go to the restaurant downtown," I said.

"That's the one I like."

"Then how about Churrascos?" I suggested. "You're usually up for South American cuisine."

"Not tonight."

"Café Express?"

"I'd rather go to Café Annie but they'll be packed by now," he said.

I threw up my arms. "Never mind, Robbie, I think I'll just whip up some pasta."

"Cream or red sauce?"

"Olive oil and spices with Roma tomatoes and feta cheese." I scanned my mind for a recipe. "Something like that."

"Sounds good. What can I bring?" he asked.

"If you wanted to come over, why didn't you ask?"

"I didn't want to invite myself," he said.

"You just did," I pointed out.

"But only after you offered to cook."

I couldn't help but laugh. "Bring a bottle of wine," I told him. "Give me half an hour, though. I've got to run to the store to pick up a few items." Yeah, like everything, I thought. And we hung up.

A warm breeze rolled off the Gulf of Mexico and stroked the city like a tender hand tousling a small child's hair. I mulled over a list of ingredients in my mind while I drove over to the market. With Perry sinking deeper I needed to hash out what was going down. But I also needed a break, something else to concentrate on to clear my mind. So it was food.

This meal would be more improvisation than by the recipe. Basil, Italian parsley, olive oil, garlic, chives, sun-dried tomatoes, and the Roma tomatoes for starters. I thought I'd use angel-hair pasta, then add strips of fresh spinach shortly before the dish was ready to serve. At the market they had a shipment of fresh jumbo Gulf shrimp, so I picked up a pound. I almost forgot the feta, which would've depressed me into lethargy. Before leaving, I collected what I needed for a Caesar salad and picked up a French baguette.

Nothing against Robbie, but this was a meal I wished I was sharing with Keely. At another time, in a different world.

I bounced the Bug into my driveway, shifted to neutral, and drifted to a stop directly in front of none other than the sons of the Third Reich. Instinctively, I threw the car into reverse. Had I not realized at the last second what was happening, I'd have been out of there before they could've jumped me.

The skinheads had Linda.

Linda was a wildcat, but here she was plain outnumbered. The side of her face was bruised, and her blouse was torn at the shoulder. She was struggling as they took her down on the grass in the backyard, a skinhead on each arm, and one tugging at her jeans. The fourth skinhead, the one with the cold blue eyes, taunted a ferociously barking Samson. The Doberman was straining at his chain, just out of reach.

With all the mental forces I could muster, I tried to will Samson loose. No such luck. And Jerry Jacoma's truck wasn't in its usual spot, so he wasn't inside calling the cops.

I threw the VW back into neutral and bolted toward them. For a brief moment I hoped to fight off the attackers long enough to steal Linda away in the Bug. A very brief moment.

The apparent leader turned to face me just as I sprinted in. Unfortunately, this time he was able to brace himself for my charge. I ducked and attempted to nail him with a low shoulder, but he managed a quick sidestep and landed a sharp blow against my back. Stumbling, I fell to one knee, then took a hard kick to the ribs that lifted me over to my back. Instead of trying to get up, I rolled, which is perhaps what saved me. He threw a leg whip where my head would've been had I risen, and missed. It sent him off balance. Sensing my chance, with his back to me, I sprang up and drilled a right into his kidney. A sharp cry of pain escaped him as he staggered and fell.

The skinhead who was working on Linda's pants

jumped up to help. Without hesitation, I caught him with a left jab followed by a hard right that felt like it broke his jaw. He twisted to his hands and knees. The skinheads who had Linda's arms pinned released her and stood.

Samson barked rancor that was straight from hell. The new chain that Jerry had bought, however, continued to prevent him from acting out his hostility.

Then, for a split second, everything froze. Like a replay from our earlier encounter, the leader had recovered and was slowly circling back to me from the left. The skinhead on my right took a martial-arts fighting stance. The one on the left crouched. The only good aspect about being surrounded was that the fourth skinhead was still down, stunned.

Hate steamed from those cold blue eyes. He continued to circle until they had me in a triangle.

"I vowed to kill you, and now I can," he growled.

"Finally work up the nerve?" I dug.

His laugh was more like a hiss. From the grin on his face I suspected the odds were good he was going to enjoy this.

And then Linda shifted the odds. Having pulled herself together, she shot up quick as a mountain lion.

"Bastards," she cried while angry tears streamed down her face. In one smooth motion, she stood, turned, then whipped a right-legged kick into the leader's groin. The shock washed the hate from his eyes and the grin dropped as he fell to his knees.

I knew Linda had a black belt to the one-millionth degree in one of the arts of terror, but this put it in a whole new, highly realistic, light.

And it was all the break we needed.

I stepped into the skinhead on my left, the one not in the martial-arts pose, and threw a left jab that caught him square in the nose. His hands sprang to his face and he doubled over. To my surprise, the remaining skinhead looked momentarily hesitant. Until the first one I'd nailed in the jaw finally shook it off and stood. Then the one whose nose I'd broken straightened, took his bloody hands from his face, and let out a horrendous howl.

You could beat these guys all night and they'd come back for more, I thought.

Linda then landed a swinging kick into the martial-arts skinhead who was concentrating on me. As he went down, I grabbed Linda by the arm. She resisted. I yanked, and we ran.

A flash of dashing to Samson and releasing him zipped through my mind. Then the image of one of them pulling a knife—whether they had them or not—and slashing the Doberman discouraged me. I couldn't go through that again.

"Where's your gun?" I demanded.

"Where's my purse?" she shot back.

"I don't know."

"That's where my gun is," Linda snapped. She wouldn't look at me.

The Bug had stalled, not that we had enough time to jump in before they reached us, anyway. I shoved the door closed as we ran by, noticing the keys hung from the ignition. A few steps later I glanced back to see if the knotheads noticed. They hadn't, and came storming after us. All I needed was for them to get a key to my apartment and The Kitchen.

Running in boots did not contribute to my usual lilt. And I was clutching my side. Linda, on the other hand, was in her Nikes and doing just fine. Well, mostly fine.

"We need a plan," I called.

"Split up?"

"No," I objected a little too harshly. "I mean—"

"Never mind."

I took us out to the middle of the neighborhood street

where it was obvious we were running for safety in hopes someone would call the cops. Also, I guided us toward the very busy Heights Boulevard.

"They're coming hard," Linda warned me.

I was a runner, but not a sprinter. And Linda was keeping up with me, not me with her. About time to pull on the reins and duke it out, I thought, when a car came to a screeching halt beside us.

"Get in," said Robbie, reaching back and pushing open the back door.

We wasted no time. He burned rubber, directly at the skinheads. They dove aside.

Together Linda and I sat gasping for breath.

"I wish you'd run them down," Linda managed to say.

"I tried."

My heart slowed to a furious race. I could almost get enough air. Slowly I came to realize how much my ribs hurt where I'd been kicked. Robbie glanced at me in the rearview mirror.

"I'll tell you in a minute," I announced with a puff.

"I know," Robbie said, then added, "it looks like a damn good thing I invited myself to dinner."

"Yeah." I tried to laugh in between my jagged breaths.

At last I stole a look at Linda, but before I could get anything out, she squeezed her eyes closed and leaned on my shoulder in trembling tears.

20

Following my directions, Robbie drove us to Linda's home in the southwest part of the city. She refused medical treatment. I debated about going by the hospital anyway, but judging from her appearance, she had a nasty bruise on her face and was subject to a close call. There were no lacerations requiring stitches, no broken bones, and there'd been no rape.

However, Linda was shaking uncontrollably.

I didn't know whether to put my arm around her or not. When she continued to cuddle against me, I decided to go ahead and try, see if my holding her calmed the shaking. It took a while to ease her nerves, though it was definitely what Linda wanted as she buried her face into my chest. I winced but bit back saying anything when she laid a hand against my sore ribs.

"My truck's parked on your street," Linda said in a quivering voice at one point after a long, silent gap.

"It'll be okay," I assured her. "Robbie and I can pick it up later."

And then nothing except for an occasional direction to Robbie from me.

Shortly before we reached her house, Linda added, "This isn't supposed to happen to me." There was the sound of failure in her cracking voice.

"I know." Linda was martial-arts- and firearms-skilled

153

and had one of the best mentors in the business—her father. An attack like that wasn't supposed to happen, but it had. I wanted to ask how. Instead, I waited.

Suddenly she pushed against me—another wince—and sat straight. "One of the only times I decide to run over and see you instead of call."

I didn't respond.

"If you weren't out trying to save the world, then they wouldn't have been there," she added.

I wasn't trying to save the world, only Robbie's friend Charles outside a bar, I thought, but kept to myself and let her tongue-lashing go.

"Where's my father?" she asked.

"Galveston. Some guy's wife is missing."

She looked directly at me. "I came to tell you that Wanda Sims swears she had no idea she was going to be fired. And she had no idea Welles was having a relationship with anyone else, including Agnes Berryman."

I nodded. Robbie pulled down a quiet residential street. We were close.

"And do I believe her?" Linda asked rhetorically.

"I'd say you do," I replied.

Then she surprised me. "I thought I did." She shuddered. Instantly, her energy collapsed, and she huddled back down on the seat. "I dropped my guard," Linda added weakly.

The street twisted at a right angle.

"I tried to push through them, and the blue-eyed devil hit me in the face. Then one ripped my purse away, someone hit me in the stomach, and they were on me, pinning me down, my clothes were being torn, I couldn't move. . . . It happened so fast." Her voice was a half whisper that choked up. No tears, this time, but enough anger, frustration, and pain to start a war.

"There, Robbie." I pointed to Linda's one-story bungalow. He swung into the empty driveway. Streetlights had flicked on, though the evening was only graying.

"I keep a spare key in the garden," Linda told us.

"That's right, no purse," I remembered. While I lifted the key from beneath a rock near an azalea, Robbie perused the area. All appeared calm. We let ourselves inside.

Linda quickly walked, arms folded, past the dining room, across the living room, and to one of the two bedrooms in back. I heard a door close and wondered if she'd return tonight.

I released a deep sigh.

"She's going to need help," Robbie said.

"Linda's strong," I told him, "but you're right."

He paced around the wooden floor in the living room and examined the abundance of Native American art Linda owned. He particularly liked the shield hanging above the couch and the rain stick resting in a corner. When he picked it up, the rain stick echoed the sound we heard from the bathroom as Linda turned on her shower.

I knew this house, having stayed a night or two the time I'd witnessed C.J. shot down during a drive-by, so I wandered to the small bar and checked the stock.

"Want a drink?" I called.

"I could use one."

"Gin and tonic okay?"

"Grain alcohol would work at this point."

I smiled, made the drinks, and handed him one. "I had such a good meal planned," I lamented.

"Damn inconvenient of those skinheads."

"A pound of jumbo shrimp and all that produce sitting in the back of my car."

"Think of how nice your interior will smell." He sank into the large chair that faced the end of a glass coffee table.

"Yeah, with the keys dangling from the ignition, that's

the least of my worries." It occurred to me to phone Jerry Jacoma and request he rescue the keys and groceries from the VW. I left the message on my landlord's machine, adding that I'd explain later.

Next I called and left word for C.J. to get in touch at Linda's. Tonight.

"C. J. McDaniels is going to kill those guys," Robbie stated the obvious.

"If Linda doesn't get them first." I paced around the room.

"What prompted the skinheads to crawl out of their hole now?" he asked.

"C.J. wanted to shake things up. Actually, smoke people out, he said. I don't figure he had those roaches in mind, though."

"Hell, you sure planted a burr on someone's butt."

I vowed to kill you, and now I can, the skinhead had said. *And now I can, and now I can,* repeated in my mind.

"You're right, of course." I told Robbie what the cold-eyed leader had said. "The sense I got was not that now he could kill me because we were physically facing each other but now he's been allowed to. Someone has been holding his—their—reins."

"And now isn't." Robbie sipped his drink.

"Most obvious candidate is the Reverend-General Gideon York. He all but announced he'd come after me."

"Why?"

"I have a bad attitude."

"I can't argue with that," Robbie said, "but I'm not trying to kill you."

"Trouble is," I informed Robbie, "Gideon has his own muscle—and I'm talking more muscle than the Dallas Cowboys' offensive line. He doesn't need the skinheads. In fact, he stressed that point himself. He has a problem with Nazi wanna-bes."

"He didn't appear to have too much of a problem with them the night they were beating Charles half to death," Robbie pointed out.

I scratched my beard and grunted. Very true, I thought.

"Who else could it be?" Robbie wondered aloud.

"The rest seem a distant second."

"Gideon's muscle sounds like a signature. You know, his calling card," Robbie tossed out. "Maybe he doesn't want to leave his calling card."

"Maybe."

Robbie kicked himself out of his chair. I followed his gaze and turned. Linda had entered the room, wearing a yellow cotton bathrobe.

"I'm hungry," she announced softly. She plunged her hands into the pockets of her robe. Her damp hair hung in dark waves. There was an element so vulnerable about her, something I never thought I'd see in Linda, that I didn't know how to respond. When Linda and I'd had our spin around the dance floor, her strength had attracted me. Sassy and exotic. But it was that sassiness, that stubbornness, the need to control that also drove me away. Now, though . . .

"We could order a pizza," Robbie suggested.

Linda wrinkled her nose.

"Well, let's see what you have," I said, grinned, and headed into the kitchen.

Fortunately, her refrigerator wasn't nearly as abused as mine. Much better fed. Enough beef, though, to give the freezer high cholesterol. Had to be the influence of Vic Hernandez, her ex-boyfriend.

I rustled out one of the sirloin steaks and thawed it in the microwave. Then I proceeded to cut it into bite-sized chunks and coated them with flour, salt, and pepper. Linda didn't have egg noodles, so I settled for a parsley-garlic rice.

Robbie refreshed our drinks and handed Linda a glass of white wine as she pulled up a stool to watch.

"What are you making?" she asked.

"Beef tips in a red wine sauce. Is that all right?"

"Long as it's not fajitas, fine." She forced a smile and sipped the wine. "I've got a bottle of Merlot in the rack behind the bar you can open."

"Thanks."

Linda was concentrating hard to remain in control. Her sentences were stiff, and her glass quivered as she continuously sipped from it.

Robbie fetched the red wine and opened the bottle.

I diced an onion and minced a few cloves of garlic, then heated a cast-iron pot with part butter, part olive oil. More and more I found myself using olive oil, if not exclusively then cut in half and half. Where before I might've strictly used butter, the olive oil was healthier, and I was liking the taste.

"I left a message for C.J. to contact me here," I told Linda as I started sautéing the pieces of floured beef.

"That all you say?" she asked.

"Yes."

Robbie cleared his throat. "Are you going to call the police?"

Linda paused the ascent of her glass and, as I expected, gawked at Robbie like he'd been sniffing too many wine corks. Then she drank.

"I see," he said, and blushed.

As the beef started to brown, I added the onions and garlic. In a frying pan, I began to brown the uncooked rice in olive oil.

"The cops would have another charge against those skinheads," I reasoned, "besides the damage Robbie and I can do."

"I don't want to handle it that way," Linda objected.

"You can't just shoot them," I said.

"Who said I was going to?"

I again grunted, then using my forefinger and thumb, crushed a couple of pinches of dried thyme onto the beef and cracked in more pepper. As the rice grew tan, I added onions, garlic, and parsley. Finally I poured in a generous amount of Merlot to the beef, stirred it well, turned the temperature down, and let it stew.

"What's the difference between this and Stroganoff?" she asked.

"The wine, no mushrooms, little things, really." I added water and a cube of dried chicken bouillon to the rice, crushed in more dried parsley, then covered the pan.

"I have sour cream," she offered.

"I intend to use it."

"It smells wonderful," Linda told me.

"Yes, it does," Robbie agreed.

"That's only because y'all are starved," I responded.

"Probably." Robbie laughed.

Linda took another sip of wine. "You still seeing that professor?" she asked.

Wham, out of the blue. "I never was," I answered casually. "She's married."

Linda started to roll her eyes, then caught herself. "Okay, are you two still friends?"

"We'll always be friends."

"I mean, do you still spend a lot of time with her? Why are you being so difficult?" Anger flared.

"You're implying something that isn't there?" I noticed Robbie slip into the living room.

"What? That you slept together?" Linda waved her hands in the air. "I don't care if you slept together."

"We never did."

"Well, we did."

I stopped, stirred the beef. "And you're not married."

She ran a finger around the rim of her wineglass. "Funny thing, I figured you were a short-term relationship for me. Have some fun, date awhile, you know? Instead, you broke it off first. That doesn't happen to me much. And then it's for a married woman you only moon after and don't even chase."

Let's get off the subject, I thought. Of course she didn't hear me.

Linda relented. "I know you love her, Neil."

I didn't respond.

"You should go after her."

"I can't," I replied more curtly than I intended. "Anyway, she's leaving for California."

"Follow her."

"She doesn't want me to."

"Is that what you think? Really? Look at me."

I obeyed.

"You don't know much about women, do you? You poor fool."

I shook it off, refused to get into it any more with this woman after what she'd just been through, and added the sour cream to the beef.

Linda finished her glass of wine and wandered into the living room. A moment later Robbie returned.

I smiled.

"Be gentle with her," he said in a soft voice.

"I am."

"I mean be careful of her feelings," Robbie explained. "I couldn't help but overhear. She still has it bad for you."

"Oh, come on—"

"Then you ride in like John Wayne—"

My turn to interrupt. "And get my ass whipped. Linda got us out of that mess."

"You know damn good and well what would have happened if you hadn't arrived on the scene," Robbie stated, "and so does Linda."

"So it's a temporary shining-knight thing."

"I suspect she was smitten with you already and this exacerbated the situation."

"Exacerbated. Interesting way to put it," I commented. "Didn't realize you knew such big words."

"I know a couple of little ones, too, like, shithead."

Music rose from the living room. Sinatra. Robbie raised his eyebrows.

"I'm very fond of Linda," I told him, though I felt myself step back emotionally. "But I won't mislead her."

"No one's asking you to. Be supportive is all."

"Who made you so wise in the ways of women?" I asked.

"It's not that I'm wise," he replied, and picked his drink up from the counter. "It's that you're so dumb." Robbie tipped his glass to toast me.

"Yeah, and I've got a couple little words for you, too."

Then the front door opened and closed and knocked us back to reality.

C. J. McDaniels was about to find out what had happened to his daughter.

21

C.J. broke open a shotgun. Robbie wrung his hands together searching for someone to say something.

"What are you going to do?" I asked. "Cruise the city until you happen to cross paths with the skinheads?"

No response.

"Even the cops haven't been able to find them so far," I pointed out.

"I don't intend to go on no snipe hunt," C.J. growled.

"Then if you're not loading up for the skinheads, who are you planning to go to war with?"

C.J. ignored my question, but I could tell what he would've said: *If you don't know then I'm not going to tell you.*

Linda's back was to us. She stood with her head dipped and resting against a hand. I'd related most of the story to C.J., though Linda had explained why she'd stopped by my apartment in the first place. While rehashing the incident she'd appeared to hold up well. It was when we'd finished and C.J. had wrapped his big bear arms around her that she began to lose control of herself. A storm of emotions continued to encircle her as she fought for calmness in the eye of her hurricane.

"Okay, let's do process of elimination." I was buying time until I could hit on the right words to say. "Agnes Berryman? Possible, though she doesn't strike me as the

162

kind of woman who'd know where the likes of the skinheads hide out. Wanda Sims? Naw, she's too busy crying. Conrad, our unfaithful dishwasher? Getting warmer. He could be acquainted with the Nazi crowd. Nathaniel York? Have met the man only through pen and rumors. Keep that line open. So who's left?"

"Warren Clay," Robbie offered.

"An attempt at humor," I said. "Clay's the type these skinheads enjoy knocking around."

"So is Nathaniel York," Robbie countered. Good, finally I wasn't just talking to myself.

"On one side of his life, true. But perception, remember. I still say keep that line open."

The thought seemed strangely plausible. Gideon York had his muscle. What would he need with creatures of hate such as the skinheads? Dumb question, Neil. Rhetorical. Still, if they weren't connected with the reverend, then who would be a likely alternative? Someone insecure, unable to come to terms with himself—someone who understood bursts of anger and hate. As in deriving from self-hate? As in Nathaniel York? Worth keeping in mind.

"You're forgetting who we were talking about earlier." Robbie leaned against the arm of the couch.

"Not hardly. Logic does point first and foremost to the militant nut in the bowl. I've been weaving my way toward him."

A predatory look glazed C.J.'s eyes. He dropped in a couple of shells and snapped the gun closed.

"You're going to drive with that thing loaded?" I asked, scanning my mind for something that would break his focus. "Or is it going to be a drive-by?"

"I appreciate what you boys did," C.J. muttered, and made for the door.

I followed. "We don't know Gideon York was behind the assault," I told him.

"I'll sure as hell find out."

C.J. wasn't bluffing. I'd once seen him lay his sledge-hammer fists into a man who wouldn't tell him what he needed to hear. And that was in front of a cop. No telling what he'd do without the police present to temper his actions.

"Look, I know I pushed his buttons, threatened his manhood or something, but think about how anti-Nazi he was," I argued.

"Mercenaries are mercenaries," C.J. cracked.

"Okay, then *we'll* find out," I said.

"You ain't invited."

"I wasn't asking."

"Don't cross me, Neil."

Before I could go on, though, Linda stepped up to her father.

"This isn't the way," she said. "At least, that's what you once told me."

"You didn't listen."

"I should have," Linda responded. "It didn't bring her back."

The muscles in C.J.'s neck tensed. "When all was said and done, I was glad."

"I was lucky."

"No, you're good," C.J. told her, "almost as good as me."

There was more passing between them than a few cryptic sentences. The replay of a painful time gone by. A connection where silence crackled and secrets were only emotions without words.

Instinctively, I knew they were referring somehow to Karla, C.J.'s late wife, Linda's late mother. I imagined that one day I would learn the whole story. But not today.

"Yeah, well, I'm not feeling like I'm all that good right

now," Linda said to split from the past. "Wasn't right then. Still isn't."

C.J. hesitated.

Without warning, fire ignited the black in Linda's eyes. She struck out like an uncoiling snake and grabbed his shirt. "I want them. I need to bring those assholes down, not have you do it for me," she said fiercely.

A deadpan expression met Linda's words. Anyone else would've felt the shotgun butt square up the side of their head by now.

"I'll be all right," Linda added more reasonably, "if we do it my way."

"What's your way?" he demanded.

She released him, lifted the gun from his arms. I thought Robbie was going to soil his pants when she tossed the loaded firearm to him. He caught it softly with both hands, then stood with the gun resting on his shoulder like he was Wyatt Earp to compensate for the momentary wobbling in his knees.

"Simple," Linda explained. "Continue your investigation, but leave me free to roam."

"Roam where?" C.J. asked.

"Neil's right," she said, "we're not going to bump into them at the local doughnut shop or strolling through the park—"

"Unless they want to," I broke in.

She bit her lip to maintain composure. I should've bit my tongue.

"So, I roam from suspect to suspect," Linda went on, "to see if any of them have connections to those vermin."

"And what if it was a random hit?" C.J. asked.

"Be rather coincidental." I took up the cause for Linda. "You shake an apple tree and fruit falls."

"He's right," Linda stated through clenched teeth. "The only thing coincidental was me being there. But if there is no God and it was random, you still have me poking around in all these people's lives. No telling what I might find."

C.J. thought a moment. "Where would you begin?"

"Neil's assessment sounded pretty good. Start with Reverend-General Gideon York and work back."

I pictured the thugzillas. C.J. sensed what was going through my mind.

"What do you propose to do?" He fell into the cushy chair.

"Stake him out," Linda replied. "If he's connected with the skinheads, then sooner or later there will be contact."

"What if it's by phone?" I asked.

"What if?"

I didn't follow. C.J., squinting, apparently did.

"I've got a couple of favors to call in," she explained to her father, "and it's better than shoving a shotgun in his face."

"She has a point," I agreed. "I don't think the reverend's deacons will casually stand by and allow you to conduct your interrogation."

C.J. steepled his hands.

"Linda shadowing York makes the most sense," I added.

He brought his hands slowly up and rested his chin on his thumbs. The image of a praying Buddha flashed before me. Far from reality. Linda sat on the arm of the couch.

"Why?" C.J. asked me.

"We need to be available for Nathaniel York to find," I reminded him. "You're smoking him out."

C.J. mulled the idea, then blew against his hands and pushed himself up from the chair. "Goddamn, I want a cigarette," he complained.

We waited.

"Your way," he told Linda, "on one condition. Do not, under any circumstances, confront any of them yourself.

Not the reverend-general, not his goons, and most of all, not the boneheads who attacked you. You can take pictures, tape conversations, follow them to hell and back, but no face-to-face. Understand?"

"Understand," Linda agreed.

I tried to read if she was shelling out an *I'll humor you and agree* answer or if she was sincere. When they locked in that zone again, I leaned toward sincere.

"You want some dinner?" I asked. "Hopefully it hasn't burned or separated."

"Appreciate it, but thank you, no. I had a po' boy in Galveston." He smiled.

"How'd it go with the guy with the missing wife?" I asked.

"Hell, she ain't missing." C.J. ripped open a piece of Nicorette gum, not attempting to hide his irritability, and chomped. "He lured me down there on false pretenses."

"Meaning she's run away," Linda stated.

"Yep."

"So you chucked him," she followed up.

I wandered into the kitchen to retrieve my drink and check the beef tips in red wine sauce. The rich aroma filled the room.

"Normally I would have," he replied. "But this fella's name is Everett Baker, married to Wanda Baker. Wanda Sims Baker."

"You're kidding," said Linda.

I poked my head out. "I second that."

C.J. flipped open a small notepad. "Seems Wanda ran off about three years ago—"

"And he's just now looking for her?" I rejoined them. "Coincidentally calling you?"

"Again there's no coincidence here. Hush up and listen. She leaves him a note saying adios so the cops have no interest in trying to locate her. Baker's a writer, unpublished"—C.J. glanced at me—"living some poverty-level romantic idea of the suffering artist. Needless to say, he doesn't have money for the likes of me. He pokes around himself but discovers tracking a person down is harder than he thought, especially since he has no experience or contacts."

"So he decides to suffer." I filled in his pause.

He smirked. "Then one day he sees her—"

"On TV," we chimed in.

"Brilliant deduction, children," he complimented dryly. "Baker drives to the station to confront her. At first he claimed that, as it was obvious she wanted nothing to do with him, he simply asked for a divorce."

"What did he say after you insisted on the real story?" Linda picked up her glass and swirled the wine around the bowl.

"He gave me the rest of the truth." C.J. closed the notepad. "Wanda could have an uncontested divorce if she paid him off."

"How much?" Linda asked.

"Twenty Gs."

"Gives writers a bad name," I commented.

"Don't worry," C.J. consoled, "he's no longer a writer. Now he sells T-shirts down on the seawall that say things like 'Born to Toke' and 'Best Booty on the Boardwalk.' "

"Glad to see he didn't squander his literary talents." I noticed that Robbie had taken over tending to the beef and rice.

"She pay him?" Linda asked.

"That's how he started his little T-shirt business."

"Why'd she give him a dime?"

"My guess is she didn't want her reputation damaged while chasing Sherwood Welles."

"Could not have been very easy for a poor runaway

wife-turned-model-turned-chef's assistant," Linda observed. "She must have borrowed the money."

"A safe bet."

"Now for the *Jeopardy!* question of the day," I said. "Why did Baker tell you this? First off, you and not the cops?"

"He says he has a phobia of cops. From the way he reeked, I wouldn't be surprised."

"You bought that?"

"Partly," said C.J. "But I'll get back to it. He also wanted to know if there was a reward for information that would help crack the Welles murder."

"A reward?"

"The man's got a marijuana leaf burned into his brain. But think about it—"

"Baker's saying he has information about the murder of Sherwood Welles," Linda broke in.

"How?" I asked.

C.J. began, "He was at The Bath House—"

"The Bath House?" I confirmed. "You're talking about the gay whorehouse?"

"Officially it's a spa," C.J. clarified.

"In underground levels, it's a whorehouse, right, Robbie?" I called.

"A spa-bar with private rooms," he replied, and peered around the corner. "But I don't go there."

"I didn't mean to imply you did," I told him.

"The only time I stepped foot inside that dive was when I caught my slutty ex cheating," he added, and returned to the food on the stove.

"No wonder Wanda left him," she said. Somehow that seemed to make her feel better about the woman.

"And no wonder she didn't want Welles to find out she'd been married to Baker," I added.

"At this fine establishment," C.J. continued when we

were through, "Baker hit on a very intoxicated patron because he looked like money. Later, when they were both wired, the man bragged he knew who murdered Sherwood Welles, but he wasn't going to lift a finger to help the accused. I won't go into the lurid, ah, details concerning his feelings toward Mr. Stevens. But according to Baker, the man indicated even I couldn't help Stevens."

"Which is how he got your name," Linda said.

"Apparently."

"Nathaniel York?" I ventured.

"Baker wouldn't name names," he said. "Not for free. York, however, was my first guess."

"There's something screwy about this," I said. "Wanda Sims's ex-husband meets up with Nathaniel York and not only do they get wired—which would cast a little doubt on his word—but he implies York could spring Perry but won't? Come on."

"How about on the prowl?" Linda suggested. "Maybe Baker had seen York at the station when he'd shaken down Wanda. Then catches him out at the cathouse a few times. Finally, he sees him after Welles has died. He knows his ex was involved with Welles, so he chases York the next time they cross paths to find out if he can use the situation for his own profit."

"That being the case," I said, "then why hadn't he squeezed York's reputation?"

"I don't know. Except maybe he didn't know that could be a problem."

I shook my head. "This is too convenient."

"Which is why I didn't pay him anything. Or promise to."

"Couldn't you get Alice to subpoena him?" Linda asked.

"Crossed my mind," said C.J. "In the meantime, though, I think Neil and I should pay a visit to Wanda Sims ourselves. You keep in mind what I said, Linda, when tailing the elder York."

She nodded, hands clutched together, and closed her eyes. Focus, I thought, focus on the eye. The eye of the hurricane.

"I look forward with great anticipation," C.J. added, "to finally meeting the younger York.

"Damn soon," he growled.

22

I awoke feeling like a side of beef Rocky Balboa had pummeled in the meat locker. Only one kick, I chided myself, the idiot landed only one kick. But it left me with a nifty bruise and some tender ribs. Oh, cowboy up, Neil.

As usual, it was early. The jogging hour. Stumbling to the kitchen for a glass of ice water, I had a strong feeling I should blow off the run. What if I'd fractured a rib? Bouncing around out on the street wouldn't be the best therapy. More important, I might also run into a situation where I got more of my ribs busted up. The sense I had was that the skinheads were wild dogs on the hunt now. And I was alone. I showered and dressed.

There was little doubt in my mind that Linda had wanted me to spend the night, even after C.J. had announced he was going to sack out in the spare bedroom. I had given it heavy consideration. A strong part of me wanted to curl up with Linda, hold her, protect her—perhaps more, in which case I'd have followed her lead. After the months of iciness between us, though, the timing felt wrong. Over and over I'd told myself I wouldn't mislead her. Considering her vulnerable state, how could I not have misled her by staying? How would I not be taking advantage of her weakened condition? How would I not have been preying on her—I stopped myself.

Okay, so I felt guilty. I should have stayed, been supportive like Robbie had said. Perhaps it was the fear of getting close again that pushed me away. Or the thought of Keely. Maybe closer to the truth, as Robbie so eloquently stated, was that I was just plain dumb when it came to women.

The phone rang as I was stepping out the door. I quickly grabbed it.

"Neil?"

I couldn't place the voice.

"Yeah?" I didn't try to disguise the wariness.

"It's Warren, Warren Clay."

I almost laughed. My right hand was balled in a fist as if I could ward off the tension I'd expected to rope me through the phone line. C.J., Robbie, Alice, Linda, any of the above could be calling this early with God knew what news. But Warren Clay? Still chasing. I didn't exactly relax, but the tension shifted to irritation.

"Warren, it's barely seven."

"I didn't wake you, did I?"

"Well, no," I admitted.

"I knew you were an early bird. Listen, I have an idea, or, er, rather, a proposal, okay?" He was sounding awfully nice after being rather snooty yesterday.

Overcoming my reservations, I said, "Go ahead."

"I saw last night on television that Perry Stevens is being held without bail for the murder."

"Yeah?" Wariness returned.

"So he's not going to be able to get out to do it, is he?" Clay stated with great importance. I really wished he'd drop the declarative-interrogative crap.

"Do what?" I was almost afraid to speculate.

"The crawfish boil, Neil," he told me as if I had swamp grass for brains. "You remember it, don't you?"

"The crawfish boil is not foremost on my mind," I said firmly. "Nor do I suspect it's on Perry's."

"Robbie said he hadn't canceled the two hundred pounds of crawfish."

"When did you talk to Robbie?"

"At lunch." Thick swamp grass for brains. Though I had to admit he left off one of his little pet names for me. *At lunch, stupid.* Or, *moron.*

But I didn't recall anything being said about the boil. Not in front of me.

"Proceed." As in, let's get this over with.

"How about we throw the crawfish boil together?" he offered.

Why'd I know that was coming?

"I don't think that's such a great idea, Warren."

"Why not? We could combine client lists—"

"The alleged murderer's and the victim's? Why don't we supply boxing gloves, too, and let them duke it out."

"Be serious," he snapped.

Oh, I am, I thought.

"It could be a kind of memorial gathering for Sherwood," Clay continued. "Kind of a healing party."

"A crawfish boil?" The guy was an entrée without taste.

"It's a good idea," he added.

"No."

"What are you afraid of? You afraid I'll steal all of Perry Stevens's clients? They're going to come to me, anyway."

"Bye, Warren. I'm going to hang up now."

"This is your last chance."

"I thought yesterday was my last chance."

"You're throwing away a great opportunity for some good publicity. After all"—he laughed at his own dig—"y'all are going to need it."

"From what I understand, you're going to need a bit of

publicity, too," I shot back, "seeing as you're not getting your TV show."

He growled, "Where'd you hear that?"

"Word gets around even in this neighborhood."

"Well, I'm not finished working on her," he declared. "You'll see me on TV yet."

I didn't respond, not even with the potential slam about Perry being Berryman's first choice. Let Agnes mop up Clay.

"Good luck, Warren."

"Marshall—"

I punched my cordless off.

Not all fruits and nuts come from California, I thought. Down here in Texas we got 'em wrapped up in a single package.

I pushed Clay out of my mind and refocused. My VW had gone untouched. Sadly, that meant the groceries, too. Jerry's truck was here, but he must have gotten in late and not checked his messages. The keys hung from the ignition where I'd left them. Food in the back. Shrimp bad. Spinach and basil shriveled. I rescued the nonperishables and some of the produce, such as the Roma tomatoes. On a slightly positive note, given that the car was intact, it was obvious the skinheads hadn't returned. Hard as it hurt to see food wasted, I'd rather it rotted on the back-seat of the VW than end up in the hands of those culinary Neanderthals. I could picture them staring perplexed at the feta cheese while trying to smoke the basil.

Deciding it was worth the risk, I grabbed the .38 Smith & Wesson, tucked it under my shirt, then under the passenger's seat once I reached the car. I'd installed a strap to the underside of the seat to hide items I didn't particularly want in full view or rolling around the floor.

The Bug chugged by Linda's truck. I knew that C.J. would drive her out to pick it up later, and I surprised myself by sending a silent word into the ether for her to be strong and heal quickly. Been a while since I'd done that. Not that I wasn't religious, but despite—or maybe because of—my knowledge of the Good Book, I wasn't a church-goer. Large organizations—i.e., organized religion—made me nervous. The politics. Control. Whatever. God understood. For that I appreciated Him. Then I laughed, thinking of my New Age friend Trisha. For, as Trisha always said, appreciate *Her*.

I grabbed a couple of breakfast burritos and coffee at The Flower and pondered what to do. C.J. was supposed to pick me up when he brought Linda to her truck. But I had time. Conrad had been needling my mind as of late, and I couldn't finger why. Except I believed he was spouting half-truths. Enough reason to pay a courtesy call.

I'd catch him early.

In less than ten minutes I was down the street from Conrad's house. I drifted to a stop beneath a large pecan tree. The house appeared quiet—quiet as roadkill. I doubted that place would ever survive a face-lift. Any attempt to scrape away the wrinkles of paint would probably send the frame tumbling down. I took a few minutes to watch the house cling to life as I organized my thoughts.

For a short while, I realized, the attack on Linda had overshadowed Perry's situation. Though he'd been in custody barely two days, it felt like two weeks. And now he was downtown, in a prison jumpsuit, awaiting trial for murder.

Okay, Neil, how did the murder weapon come to be in Perry's car? Perry either really committed the crime or it was planted. I preferred to believe the knife and towel were planted and Perry lost control when he discovered them. Brilliant deduction, Neil, now answer this—planted by whom? Someone who had access to his car. Such as? Such as me—and I preferred to eliminate myself—and Robbie. No way. Who else? Mattie. Not that angel. Claudia. The old, battle-weary kitchen manager had been home nursing herself. Con—

I leaned back in the seat, crossed my arms, and concentrated carefully on the house and my thoughts.

Sure, Conrad had access to Perry's car. In fact, he often ran errands in it, washed the Lexus weekly, and took care of all the servicing. But Conrad walked off the job the day before Sherwood Welles was murdered.

Still, no one had assigned Conrad a set of keys. With all the running around he did, though, he could easily have made a copy.

"Why?" I asked aloud.

To help himself after hours to some of The Kitchen's inventory? Kinda funny how that fit together.

A nagging voice that strongly resembled C.J.'s resounded in my mind. A thunderous devil's advocate. *We have to face the possibility,* I imagined C.J. telling me, *that Perry stashed the knife in the trunk himself.*

Not yet, I thought.

I'd spent enough time admiring the view. Closing the door gently, I made my way to the overgrown walkway that led to his small porch. I was unsure how to approach him. A bluff? We've learned of another witness, so you'd better come clean? Sounded weak.

This time Conrad didn't step out. Still sleeping? Probably. Then why did I have the creeps? A feeling like someone had a gun pointed my way. Was I jumpy or what?

The .38 was in the car, I reminded myself. Hesitated. Then plowed on up the steps. Conrad wasn't going to take a potshot at me. In fact, being an ex-con, if he was even caught with a gun, his ass would be back in the slammer.

I was about to knock on the frame by the screen when the front door, swinging free to the inside, drew my attention. Actually, startled me. The screen was so dark I hadn't noticed until I was right on top of it. But no one was there.

The door shook gently in the cross breeze. I went ahead and rapped on the frame.

"Conrad," I called. "Neil Marshall. I need to talk to you."

Nothing. I wondered if his wife had flown the coop. He'd made that comment when he stormed out of The Kitchen about not being able to support his family. Which suddenly brought things into focus a little more. What if she had left and he was blaming his wife's running off on Perry? A good motive for revenge. I knocked louder.

"Hey, Conrad."

I heard a rustling at the back of the house. A jingling and a rattling like someone was trying to turn a broken doorknob.

"You okay?" I called.

Then there was a crash. Glass breaking, something heavy falling, multiple pounds against wood. I opened the screen door.

"Conrad?" I wandered inside. "Where are you? You okay?" Trash heaped out of a can in the kitchen. Dirty dishes filled the sink. An empty bourbon bottle—our stock?—beside it. Beer bottles—many of which were Heineken, which I was positive came from The Kitchen—and opened cans of half-eaten chili, complete with spoons sticking out, covered the counter. I knew Conrad was a mess, but I hadn't pictured it this bad.

"Conrad?" I called again, and passed through the doorway on the right, then turned left into a small hall. A door was open to the right. The bathroom. A pair of sneakers, laces tied, dangled from the shower curtain. Pants soaked in the sink. I was about to inspect them closer when I caught an image in the corner of my eye.

In what looked to be the living room, a desk that had held a collection of tools was turned over, a shattered lamp beside it. Soiled, torn curtains billowed from a broken window above the desk.

And on the floor, curled in a fetal position in a pool of blood, lay Conrad.

He was dressed in the same T-shirt and jeans I'd last seen him in. No shoes. I knelt beside him. He had a weak pulse. And a knife in the gut.

There was short, choppy breathing. Mine. I steadied myself. Stood. Ignored the blood and found a phone. Dead. Damn it, Conrad.

I stumbled out of the house, choking back breakfast as I retraced my steps, and ran to the house on the right. My pounding on the door sent a Hispanic woman into hysterics. We could see each other through a small window. A man ran up to her and pointed a gun at my face.

"No," I tried to explain. "The guy next door, Conrad, your neighbor, he's hurt bad and needs an ambulance. Call 911. His phone's off."

He waved the gun at me, said something in Spanish. I didn't argue. I jumped off their porch, identical to Conrad's, and looked around.

An old man across the street smoking a cigar and holding a newspaper wandered from a lawn chair toward me. "What's that you say, boy?"

I repeated what I'd told the Hispanic couple. He rushed inside his house to make the call.

The effort proved futile. By the time I forced myself back into the small house, it was too late.

Conrad was dead.

23

"If you think this is going to get your boss off, Marshall, then you've blown a piston or two," Assistant District Attorney Ed Krieger bellowed. Though he was good at little else, he was very good at bellowing.

C.J. had recently arrived. I leaned on the hood of his Mustang and sipped from the large Styrofoam cup of strong black coffee he'd brought me. The old man across the street had kindly let me use his phone to call the private detective.

I saw nothing to gain by arguing with Krieger, so I stood my ground and endured the bluster.

"We still have the blood," he declared, and pointed at me. "You can shut up his witness, but you can't deny the blood."

I wondered if Krieger realized the double entendre, or that what he'd said was very Shakespearean. I doubted it. For all his hairiness and adorable temperament, Krieger reminded me of the militant, narrow-minded gorillas from *Planet of the Apes*.

He pounded on the hood of the Mustang. "You've lassoed a heap of trouble this time, boy. And your ass is in the noose."

"That's my car, Krieger," C.J. warned. He'd come out of the house with Lieutenant Gardner.

"I get the distinct impression the assistant DA believes I had a hand in Conrad's death," I told Gardner.

"Did you?"

"No."

"Has anyone checked to see if he has blood on him?" Krieger demanded.

"He's into blood these days, isn't he?" I observed. Oh, God, I thought. A Warren Clay declarative-interrogative.

Gardner remained straight-faced.

"I don't have blood on me," I explained, and waved my free hand toward the ground. "But even if I did, it would be because I knelt next to Conrad and took his pulse."

"And?" Gardner prompted.

I repeated the events. Again.

"Not many killers report their own crimes," Gardner told Krieger.

A blue jay rode the warm breeze and landed in a nearby beech tree. In the starkness of Conrad's yard, the early-morning sun bore down hard. Still, I drank the coffee. To be in the shade would be much more pleasant. While Krieger gave me the evil eye I wiped a film of sweat from my forehead.

"You'll get yours," he threatened me.

"Why were you here, Neil?" Gardner asked. Ever polite, ever classy, ever dangerous.

"I had a question for Conrad," I replied.

"What?"

C.J. nodded.

"I wanted to know why he was giving you only half the truth," I told the lieutenant.

No change of expression.

"Half the truth," Krieger bellowed.

Gardner put up a hand and stopped him. "Do you know something we don't?" he asked.

"Well, ah, no," I hemmed and hawed. "It's just that in my gut I know he wasn't telling the whole truth."

Gardner's eye twitched.

"Sherwood Welles said 'voices' and 'they' during the 911 call," I pointed out, "and even the news reporter mentioned a 'group of assailants.' Therefore, it doesn't take a genius to conclude Conrad witnessed more than he was letting on."

"Witnessed something you were afraid would come out," Krieger charged. "Is that why you confronted him?"

My blood pressure soared. I focused on being calm. "I didn't confront Conrad," I told him. "And you're missing my point. I wanted the missing information to come out. Who else could he have seen? I don't care what you think. Perry doesn't have the muscle to vandalize property in the manner Welles's kitchen was hit, never mind murder anyone."

Krieger opened his mouth but Gardner again stopped him.

"You don't have any new evidence," he stated.

"No."

C.J. shook his head.

Following his lead, I kept the Everett Baker–Wanda Sims deal and the Berryman-Welles-Sims triangle to myself.

Gardner tried another tack. "Out of professional curiosity, who else could have been at Welles's kitchen the night he died?"

"The skinheads," I replied. Something suddenly struck me. On the 911 call, Welles had made the comment *Let me get to the desk*. That wasn't aimed at the dispatcher. Under his breath, to himself, then? Or had he not been alone? Surely the cops had picked over every word Welles had muttered better than fire ants on a half-eaten drumstick. Still, I added it to my mental list to run past C.J.

"We've been through that," the lieutenant said. "We're searching for them."

Throw me out as bait and you'll get a strike, I thought.

"Who else?" he asked.

"I don't know," I said, "but I think whoever it was convinced Conrad—"

"Convinced?" Gardner asked. "You mean paid off or scared into?"

"Probably paid off." I finished the coffee. "Conrad didn't frighten easily. Even the skinheads wouldn't have rattled him. He'd have gone at them like a wolverine against wolves."

Gardner was listening. "Continue."

"So Conrad's paid off to testify to one thing. He saw Perry and Welles argue. Then, supposedly, Conrad left."

"Think he did?"

"Maybe," I replied. "Maybe he waited until Perry left and then helped trash the place. I could see Conrad doing that."

"So you're saying he knew who the killer was," Gardner charged, "that, in fact, he was an accomplice."

I hesitated. No, that didn't sound right. Conrad would go far enough to lie, to accept a bribe, or even to blackmail. *Click*.

"Perhaps Conrad did leave." I retreated. "But when Welles ended up dead he cranked up the heat on whoever paid him to testify. My guess would be for more money. Too much. And so this." I gestured at the house and the activity around us.

"Nice theory," Gardner finally stated, "but no evidence. And the two we know of who could set the record straight are dead." He paused. "Unless there's another name I should be aware of."

"Not a name you haven't already checked."

Gardner thought a minute. "What led you to this theory?"

"An overactive imagination," Krieger spoke up.

"Since Perry Stevens didn't murder anyone, I want to know who did."

"That doesn't answer my question." Gardner tilted his head back.

"Is anyone here being charged?" C.J. spoke up. Meaning, of course, me.

"Did you touch the knife, Neil?" Gardner asked.

"No."

"He could have worn gloves," Krieger pointed out, "and hid them. Besides, I think I can make a case of this. Employee who points the finger at boss for the murder of stepbrother now found dead, impaled by a chef's knife, by employee—who happens to be a chef—loyal to boss. Loyal employee is also a widely known amateur shamus with a questionable track record."

"Then make a case," C.J. challenged.

He didn't have to be quite so macho with my fate, I thought.

"I'm going to take it to the DA."

"Do it." C.J. began to slowly chew a piece of gum. "In your infinite decision making, though, think about this. He wore gloves but left the murder weapon? A weapon that would directly imply say, a chef such as Neil?"

Krieger balked. "I can make a case."

"Whoever committed the murder," Gardner stated, "left via the back window, turning over the desk and lamp in the process. We found fresh footprints in the backyard." He looked at me. "Do you mind?"

"The old man across the street saw Neil stumble out of the house," C.J. said. "To make the prints he'd have had to turn over the desk, hop out the window, then jump backward into the house. There are no footprints leading up to the window, only away."

"Maybe," drawled Gardner. "Humor me."

Krieger sulked.

I had nothing to fear, and we moved to the backyard. A decaying wooden fence provided as much shelter from neighbors and the streets as the Alamo did against Santa Anna's troops. As it turned out, the footprints were narrower and smaller than mine. Gardner conferred with Krieger.

"But what about checking the pants for blood?" the assistant DA complained.

He broke from the lieutenant before Gardner could respond.

"I want those pants checked out," he demanded.

I rubbed the back of my neck. "For Christ's sake."

"Now!" Krieger pounded a hairy fist against a fleshy palm.

"Fine." I'd had enough of this, so I stripped to my boxers and tossed the khakis to Krieger. Knew I should've worn jeans, anyway—I guessed I'd run and put a pair on. "Want the shirt, too?" I added smartly.

"That won't be necessary," replied a seldom-shocked Lieutenant Gardner.

"Can I get a receipt?"

"I'll send it to you."

Without another word, I marched, eyes forward, to the sidewalk and my car.

"Kid, you've got moxie," C.J. said, catching up. "But we need to talk." I caught a hint of irritation in his tone.

"Do you mind if I stop by my apartment first?" I asked, matching his irritation and raising him a sawbuck's worth of aggravation.

"I'll follow."

"I guess they're not going to arrest me," I called.

He ambled closer so he wouldn't have to shout. "I don't think they will unless they find your fingerprints on the knife, or the gloves, and can link them to you."

"Won't happen."

And no one tried to stop me.

For now.

24

I dug out a pair of black jeans to go with my white polo shirt and then met C.J. as he waited in his car. He must be irked, I thought. He didn't even get out to pet Samson.

We cruised a few minutes before C.J. said, "You gave the cops evidence."

"What choice did I have?"

"One blockheaded prosecutor hopping like a baboon doesn't mean squat."

"I don't think it's a big deal." I lowered the window a few inches for some fresh air. My hair was tied back in a ponytail to keep it from whipping around in wild strands.

"No, you don't think," he grumbled. "You gave Krieger something he can use against you. Wait," he protested when I opened my mouth, "I've not said my piece yet."

I chewed on my lower lip and listened.

"By now you know the likes of Krieger. He ain't scouring this world in search of truth. He's out to win an argument, build a career, and advance his hairy ass up the ladder of power. To make himself look good, he'll create any perception that'll help. We've talked about this before. Lawyers sell illusions. They sell it to juries, judges, and the public. Think about the case he was staking a few minutes ago."

"Gardner doesn't buy it," I stated.

"Don't be so all-fire sure," he admonished me. "Even if

you're right, when it comes down to feeding time, what Gardner thinks doesn't mean a damn. He's not the jury or the judge. He's one cop who'll have to answer questions lawyers propose to twist out the shade of truth they want."

I fidgeted in the seat to get comfortable. "All right, I acted stupid," I admitted. "Sorry."

C.J. let go a deep breath and chewed the gum deliberately, eyebrows furrowed. "Gardner was fishing," he said, a decibel lower.

"Did I bite?"

"Not until your striptease act. And even that, I guess, was a nibble, a taunt. But don't do it again."

"I promise I'll never take my pants off and throw them at the cops again," I told him.

A slip of a smile touched the corners of his mouth. "Besides trying to learn something new," C.J. explained, "Gardner was out to catch you contradicting an earlier statement. He wanted to see if your information was consistent.

"As far as Welles's murder," he continued, "the cops are trolling for the accomplice. I should've known. Damn." He paused, shook his head.

"Damn what?" He was making me nervous.

"You're big enough, Neil," he reasoned, "to do serious damage if you went on a rampage through a kitchen. And you're loyal. Now you've set yourself up to be Stevens's accomplice. And Krieger's coming after you."

"I was with Robbie Persons the night Welles died. Stayed at his place."

"Is that something you often do? No," he answered for me.

"But I had a good reason—fear of the skinheads."

"I know. Krieger will either play that down or use the incident as proof of your violent streak. And he'll still point out that usually you spend the night at your apartment, alone."

Did he have to stress alone? I thought.

"Krieger will further say you set an alibi up for yourself. And with another company man."

C.J. was depressing me. I fought it. "There was something else on the 911 tape, if you recall. Welles's reference to letting him get to the desk sounds like he was talking to someone."

"Like who?"

"I don't know. Conrad?" I tried, though had major doubts. "Maybe Welles was interviewing him."

"That doesn't set right. You go on those lines, *if* your hunch is right, it could've been Perry, too. He hasn't exactly shot on a straight line from the beginning."

Not a welcome thought. "Perhaps someone else was there we don't know about."

"Then why hasn't he come forward?" C.J. asked.

"Because he, or she, was somehow involved with the murder," I offered.

He took a left through a yellow light. "Or another person's presence was coincidental."

"Like you said, then why not come forward?" I wondered.

"Or have ended up dead, too? Still, you sound like you're grasping."

"Seems to be all we have."

After a patch of silence, C.J. added, "The cops will haul Robbie in for questioning soon."

"I'll give him a ring. I need to tell him about Conrad, too."

C.J. drifted past the bustle of the Farmers' Market to the freeway then fired west down Loop 610.

"Cops will tell you most murders aren't complicated,"

he said after a while. "Often it's someone close to the victim, someone who has motive and means."

"And unfortunately I fit the bill as a loyal accomplice who whacks Conrad."

"Yep."

"Shit." Despair was beginning to shred my confidence.

"What's the plan?" I asked. The loop swung to the south. As we rode on the overpass above I-10, I gazed at the skyline in the distance. From this angle downtown appeared compact, tight as a bundle of pens. Mont Blanc and such. The view was crisp, without the dense haze that would settle around it come the summer heat and humidity.

"Stay the course," C.J. answered. "Keep you active and hard to get hold of."

"To Wanda Sims?"

"I'd like to hear what Ms. Sims has to say about her ex," he told me.

"Stay the course," I repeated softly. Then thought: "Just wondering, but why didn't you say anything about yesterday's reappearance of the skinheads. I mean, with attacks like that, isn't it obvious we're rubbing someone the wrong way?"

"Obvious, no—you drummed it into my head the Nazi thugs could be working on their own. And it's very possible they're not. I didn't say anything because I don't want Vic Hernandez to disrupt Linda's surveillance. I know Vic. He would track her down to make sure she's all right. And to protect her."

Surprisingly, I felt a twinge of jealously at the idea of Sergeant Hernandez protecting Linda. I'd been there to help her. She was okay. For the most part.

Just beyond the Galleria, and before Highway 59, we exited on Richmond Avenue. A great portion of Richmond was commercial. Clubs, restaurants, car repair shops, and one of my favorite places—The Richmond Arms. The Ale House's west-side sister.

But we weren't going for a brew at The Arms. Well before the pub, C.J. turned into a pocket of apartments and town houses.

"I still don't know what to make about that morbid recipe," I mentioned. "Would Sherwood Welles stoop to that level?"

On a narrow drive, he stopped in front of a redbrick town house.

"He was paranoid, had problems with his stepbrother's sexuality, and feared his chef was jumping ship—to his stepbrother's company. Then they stop when he dies. Sounds like a wrap to me."

A young magnolia in a small plot of soil whispered close to my head as I stepped from the Mustang.

"But why go to the trouble to send trash like that in the first place?" I asked. "What's the point?"

"Make Clay nervous about switching allegiances." C.J. rang the bell, thus ending the conversation. He was satisfied. I wasn't, as I hadn't pegged Welles as that insecure and psychotic. We'd talk later. C.J. announced who he was into the intercom, and we were let in.

Wanda Sims was an adolescent boy's wet dream, a man's desire, and an old man's memory—a Garbo-like face with high cheekbones and a figure that could stop traffic on the Southwest Freeway. Though judging from the red around her green eyes, the disheveled blond hair, and the slightly swollen, sultry lips, it was obvious Linda hadn't been exaggerating about the tears.

C.J. appeared unfazed. I followed his lead.

"I appreciate you seeing us," he began. "I know you've talked to one of my associates—"

"Twice." She wiped at a piece of lint on the raspberry nylon sweat suit she wore.

"Yes, ma'am."

"I don't know what else I can tell you." She turned and we followed. The small foyer opened onto a stairway that wound to the second floor. To the right was a small formal dining room. An oak table with a silk flower arrangement on top. We entered the living room to the left. Modest in size, the area held a black leather couch with a metal frame, a matching chair, a large TV in one corner, and a couple of glass end tables. The track lights were off but the mini-blinds that hung across a sliding glass door were opened and allowed plenty of sun into the room.

"I've just stopped crying," she told us, sniffling, "constantly crying, that is."

"I'll be brief," said the private investigator.

"I stopped crying, all right," Wanda Sims repeated, "right after Miss Garcia told me Sher was going to sack me."

Sher? I thought.

"I got angry, you know." She walked to us from the screen door. "But then I called the Berryman bitch, and she said it was true. Then she said some other things I couldn't believe." She choked back more of the waterworks.

C.J. must have thought she was doing fine, for he didn't ask her any questions.

"And I cried, all right," she said, and moved to within inches of C.J. "But I cried for me, for being so stupid. That son of a bitch was just using me. God, and I fell for the no-fraternization line. What a cover. All along I was nothing more than his, his—"

She couldn't say it. Now C.J. spoke.

"What did Agnes Berryman tell you?"

"That Sher loved her, that they were going to be married, and I was only his appetizer before the main course." The more she said, the louder she seethed. Her hands were balled by her sides in tight fists. I hoped she didn't thank C.J. for bursting her bubble by socking him one in his spacious gut.

"I'm sorry," he said.

"No, I'm sorry. I'm sorry for the time I wasted on him. I was stupid. I hate him. I hate him. But I miss him." Pause, another sob. "Damn it, I loved him." Fists went to eyes as the tears burst out, and she backed around to the sliding glass door.

C.J. and I stood in silence and waited.

Finally, a weak voice asked, "Would you like any coffee? I forgot to ask."

"Thank you, no, ma'am," C.J. answered for the both of us.

Her back still to us. "I'm sorry," she said. "You didn't come here to watch me have a nervous breakdown."

After a thick breath, she turned and forced a smile. "Well, yes, now." She hesitated. "Ah, have a seat."

I took the couch, C.J. the chair. Wanda sat on the elevated brick base of the fireplace. She patted a pocket, pulled out a cigarette, and lit up. I thought C.J. was going to have a spasmodic fit.

"Want one?" she asked, reading his face.

He studied my hair then declined.

"I'll try to help you," Wanda told us, having hit the calm after another emotional storm.

"Actually, it's about your ex-husband," C.J. told her.

"I beg your pardon?"

"Everett Baker."

"Who?" she asked. Seriously.

C.J. jerked back like he'd been slapped. "Your ex-husband, Everett Baker," he repeated as if she hadn't understood.

"I don't have an ex-husband," she announced.

C.J. said nothing.

Wanda looked from him to me and back. "Look," she

declared, opening up her arms, "that's the truth. I've never been married."

"Then were you and Everett Baker ever—"

"I don't know any dude by that name," she broke in.

"In Galveston. He was a writer, now sells T-shirts." I filled in the silence.

"Oh, sounds like a winner for me." She took a long drag. On close observation, I noted that Wanda Sims was younger than me. By probably four or five years. Which, as Welles was forty-three according to the news, put him a good fifteen-plus years older than her. What did she see in him? I wondered.

C.J.'s silence was difficult to read. Did he believe her? If not, why was she lying? If so, then who the hell did he meet with in Galveston, and why?

"You're an investigator," Wanda Sims told C.J. "Look it up wherever you look these things up."

"How old are you?" C.J. asked.

"Twenty-six."

Four years younger than me.

"I was born in Houston," she was telling us, "have always lived in Houston, except for the nine months I hung around New York City trying to break into modeling. That didn't pan, so I got a job down here. And I've never been married," she repeated. "Not in Houston, or Galveston, or New York, or Vegas, or L.A. or anywhere."

I was convinced.

"How did you come to work for Sherwood Welles?" he asked.

"I've already answered that question. Don't you and your associates talk to each other?"

"I beg your forgiveness," he replied smoothly, "but I'm getting old and my memory just ain't what it used to be. And my notes are at the office."

She sighed. "The agency sent me."

"With no cooking experience?"

"Sher wasn't looking for cooking experience."

"You interviewed with Mr. Welles?" C.J. asked.

"Yes, and he hired me."

"When did he begin to show interest in you?" he continued.

"From the beginning."

"Of course you had no reason not to trust him." C.J. was doing a pretty good dance. For what, I didn't know.

"Yes, Mr. McDaniels, I trusted him. He was wonderfully open with me." A hitch in her voice. "Or so I thought."

C.J. waited.

I could certainly understand the pain, at least to a degree. The girl'd had her insides ripped out with Welles's death, and then run through a shredder as if they'd never existed. It occurred to me, also, that Wanda Sims wasn't the evil hussy Agnes Berryman had made out. And quite likely she was chased by Welles, not chasing him.

"Did you know that Perry Stevens was his stepbrother?"

Wanda shook her head. "Only that he was a rival."

"Do you recall anything said about Mr. Stevens?"

"Only once," she said. "Something like, 'I'll be damned if I'm going to let that fag ruin me.'

"Sher was pretty upset," she added, "but he wouldn't talk about it."

"You ever notice any mail correspondence between Mr. Stevens and him?" C.J. asked.

I watched carefully. It was worth a shot.

She looked confused. "Mail?"

"Letters, cards, anything."

"No, but then I didn't handle his mail."

He nodded then switched gears. "Do you know of anyone in Galveston, or anyone at all, who'd claim he was your ex-husband? And why?"

"If you mean an old boyfriend, some secret admirer, or

an obsessed wacko, no. I don't receive weird phone calls or dirty letters, and as far as I know there's isn't anyone stalking me."

"Thank you for your time," C.J. said, and rose.

Wanda Sims escorted us to the door. "Sorry I haven't been any help."

C.J. smiled. "Yes, actually you have."

Once the door closed behind us he said, "We'll check out her story, but—"

"She's telling the truth," I finished.

"It'd be a damn sight easier if she wasn't."

"The jealous girlfriend done wrong. Who better to get close enough to plunge a knife in a man than her? But, C.J., she didn't vandalize his kitchen without help."

"You're right. And if she's feeding us a line, then she should've tried Hollywood instead of New York."

Yet, I saw his mind click, and he filed that notion away just in case.

25

We regrouped at C.J.'s office. Instead of moving forward, I felt like I was slowly trying to walk up the down escalator. Conrad was dead. I was a suspect. And, from all appearances, someone had dished us a bogus lead on Wanda Sims.

I left word for Robbie, informing him of Conrad's death and tipping him off that the police would be around at some point to ask a few questions. Also, I reminded him to cancel the crawfish order. From these tired eyes, the party looked dead in the water. As I reached Call Notes instead of Robbie, it occurred to me the cops might already have corralled him.

"Galveston." C.J. dug out an area directory. He spent so much time at Linda's desk I wondered why he bothered to keep his own in the back. Except maybe to hold all his junk.

"No Everett Baker listed. Guess I'll go down there."

"Could be a wild-goose chase," I countered.

He turned the phone to face him and punched in a number.

"Brad? McDaniels," he said into the receiver. "I need a favor.

"Don't give me that bullshit," he continued. "You sit on your bureaucratic ass all day letting your mind go flabby. Here's a chance to do something real.

"What? No, Linda's on a stakeout, and I don't have time. Ah, Brad"—his voice went low for effect—"remember that little incident in special collections?"

Pause.

"Yes, enough said." C.J. reached out to where the ashtray would be, caught himself, and brushed at the desk. "I need to know if a Wanda Sims of Houston, age twenty-six, ever married an Everett Baker of Galveston. Or if she ever married at all and anything you can find out about Everett Baker. Yes, that is all. Thanks."

"What incident in special collections?" I asked when he hung up. "And who'd you call?"

"A friend who, ah, borrowed a rare book only to have it lifted from him. I got it back before the shit hit the fan."

"Rare book?"

"Very," he confirmed.

"What division does he work for?" I was confused.

"The main library downtown."

"You were talking to a librarian?" I asked.

"Hey, those people are great, know everything. And in this age of communication, they can find anything out. 'Course, Brad also did a stint as a researcher for the CIA, so he may have a couple of extra tricks up his sleeve. Still, you want to find something out, ask a librarian any day."

Somehow I couldn't imagine hearing the same pep talk from Sam Spade or Philip Marlowe.

"What now?" I asked.

"We wait for Brad." He walked over to the cabinet by the open window and poured us each a mug of coffee from a freshly brewed pot.

"Linda's covering the reverend?" I accepted the coffee.

"For the time being."

"She all right?"

"Figures to be."

Meaning, *Not really but she'll manage.*

"You got a stomach for lunch?" C.J. asked, and clicked on the radio.

"A bit early, don't you think?"

"I like to plan ahead."

"I can eat," I told him.

"Let's buzz by Poppa Burger," he suggested.

Talk about a retro eatery, I thought, Poppa Burger was a hamburger stand right out of the Fifties. A long, white building looking a little worn-out—having not gone uptown like the Avalon Drug Store—it was somehow a refreshing step back in time for an old-fashioned greasy burger. How it managed to survive the stranglehold from the Golden Arches, I didn't know. I was just glad the place did.

But that would be two heavy doses of cholesterol in two days. What the hell.

"Fine," I said. "You hankering to visit your past?"

"Then we'd have gone to Prince's drive-in, if it was still open on Main Street."

Closed by an area deteriorated by crime, another piece of history was lost. And actually, it was me visiting the past before it all was lost. My grandmother had a stand similar to Poppa's in the Fifties and Sixties. Having been born near the end of its run, I didn't recall the eatery all that well. But seeing the people in Poppa's, I could picture my grandmother cracking the whip, my mother and her sisters griping in between taking orders and flipping burgers.

The opening and closing of the downstairs door broke my reverie.

C.J. read the concern on my face and scowled. He patted the air with one of his thick hands as if to say, *Get a grip*. Though he opened a drawer, drew out the .357—in case the visitors were actually crazed elephants, I supposed—and rested the huge gun in his lap.

Slowly, two sets of feet ascended the stairs. No talking. No attempt to disguise the fact they were coming. And no knock on the door.

The handle turned and in stepped Nathaniel York with a trim, hard-edged man dressed in a power blue suit the pinstripes of which were worth more than my VW.

"McDaniels," York said sharply, not bothering to introduce himself. C.J. didn't let that slide.

"And you are?"

"You know damn good and well who I am," he snapped.

Aggression sparked off him like mean from a pit bull. Hardly the toady I'd been lead to believe he was, but then again there was nothing wimpy about his writing. Perhaps the passive side was reserved for Agnes Berryman. Still, this bulldog shaped like a rhinoceros didn't look like someone who could be easily thrown through television staging.

C.J. wriggled a finger at him, which only further infuriated York. "Amenities need to be observed."

York turned to his associate then seemed to see me for the first time.

"Neil Marshall," I said, and broke the ice.

He swallowed hard. "I know."

"You're Nathaniel York," I continued. "I read your column."

"And you're Perry Stevens's chef." He swaggered a couple of steps in my direction. "Did you help plan the menus over there? I hope not. I mean, they're adequate but hardly exciting."

I held his gaze, the anger steaming off of me, until he refocused. A funny feeling hit me that I'd stared him down. Perhaps this blowhard act was just that. His silent partner appeared to be another story.

"I'm McDaniels. Who's the guy in the Corleone suit?"

"Mr. Fischer, my attorney," York replied.

Fischer showed no indication he'd been introduced.

"Mr. Fischer? I see." C.J. rested his elbows on the desk and steepled his fingers together. The .357 wasn't in view. "Do you talk, Mr. Fischer?"

He didn't.

"How unique." C.J. addressed Nathaniel York. "A lawyer who can hold his tongue. Is that because he has a limited vocabulary and doesn't want to embarrass himself?"

Fischer wouldn't rattle.

"I talk, you listen," York stated.

"I'm not going to stay out of your business," C.J. calmly told him.

York's mouth opened but nothing came out. C.J. had cut to the thick of it and in the process stolen York's thunder. With a gesture reminiscent of his father, Nathaniel raised him arm and pointed at C.J.

"I'm warning you," he said. But there was no power behind it, no Old Testament vengeance to contend with.

"I don't care if you're a closet queen," C.J. responded, "and I don't care who does and doesn't know. For starters, I want you to tell me about Sherwood Welles, your relationship to him, his relationship to Agnes Berryman, your relationship to your boss, what you observed between Welles and Wanda Sims, and why you trashed Perry Stevens in a magazine review."

York looked gut-punched. C.J. casually leaned against the back of his chair and folded his hands in his lap.

"You, you, you spread lies like that and I'll sue." York stumbled a step closer to the desk.

"I'm not a rag magazine and you're not Rock Hudson," C.J. answered. "So don't even go there."

"Perry Stevens said you made a pass at him that he rejected, and that's why you wrote the nasty review," I charged.

"No, he hit on me," York shot back.

It was a weak volley.

"How did you and Sherwood Welles get along?" C.J. asked.

"We had a professional relationship."

"Was that before or after he slapped you around the television station?" C.J. followed up.

York's countenance gave him away. His face reddened, his eyes shifted, but it wasn't from anger. It was nervousness. A window shade suddenly snapped open. Now he looked like someone who could be tossed into staging. And he was hiding something.

"What happened?" I demanded, and moved forward.

His *lawyer* stepped from the background to intercede.

"I have a companion," York inexplicably blurted.

"It's a show for your public image," said C.J. "Agnes Berryman already told us you weren't her type."

York puffed his chest. It wasn't working. The gangster-dude, though, was serious. He deflated York by placing a hand on him and pushing the puffy man out of the way.

"I knew we should've done it my way," he muttered. "You talk too much."

C.J. studied him as if Fischer were a curious billboard. He rubbed the back of his neck with his left hand, the right remaining in his lap.

Fischer tucked a hand inside his coat then broke the tension by tossing an envelope on the desk.

"What's that?" asked C.J.

"Temporary restraining orders. You and the punk"— he nodded at me—"stay away from my client and his father."

"And his father?" I repeated, but was ignored.

"On what grounds?" asked C.J.

"On the grounds that you're a pain in the ass." He then turned and took Nathaniel York by the arm.

"Even if these are legitimate they won't stand up in

court." C.J. pushed himself from the chair and thumped the big gun on the desk. "This is an investigation."

"The cops investigate, you don't," he replied.

"Why didn't you flash the papers earlier?" I asked as they reached the door.

When tough guy didn't respond, C.J. said, "He wanted to know our questions."

"It's a court order, McDaniels." Fischer almost shoved York down the stairs. "Read it and weep."

The door slammed shut.

26

C.J. was on the phone before a word was out of my mouth. He tried to reach Gardner, failed, then opted for Sergeant Vic Hernandez. Finding the tough homicide cop at his desk, C.J. informed him of the restraining order.

"Cut the chuckling," C.J. barked. "In over thirty years in this business—" Something the sergeant said cut him off.

I wandered to the chair and flopped down. Remembering me, C.J. switched the phone to conference call and hung up the receiver.

"—in the Blum case in '89," Hernandez was saying.

"Okay, so it wouldn't be the first time someone tried to pull this stunt," C.J. said. "But it won't work. You got anything on a lawyer named Fischer?"

"Doesn't ring a bell. Who's the judge who signed the order?" Hernandez asked.

C.J. slid on his bifocals. Staring at the document, he replied, "Donahue. Instructs me and anyone associated with me not to contact in any way or even come within a thousand yards of either York."

"Smiling Jack Donahue?" Hernandez whistled. "How'd you arrange to piss him off?"

"I only know the man by name. Never met him. Never appeared before him," C.J. said.

"What do you know of Smiling Jack?" Hernandez asked.

"He's tough."

"Sure as hell is, especially if you're not a gringo."

"Come again."

"Like Donahue's not a member of the Rainbow Coalition," Hernandez explained. "Borders on a white supremacist, unless he finds out you're a queer. Then it doesn't matter what color you are, your ass is in the sling."

A gay-bashing judge, I thought. Interesting. The modem in my mind dialed, beeped, and whirred to make the connection.

"Consistent with the other white supremacists I've come across," C.J. continued. "If you're gay, it's a flaw."

"Hey, if you're anything but him it's a flaw," Hernandez responded. "Donahue even likes that crazy old man from back east, the one who ran for president around Reagan's time—"

"Lyndon LaRouche," I said. "Donahue's probably a John Bircher, too."

"Marshall, *pendejo*, I didn't know you were slumming."

"I'm slumming all right."

"You're also restrained, eh?" A slight chuckle.

"Only happens to the best."

"Such a good Irish name, too," C.J. lamented. "How'd Donahue end up on the bench?"

"It's America, man," Hernandez stated.

"Yeah, a good economy is the opiate of the electorate," I put in.

"So, true, señor. No matter the complaints against Donahue, he remains on the bench. It was in the *Chronicle* where the guy even goes to some wacked-out church, but no one seems to care."

"Whacked-out church?" I repeated. There was the connection—lightning bolt, checking password.

"Do you know the name of this garden of worship?" C.J. followed through.

"Not exactly," Hernandez told us. "Some paramilitary outfit where the padre calls himself a general and offers Communion from an army Jeep."

Password accepted. We were on-line.

"Thanks, Vic."

"I don't know what for, man. But, McDaniels," he said before we disconnected.

"What?"

"Watch your step till you bust that restraining order. Donahue ain't the man to screw with."

C.J. grumbled in a tone semiaffirmative then cut the line. He paged Linda. "Best let her know what's going on."

"You going to pull her?"

"No, not yet. But now they'll be looking for a tail."

"Me or you," I pointed out. "Not that there won't be trouble should she get made."

"Linda's good. I'll leave it up to her."

C.J. would usually have announced what everyone's job was. Now he was leaving it up to her. Still shaken, too, I thought.

The phone rang. It was Brad the friendly librarian. He quickly informed C.J. that Wanda Sims had not married anyone by the name of Everett Baker or anyone else as far as he could tell. Over the speaker he announced that Sims was a graduate of Bellaire High School, had taken a few classes at Houston Baptist University but never completed her degree. Tracing her Social Security number—which I didn't know how he acquired, as we hadn't given the number to him—he discovered she'd worked as a waitress for a while in New York City, and then back here at the Lonestar Model Agency.

Everything pretty much matched what Wanda had told us. C.J. went on to Everett Baker, a name for which Brad declared he'd found only three possibilities in the Houston-Galveston area. Number one was born in Houston in

1922, to which C.J. stopped him right there. The next was a forty-six-year-old California transplant. Strike two. And the last a thirty-two-year-old Galvestonian.

"That's him," said C.J.

"So Baker's claiming it was a mixed marriage," Brad said.

Another road bump.

"Are you saying this Baker's—"

"African-American," Brad completed.

"How do you know?" I asked.

"Who's that?" Baker asked.

"A friend," C.J. said. "How do you know he's African-American?"

"This Everett Baker sells real estate. Has his own Web page on the Internet, complete with picture."

"You bother to check any Bakers with Everett as the middle name?" C.J. asked.

"I don't have all day to be running after your dirty laundry, brother. But it just so happens I picked up two potentials. Unfortunately for you, neither turned out to be under forty."

"Thanks, Brad."

"Now you keep mum on that special-collection shit."

"Brad," C.J. drawled the one-syllable name out to around three, "you know I wouldn't have poked a stick in that hornet's nest."

"No, you'd have kicked it wide open."

C.J. picked the receiver up, then placed it back in its cradle to hang up.

"I was sucker-punched," he announced with disgust.

"You'd have gone to Galveston to scope that case anyway."

"The idea was to turn my focus to Wanda Sims."

"And away from whom?"

C.J. smirked. "Yes, whom?"

27

After Linda's call, which C.J. took privately, we ran out for a burger and a bull session. Linda wouldn't hear of pulling out. Actually, she was delighted with the restraining orders. Her time staking out York—and she'd chosen to begin with the elder—wasn't a waste. C.J. had told her keep a low, low profile, as it appeared they had a judge on their side.

We collected our burger baskets then sat at one of the picnic tables positioned beneath an overhang.

"Basic questions," C.J. announced.

"Who murdered Welles and Conrad?" I took a big bite, allowed the juices to drip onto my fries.

"Not that basic."

I surveyed the area and wondered if we were being watched. Despite the weatherman's promise of rain later, the day remained beautiful. Balmy but not humid. The downtown lunch crowd getting out to enjoy it. Smartly dressed. Spirits high. Enough pretty women to bring a case of spring fever to the intensive-care unit.

"I didn't spot anyone," C.J. said, observing me.

"Okay, basic questions," I echoed. "How did the blood-laden knife find its way into Perry's car?"

"Good," C.J. said. "Add to that, who would want to frame Perry? What would he or she get out of it? Was it a plan to get rid of him or improvised to draw suspicion from the guilty party?"

"Taking into account the threatening messages makes me wonder."

"Maybe. But they fit in somewhere. As does the restraining order."

I sipped my Coke. "How about a 'what if'?"

C.J. bit into his cheeseburger and beckoned me to continue.

"We know Gideon York's a militant. What if he went after Sherwood Welles, the situation got carried away, and Welles ends up dead? He knows through Conrad that Perry was there, so he arranges the setup with Conrad's assistance. Conrad gets greedy and wants more than whatever he was promised. He pressures until he receives an early-morning visit. The visitor gives him something, all right, but not what Conrad expected."

C.J. listened carefully. "A big problem. We've established that Welles isn't gay, so why would Gideon go after him?"

I set the burger down and sagely raised a finger. "The fisticuffs at the studio," I said. "We've been looking for a reason tying motive back to prejudice. What if that's not the case?"

C.J. set his lunch down and crossed his arms.

I anticipated at least one of his questions and told him my thoughts about Conrad's access to Perry's keys, the possibility of copies.

"Tricky. He'd walked off the job," C.J. reminded me.

"But it's possible."

"That would mean Conrad was present at Welles's death, or at least inside the building between the time the 911 call was made and the police arrived. A small window."

I held up my burger with both hands and ate.

"That also means he collected a sample of blood," he added.

"Or it was accidental."

"And he had the forethought to plant it?"

Stumped. I picked at a fry.

"And where does Wanda Sims fit in?" he asked.

"Why couldn't Gideon set up a diversion to send you barking down the wrong trail?"

"And how is Nathaniel York entangled?" C.J. thought. "I like the angle with the television-studio fight. Gideon could've sent someone out to rough up Welles. But something's still missing. Nathaniel York acted strange. He was like a bull having a nervous breakdown. And then the lawyer took over."

"Fischer would be a lawyer Gideon would have."

C.J. wolfed down the remainder of his burger then chewed on some fries. I decided not to share my theory on the perfect french fry with him. Besides the timing, the audience wasn't quite right.

"Another 'what if,' " I suggested. "Say Gideon's goons were out to trash the place. Then Welles appears and chases them off."

"How?" He pulled on the straw of his Coke. "Gideon's army doesn't scare easy. Not to mention they enjoy scraping their knuckles on people's noses and would probably have beaten him senseless before hightailing it."

"Welles charges down from his office brandishing a weapon," I proposed. "And the only kind of weapon that could chase a bunch of thugs off would be a gun. Why not? He'd be the type to keep a gun in his office."

"Don't recollect a mention of any gun being found," C.J. said dismally.

Stumped again. "What if he uses the chef's knife?"

C.J. looked doubtful.

"Let's come back to that."

"For a stretch of the imagination," C.J. allowed, "say Welles did chase them away. Then who could've stuck the knife in him?"

"Someone he trusted. Someone who could've gotten close."

C.J. perked. "A lover? We have the choice of two."

"A classic triangle," I said. "Like you told Berryman, love has raised plenty of gravestones."

"Back up a minute and say Welles had a gun. Where is it?" he pondered.

"Or who took it?"

"Or did a gun even exist? Are you fabricating evidence?"

I caught that. Not *we* but *you* as in *me*.

"Damn Conrad for being dead," cursed C.J. "He knew and it cost him."

"Well, he is." I left about half of my fries untouched. "Where do we start?"

"Who would know if Sherwood Welles kept a gun in his office?"

"Agnes Berryman. Or Warren Clay, his chef." Fabrication or not, I guessed he figured it was an avenue worth traveling.

"I hate to split up," he said, "but you know Clay. Talk to him. I'll question Berryman."

"Why do you hate to split up?"

"Think about it, kid. Someone's going to come down on you. Be it the cops or who knows what thugs. And you're not equipped for either."

A sobering thought. "But we're running out of time," I added.

His Coke ended with a slurp, and he nodded.

28

I traded shotgun in C.J.'s Mustang for lead in my VW and wrangled my way over to see Warren Clay. I hadn't bothered to call ahead, partly because C.J. had dropped me off at the Bug and sped right away. So much for worried about my welfare. The thought of hanging solo any longer than necessary—like taking the time to slip into my apartment just to use the phone—had very little appeal. Another close encounter of the Nazi kind was best avoided by staying on the move.

Not having Clay's home address, I naturally headed for Welles's kitchen. I remembered Clay was fulfilling commitments that remained after his boss's death, so it was a good bet he was there. I guessed that being the victim meant something solemn. One only canceled on the accused.

Now, don't be bitter, Neil. I took a deep breath to center myself. At this point I could've used a healthy dose of Trisha's New Age philosophy.

Or Keely Cohen's understanding. Support. Strength.

I was spiraling down and needed a kind word. When Keely had told me last Christmas she was leaving, it hadn't hit me at first. It took her being gone for the reality to set in. The emptiness of losing a friend. Of course, I'd lost my best buddy when Jason Keys had died. With Keely, though, it was more. I'd wanted more, in spite of my denials. The naked truth was, I was facing the end of a dream. A wonderful, foolhardy, romantic dream. And, with love reduced to loss, the end of a dream left nothing less than a hole in your heart.

And, as Billy Joel sang, so it goes.

I bit my cheek, shook my head, and focused on the building I approached. The police tape was gone. Nestled in an area slightly southwest of the Galleria, the neighborhood was a tad more upscale than The Kitchen's—meaning, at least there were no hookers prowling the street—and quiet. The house-turned-business was two stories and quaintly Victorian in flavor. There were half a dozen steps that rose to a porch that ran the front of the building. Curtains were drawn on the two windows I faced, as well as on the door window. Same upstairs. A BMW and an Escort were in the driveway to the right. I hoped Clay wasn't entertaining a client.

Something told me to park and give it a few minutes, which I did, a couple of houses down on the opposite side of the street. Perhaps it was a case of paranoia, but nobody needed to know I talked to Clay. God only knew who would catch wind of it, and I didn't need anyone shaking down Clay to find out what I wanted. When the visitor left, I'd slip in.

I realized this place wasn't far from Wanda Sims's town house. Maybe a five- or ten-minute drive south. What was that about someone Welles trusted planting the knife in him? Someone in the direct vicinity?

The street was lined with live oaks, large limbs with thousands of small leaves that rustled like the sleepless tossing and turning between a set of fresh sheets. After a long ten minutes I almost left the sleepless and began to doze. Then the front door opened, and what I expected to be a businesslike departure was scarcely that at all.

Agnes Berryman stormed down the porch stairs with Warren Clay in hot pursuit. I slouched down in the seat and listened through the open window of my Bug. Their words were no more distinguishable than the rustling leaves, though the tone was perfectly clear. There was enough thunder and lightning between them to scar a lovely day. Then the volume rose.

"It's my right," Clay half screamed, half begged, "I've earned it."

"No, it's within my rights."

Clay waved his hands up and down. For a moment I thought he was going to stomp the ground, too. "Don't you understand? Everything I've worked for will be gone!"

"Keep your voice down and stop acting like a fool."

That loud voice is giving advice? I thought. Then she re-grouped and paused. Slapped Clay with a few more words that I couldn't make out, then jumped into her BMW. Dark blue, not more than a year old, I'd bet. She left Warren Clay standing hunchbacked, shaking, the picture of frustrated anger. It wasn't until her taillights were around a corner and out of view that he stiffly went back inside the house.

Falling back on my keen ability to read people, I let another ten minutes drag by before I considered approaching Warren Clay. Asking a furious man about the possible existence of a gun was not wise.

I wondered what they'd been arguing about. Two-to-one odds said the television show, though Berryman had mentioned she'd already turned him down for the spot. Could Clay have been trying to woo her with a lunch, a demonstration, a late-inning rally?

When I could no longer sit still, I abandoned the Bug, quietly closed the door, and made for the house.

The front door was locked. I rapped on the window and drew Clay's attention. He seemed hopeful at the approach, then frowned when he saw it was me.

"What in the world are you doing here, Neil?" he asked as he opened the door. "Have a change of heart?"

"No, Warren, I was hoping you could help me out."

"What, you need a cooking lesson?"

And he thought he was funny. Even his effort to crack a smile was strained.

He closed and locked the door. I glanced around. The workspace was smaller than ours at The Kitchen, as the structure focused upward as opposed to sprawling out. A couple of stainless workbenches were in the middle of the black-and-white tile floor. A utility rack hung above. The commercial stove and oven rested against the wall to my right. To the back was the wash area. Opposite the stove I noticed a door for a walk-in cooler—a luxury we didn't have. I wasn't sure where the freezer was, but when I stepped farther inside I noticed a line of storage racks in a small alcove to the left. A couple of them were pretty banged up. The stairway was also to the left, though near the front of the house.

Nary a sign a man had been murdered here, I thought, or that the kitchen had been trashed.

"Seriously," Clay said, "what can I do for you?"

"This is probably going to sound odd," I told him. "But it could be important."

"Shoot."

"Good lead-in."

Clay looked at me more dazed than usual.

"Do you know if Sherwood kept a gun in his office?" I folded my arms and leaned against one of the tables.

After many blinks, Clay slowly confirmed what I'd said. "You want to know if he kept a gun in his office?"

"Yes."

"Why?"

A simple question, I thought, why not simply answer it? However, he'd been through the wringer with Agnes Berryman, so I played it cool. Itching as I was to ask what went on between them, I didn't. Instead, I answered directly.

"The private investigator who's helping with Perry's defense," I said to stress the importance of his answer, "speculates that Welles ran someone, or someones, off before the real killer finished the job. In order to accomplish that, he wondered if Welles kept a gun handy."

"Kept a gun handy?" he repeated, suspicion clouding his face. "Why isn't this investigator asking me himself?"

Oh, the delicate ego. "I volunteered," I told him, "as I know you and all. And C.J.'s got his own ground to cover."

Hem and haw, then: "Why should I help the man who killed my boss?"

Oh, God, don't go there, I thought. I wanted to point out that he wasn't exactly loyal by trying to enlist Robbie and me in an independent venture. But the possibility that he felt guilty about jumping ship and would therefore become angry and throw me out held me back. I chose a more standard approach.

"Don't you want to find the true murderer?"

Clay walked to one of the front windows and flicked at the blinds. "Right, I forgot you thought he was innocent."

"I believe he is," I replied in earnest.

He turned. "You would, wouldn't you?"

"No, Warren, he is."

"Aren't you in tune with the police investigation? If you were then you'd know Sherwood had some sort of handgun registered, but it's not here."

"Did he stash it in his office?"

"I don't know where he kept his gun," he said indignantly. "The cops only came across a box of bullets in their search."

"A box of bullets?"

"Isn't that what I just said?" Tone meaning, *moron*.

"Where did the cops find the bullets?" I pressed.

"In his bottom desk drawer."

"What caliber?"

"I don't know." Clay was wringing his hands together. "And I don't know about you, but I haven't found much use for guns when I cook. The meats I work with have already been processed when they come in. I don't have to slaughter a single cow or chicken. Do you? I also don't tenderize my steaks or briskets with bullets. I use a mallet. Other culinary instruments I reach for include whisks and spoons and knives. Not a single recipe that I've come across in *The Joy of Cooking* calls for a gun. So I've never needed to borrow a pistol, a rifle, or an Uzi, not even Sherwood's .38."

"Thirty-eight?" This tirade had begun by him saying he didn't know the caliber.

He was pacing haphazardly, a little crazy, and to say the least, his dander was up. The sound of my voice caught his attention. "What?"

"I thought you didn't know the caliber."

Suddenly he seemed as surprised as I was. "You know, come to think of it, Sherwood referred to his handgun as 'my .38.' Guess I'd forgotten that."

I should've laid off, but now I wondered what pushing him further would bring out.

"Can you think of a time when he referred to his .38?"

He pushed on the bridge of his glasses, concentration quickly twisting to irritation. "I don't know, okay?"

"Under a little pressure, are we?"

Clay heaved a sigh.

"Haven't you convinced Agnes Berryman to let you be the next TV celebrity chef?"

Clay's aura smoked like a grease fire. "No, it's worse—" he started, then stopped.

"What's worse?"

He waved a hand. "Nothing."

"She's offering the show to someone else," I prodded.

"I don't know what the hell she's doing!" Clay's sudden shrill just about sent me through the ceiling. "With the show," he added. An afterthought with a threadbare feel, too sheer to hide the fact that he wasn't plating up the full story.

"Warren, you're ripe for a vacation," I said. "A long one."

"No, Marshall, I don't need a vacation. I need money, like most people, you know? A lot of money."

"Can't help you there, bud. What do you need the dough for?"

Again a wave of the hand, though this time it was a large, looping sweep.

I'd learned what I'd wanted to know and was now running out of questions to ask. Also, Clay, in his manic-depressive mood, was starting the slide down. I imagined Berryman's voice echoed in his mind. Had she told him she'd put aside the feud and wanted Perry Stevens for the show?

Could be why he was antagonistic toward me. Why he wasn't all that hot on helping. Like claiming not to know the caliber then it slips out?

"Thanks, Warren," I said, and headed for the door.

"That's twice you've pumped me for information," he announced. "Remember that when I need help."

"You bet." I touched my forehead then rolled my hand down through the air as I bowed slightly.

"Don't mock me, I mean it."

"I'm not mocking you."

He grunted.

I yanked on the door. It didn't budge. Feeling a shade redder, I twisted the lock open then stepped out onto the porch and into the lovely day, my lungs welcoming the fresh air, and my mind scraping off the soot of Warren Clay's aura.

29

I dropped by The Kitchen on my circuitous route to
C.J.'s office. As Agnes Berryman had left Clay's company
a short time ago, I had a hunch the big detective was either
still talking to her or had yet to track her down. This allowed me time to check my messages—or threats—and
catch Robbie up to date.

To my surprise, Robbie wasn't alone at The Kitchen.
Mattie and Trisha were also in. And they were happily
working as if the drought was over and the crops were
saved. No one had told them about the oncoming locusts.

"What's all this?" I asked. "You mean there's someone
who actually didn't cancel?"

"Better yet, a new client." Trisha beamed.

"A friend of yours?"

"No, of my parents," Trisha explained. "It's a last-
minute dinner party sort of thing, so my mother directed
them to me. Isn't that something?"

"Manna from heaven."

"Yeah, it is." She squeezed a pastry bag and piped the
finishing touches of chocolate buttercream onto a fudge
brownie cake. "And, Neil, visualizing is only a step before
realizing."

"Whoa, I'm coughing dust, kid."

"Can't follow me, huh?" She grinned. "What I mean

is focusing on and visualizing normalcy will produce normalcy."

"Thus the job," I deduced.

"As you said—*sans* the sarcasm—manna from heaven."

"Talking to you, Trisha, is always so, ah, different."

"That's why you love me, baby."

I agreed and rapped my knuckles on the stainless-steel table. In back, Mattie was pounding out chicken breasts to be stuffed with prosciutto and a spinach–feta-cheese mixture.

"Everything under control?" I asked.

"My end's fine." She stopped hammering. "It's a shame, what happened to Conrad. Anyone know who did it?"

"Cops seem to be leaning toward me."

Her eyes widened. "That's plumb crazy."

"You could say that." I stole a pinch of the spinach-feta filling. There was a hint of basil and sun-dried tomato, too. Good. "Before Conrad walked out, did you notice anything unusual?"

"He was pretty unhappy. Complained about having no money. Kind of acted like the rest of us is stepping in high cotton."

"That's not unusual."

"No, but—" Mattie spread another chicken breast out and whacked it a few times with the mallet.

"But what?"

She grimaced, appeared sheepish. "I should've told you before."

My heart quickened. "Told me what?"

"I came up here last Saturday morning," Mattie began. The morning after Welles's death, I mentally noted.

"You see, I'd forgotten my sunglasses on the front table and J.J. and I were driving to Galveston to spend the day at the beach, so I wanted them. I tried reaching you—"

"But I wasn't home."

"You didn't pick up all's I know. Same thing with Robbie, I got his message service. Last I called Perry."

"I need to make you a set of keys," I commented. Outside of Perry, only Claudia, Robbie, and I had them.

"It'd be nice. Seems like I'm the only person who doesn't have keys. I think that's discrimination against a poor black woman." Mattie pounded a chicken breast for emphasis while peeking out of the corners of her eyes at me and grinning.

"Then I best rectify the situation before you file yourself a lawsuit."

"Good." She nodded, and whacked the chicken with the mallet. "Anyway, Perry'd planned on coming up here to finish some invoices, so he said he'd meet me." She cleared her throat. "Well, I drive over and who should I see but old Conrad."

"Waiting outside?"

"No, he was turning off the inside lights and locking up. That's what I mean about those keys. You pass them around to anybody."

"Conrad was never issued a set," I told her.

The lights clicked on. "I see now. I wondered why you'd give him keys. And him inside helping himself to things."

"What do you mean 'things'?"

"He was stealing, Neil. Eggs, a slab of bacon, fruit, bourbon, a case of beer. Food and"—she turned up her nose—"drink."

So I'd guessed correctly, Conrad had made himself a set of keys. Also, that explained the discrepancy with the inventory. Conrad was compensating for his low pay, and I was sure his thievery was perfectly justified in his mind.

Then something hit me. "Conrad didn't own a car. What was he putting this stuff in, a shopping cart?"

"The van," Mattie replied.

"You mean our van?"

"Yes, the company's. Conrad tried to shuck me with a lame lie that Robbie called and asked him to help take care of some rental orders. Like I wouldn't check on his story with Robbie." She scowled and thumped another chicken breast. At first glance, Mattie came across as a rather delicate woman. And when I first met her, she was. Since the battle with her ex-boyfriend—when he had wanted, among other things, their son, J.J.—timidity had given way to tenacity.

"And you told Conrad as much," I prompted.

"Darn right I did. I told him I wasn't no fool. The van door was open and I saw the booze and food and knew he was thieving. Then I told him Perry was heading over to catch up on them invoices.

"When Conrad heard me say that," Mattie continued, "he got real nervous. Mumbled he was leaving, slid the van door shut, and then walked away. Left the food and the booze sitting in one of those white tubs in the van."

Conrad was using the van to transport his pilfered goods, I mulled. He probably drove to his house, unloaded, took the van back, then walked or bicycled home. And if he had keys to the van, there was no reason not to suspect he had keys to Perry's Lexus. Stop by the dealer, say you need a spare set. *Voilà.*

The sheepish look returned to Mattie's face.

"You're doing fine, Mattie," I encouraged. "This is important."

"Next I kind of felt sorry for Conrad. The dude hasn't had many breaks, and like I said, he's got money and marriage problems. So I didn't say nothing. At least not to Perry—I was afraid he'd have a holy hissy fit. I figured you or Robbie might handle Conrad better. I intended to tell you sooner," Mattie concluded, "then all this with Perry went down and Conrad's skimming seemed small."

"That's okay. I'm glad you did." I ran the sequence of events over in my mind before I asked anything.

"Perry didn't know Conrad was here?" I confirmed.

"Right."

"And The Kitchen was locked when he arrived."

"Everything was the way it should be," she affirmed. "Except for the food and booze in the van."

"What happened to it?"

"I don't know," Mattie replied. "If I'd had the chance I'd have put it up. But I didn't do nothing in front of Perry because I didn't want him to think I was robbing the henhouse. 'Sides, I'd have to do all that explaining about Conrad, which, like I told you, I was hoping to avoid. So I left the stash, thinking if anything I'd mess with it Monday."

"Did you mess with it Monday?"

"No, all the stuff was gone."

Neither Perry nor Robbie had said anything about finding groceries in the van. Which meant they didn't stumble across them, either.

Which meant Conrad had come back.

"Did you notice Conrad hanging out on the street or down at the convenience store or anything?" I asked.

"No," Mattie responded, set the mallet down, and wiped her hands with a white kitchen towel. "A matter of fact, that was the last time I saw Conrad."

"If Perry was invoicing clients, then, as of Saturday morning, he hadn't learned of Sherwood Welles's death," I observed. "He was knocked into a tailspin once the news reached him, and he hibernated at his town house."

Mattie placed a piece of prosciutto across the tenderized chicken, trimmed any excess, then added a few tablespoons of the cheese filling and folded the breast over.

"What happened after Perry arrived?" I asked.

"He unlocked The Kitchen, and I retrieved my glasses," she said.

"Where was his car parked?"

"Under the live oak," she replied.

"On the street?"

"Yeah, I'd pulled into the driveway in front of the van," Mattie explained.

Okay, I thought, there was the opportunity for Conrad to have access to the car. But he wouldn't have known Perry's Lexus would be parked there, or else he wouldn't have been ripping us off. I needed to talk this through with C.J.

I started to walk away, then stopped. "Did you notice if Perry opened the blinds in the office?"

"I don't know. They were drawn when I left."

He usually didn't, especially when he was alone. Perry would lock himself in and concentrate on his work. Therefore, if Conrad tinkered with the car, Perry wouldn't have noticed.

I thanked Mattie. She apologized again for not having mentioned the incident sooner, but I assured her that everything was all right. She'd told me in time.

I prayed.

30

Robbie was in the office working on the rental order for our new client. After he greeted me I asked if Mattie had told him about Conrad's sticky fingers. He nodded solemnly.

"He planted the knife in Perry's car," I said. "I'm sure of it."

"How?" He tucked a pencil behind his ear. "He walk around with the bloody knife strapped to his belt just waiting for the opportunity to frame Perry?"

That made me think. I picked up the phone and punched in Alice Tarkenton's number. Her secretary told me Alice was busy.

"Inform Ms. Tarkenton this is Neil Marshall and it's very important."

A few seconds later her craggly voice barked, "I'm in a meeting, Neil—"

"I know who planted the murder weapon in Perry's car," I interrupted.

"Really? Can you prove it?"

"Almost." I stretched the truth.

"Almost? What the hell does that mean?" She hacked. "No, never mind. Call me when you hit a ringer, none of this almost crap."

"Wait," I hollered. "Did the police find blood anywhere other than the trunk?"

"Christ, Neil, you about busted my eardrum."

A recent bad habit. "Sorry, but this could be crucial."

"Oh, goddamn it, how dramatic." I was clicked onto hold. She had music on her line. If you could call it that. Some pseudo-symphonic, papier-mâché version of "Let It Be."

"All right," her voice returned, "I've cleared my office for thirty seconds, so listen carefully. You know about the evidence in the trunk. Well, another sample was found on the driver's-side floor. They believe he tracked it in on his shoes. In fact, the cops got another warrant and are searching his town house for the shoes, or any clothing that might also have samples. Now, who do you think tracked it in there? The dishwasher?"

"How'd you guess?" I was unable to hide the surprise in my voice.

"I'm so goddamn smart I amaze myself. Why can't you prove it?"

"Conrad's dead."

"I know he's dead," Alice yelped. "Krieger's pretty pissed off his witness was whacked. So much so he's trying to pin that homicide on you."

"I know."

"Then get busy."

"I'm trying," I told her. "Are the cops at Perry's now?"

"Don't you go near that place," she ordered.

"I won't. I was just wondering about Aspen."

"Who?"

"Perry's dog. Who's tending to him? Or is he hiding in fear from the police under Perry's bed?"

"For Christ's sake, I've got the dog. I can't believe you. Your ass is about to be hung out to dry, and—Jesus, you've taken too much of my time."

"Alice—"

She hung up. Irascible, I thought. Petulant. Cantankerous. Vinegary. And that was to her friends. Krieger shouldn't stand a chance.

But of course he did.

"Well?" Robbie asked.

I repeated the half of conversation he hadn't heard, and found myself at a pause when I thought about the way Alice had phrased a point.

"The police are saying Perry *tracked* flecks of blood into his car via his shoes."

"Yeah?"

The image of Conrad's shoes dangling from the shower curtain came to mind. "But it had to have happened Saturday morning," I told myself.

"What are you talking about?" Robbie asked, growing frustrated.

"Conrad must have gotten to the Lexus Saturday morning."

"After encountering Mattie?"

"He'd swear she watched him leave." I paced to the window and cracked the blinds. The neighbors complained just the other day about Perry parking under their shade. Not that I ever understood why, as they kept their ancient Plymouth in the garage.

"How far do you think it is from here to that oak?" I asked.

Robbie rocked the chair back on two legs to look. "Around a hundred to a hundred and fifty feet."

"Do you think Conrad would have the balls to use Perry's car right under his nose?" I asked.

Robbie shrugged, thumped the chair down on all legs.

"What if he was waiting for Mattie to leave?" I asked. "Then once she did, he checked to see if the stuff he ripped off was still in the van. It was, which means Mattie didn't rat on him. He collects the tub and uses Perry's car to run it over to his house."

"You've been reading too many comic books, Dick Tracy." Robbie took the pencil from behind his ear and made a note on the rental sheet. "Why wouldn't Conrad just use the van?"

"Too loud. Too close to the building. Perry would hear it. But his Lexus purrs, and it's far enough away for him to just start it up, slowly back away from The Kitchen, and turn around farther down the street.

"Hey, the blinds are drawn," I continued. "Perry always puts on music. How long would Conrad be gone? Fifteen minutes at the most. Perry had just arrived. He wasn't about to leave."

"How would Conrad know that?"

"Mattie told him that Perry was going to catch up on the invoices." I released the blinds and sat in one of the rolling office chairs. "So he makes off with his stolen goods and in the process tracks dried blood into the car."

"But you're also saying—"

"Conrad planted the knife," I finished. "He was angry enough at Perry."

"Then you think he murdered Welles?" Robbie asked. "Why else would he have the knife?"

I ground my teeth. Events still didn't mesh. "And if he murdered Welles, why would someone kill him?"

"Doesn't make sense," he agreed.

I rubbed my forehead, glanced through the blinds at the shade from the live oak in front of the neighbor's house. "Well, first things first." And I shot out of the office, breezed by Trisha, and jogged next door.

The yard was surrounded by a Cyclone fence and shaded by four huge pecan trees. Two empty chairs rested on the porch. The house, powder blue in color with white shutters, was well kept. I rang the bell.

The man answered. A tough-looking bird, silver-haired, about six inches shorter than me but hard, muscles still in use, and without an ounce of fat on his body.

"Neil Marshall," I introduced myself, and stretched out my hand. "I work next door."

Reluctantly he pushed open the screen door and shook. "Yeah, I've seen you."

"I'd like to ask you a couple of questions concerning my boss's car."

He stiffened. "I ain't touched it. I don't much like it parked under my tree, but I ain't laid a finger on it."

"I'm not saying you did." I raised my hands in defense. "But something happened, we think, Saturday morning."

"What?"

I deflected his question. "Did you notice the Lexus parked out there Saturday?"

"Of course I did. I was in the garage changing the oil on the Plymouth when he pulled up. I was hankering to say something, but he scooted into his place with that young black woman too fast."

The man's wife came up behind him. I'd seen her many times, though not this close. Even in the shadows of the house I could see wrinkles on her face. It was like viewing the rings on the stump of an old, old tree.

"What is it, Earl?" she asked.

"It's the big kid from next door."

"I can see that," she scolded.

"He says something happened to that Lexus that's always sitting under our tree." He talked to her but looked at me.

"What happened, young man?"

"I think somebody took it without permission."

"Why, I don't recollect that, do you, Earl?"

"No, Esme, me either." Still focused on me. " 'Less you mean that other fellow who works for you," Earl added.

Pay dirt. "Other fellow?" I asked.

"The scrawny guy with tattoos."

I described Conrad.

"Yep, that's him," Earl announced. "Looks like a street person. Why you hired vermin like that, I could never figure. You may not be the easiest people to live next to, but y'all are at least clean."

"Now, Earl."

"Don't 'Now, Earl' me, Esme." He scowled, finally glancing at his wife. "You done told me he scares you, too." He faced me again. "That fellow acted real strange."

"What do you mean?" I asked.

"Spooked. Like he was hiding. Almost thought he was stealing the car until I saw he had keys. Might not like that fancy car parked under my tree, but I ain't going to let street trash steal it, either. 'Cepting, like I said, I saw he had keys. He popped the trunk, put a white tub of stuff in, then jumped in and started her right up. Funny, he backed down almost to end of the street before he swung around and headed in the right direction."

"Did you see him return the Lexus?" I asked.

" 'Bout ten, maybe twenty minutes later."

"Thank you, sir."

"What'd that boy do to the car?" Earl asked.

I answered carefully. "Left something inside that was his, and my boss got in trouble for it."

"That so. Was it drugs? He looks like a dope addict."

"No, not drugs, but would you be willing to tell the police what you've told me?" I asked.

"The police!" He pronounced it *po*-lease. Straightening himself, he said, "It's my duty, I reckon."

"Again, thank you. I'll be in touch."

As I walked away I heard Earl tell his wife, "The police. What do you think it could be?"

"My God, Earl," Esme replied. "I hope it wasn't no dead body." The door closed.

And I thought, Afraid so, ma'am. So to speak.

Afraid so.

31

Triumphantly, I announced my findings to Robbie. He directed the computer to print the new client's invoice as I finished relating my conversation.

"You're depending on those old coots?" Robbie asked, honest bewilderment in his voice.

"Why not?"

"She's half-blind and he thinks the Holocaust never happened. Need I say more?"

Talk about knocking a man to the canvas.

"And wouldn't Conrad have noticed blood on his shoes?"

I told him about seeing the shoes in the shower. "Perhaps he didn't notice until after he'd used the car."

"Then the cops have to see Conrad's shoes—complete with a trace of blood—or I don't think you can prove anything. Maybe you can convince one of your cop friends to do whatever they do to test the shoes for evidence. Even then that doesn't prove he planted the knife."

"You're a hard case, Robbie."

"Keeping you honest, and trying to think how the police would respond. Bottom line is you're going to have to change Lieutenant Gardner's mind. No way will you get through to the guy from the DA's office."

He was right. Damn. But what other evidence could link Conrad to the knife to the murder? And then I thought

233

of the .38. Not fabricated—Clay attested to that. And in Conrad's house? I wondered.

"I don't like the look in your eyes," Robbie commented.

"Relax, Butch, just contemplating my options." Which was how I was going to enter Conrad's house unnoticed and search it.

"How come the word *illegal* is screaming in my mind, Sundance?"

I grinned but didn't respond. Instead I picked up the phone. I failed to reach anyone. Left a message with C.J.'s answering service. Another on Linda's machine. And Alice Tarkenton was out of the office. Or so her secretary said. Guessed I was on my own.

"And the phrase *loose cannon* also comes to mind." Robbie stood tall in the middle of the room, frowned, and crossed his arms.

"Your point is?"

He lowered his voice to a hush. "You go back to that house and get caught, what do you think the cops are going to think? Neil, you'll have served yourself up to the prosecutor on a freshly polished Revere tray."

"You're right," I agreed, then redirected him. "Everything okay for the job tonight?"

He released a heavy sigh of relief. "Yeah, fine. The three of us are going to work the job."

"Good."

"You fixing to call Gardner and tell him about your latest discovery?" He folded the invoice into an envelope branded with our logo then bent over to write the client's name on the front.

"Of course. Later."

"Why later?" he asked.

But he was questioning the wall as I slipped out of the room and didn't stop walking until I reached the Bug.

Robbie must've seen no use in chasing me. He'd said his

piece, and I chugged off without so much as a backward glance.

I parked a block away from Conrad's house and approached it from the rear. Using a small set of spyglasses C.J. had loaned me for a Fleetwood Mac reunion concert, I scanned the area. The neighborhood was quiet. No cop cars were parked out front. In fact, no cars were parked around the house at all. The old man who'd called for help this morning was still sitting outside. He was paging through a magazine, apparently listening to the radio. The Astros game, I bet. Moises Alou and the Killer B's. Sounded like the name of a bad heavy-metal band; I almost laughed. But I'd have given almost anything to be at the Dome right now watching Alou with Bagwell, Bell, Biggio, and Berry as opposed to undertaking this endeavor.

I palmed the small set of spyglasses and casually ambled toward the house. The sky was clouding over. I guessed the weatherman had called the late-afternoon thunderstorm correctly. When I reached the rotting cedar fence that scantily bordered the backyard, I glanced around. No one in sight, as far as I could tell. I tugged a couple of boards next to a gaping hole loose at the bottom. Carefully I lifted them up then squeezed into the yard, propping the boards in their original position.

A large hole on a back stretch of fence leading from this yard into the next told me that was where the murderer had disappeared. I wondered if there'd been anyone home in the neighboring house who'd seen anything. I made a mental note to check it out. The neighbor angle worked the last time.

Police tape crisscrossed the window the killer had escaped through. I imagined the warning tape stretched across the front, too. As I drew closer to putting my plan into action, I realized my heart was swinging faster than the Cherry Poppin' Daddies' "Zoot Suit Riot." Simply getting into Conrad's house was going to be a chore. Couldn't break the police tape. Couldn't make too much noise or the old man would alert the police quicker than a Mark McGwire home-run cut.

After easing up to the broken window, I peered inside and determined no one else, such as killer or police, was poking around the house. I pulled on a pair of black plastic gloves, the kind used for washing dishes, and tried the back door. The knob spun in my hand, broken. That must have been the jingling noise I heard this morning, the killer fussing to get out this way.

A large, wall-unit air conditioner took up too much room in the other window in back for me to get through. Staying close to the house, I edged to the corner on my left and peered around. The same rotting fence stood with determination as far as the front door then turned at a right angle that leaned against the house. There was no gate on this side, but barely enough cover to hide behind, as well.

Another wall-unit AC protruded from the side window closest to the street. But with the window nearest me, I was in luck. Not only was it unobstructed, but also half-open with only a flimsy screen to negotiate through.

I stood a moment, listened, and tried to calm the blood pounding through my veins. Any faster and I'll black out, I thought. From this angle, I couldn't see the old man across the street. Thus he couldn't see me either. Good. I could hear the radio now, turned up nice and loud. Surprisingly, not tuned to the ball game but a holy-roller Christian station. Perhaps he was trying to ward off evil spirits in the neighborhood. Hadn't worked for Conrad. However, it was scaring me to death. I even had the urge to shout a couple of biblical quotes back at the radio announcer's deaf ears.

The screened window led to a bedroom. Like the rest of

the house, it was in a shambles. A mess of tossed clothes. Dresser with drawers half-open, socks sticking out at the top like a wild Einstein hairdo. Though the frame was nailed in place, the screen was so weak that all I had to do was push to tear it away from the base. Okay, I thought, this is it. With a hop-skip, I hoisted myself up and into the house.

Immediately, my overactive imagination went to work. It was eerily quiet, with a stench in the air that made me think if fear could decay, this was how it would smell. Staleness rotting, a hint of sweat, both layered over an unheard scream. Anger slain. The pain of fear. Death.

When a floorboard creaked underfoot I almost dove back outside. I rolled my shoulders and calmed myself, then pushed on. First I toured the house, avoiding the white chalk outline of Conrad's body and the bloodstained floor, to convince myself I was really alone. I was.

While in the bedroom I poked around for the gun. Under the bed, the mattress, the clothes on the floor. Nothing. In a closet, on the shelf, behind some boots. Nothing. In a dresser. Nothing. A grubby room, but clean of the .38.

Soon the sky had grown the color of blackened redfish, making visibility in the house difficult. I sure wasn't going to turn a light on, and I hadn't armed myself with a flashlight. Moving quickly, I popped out into the hall. A clap of thunder made me jump. The second one I handled by stiffening. An improvement.

I roamed the house again, knowing this might be my only chance to search it, and I wanted to be certain I hadn't overlooked anything. Glancing across the street, I saw that the old man had made for cover inside his house. A blessing of the oncoming storm.

A few heavy drops of rain slammed down in warning. Streetlights clicked on to cut the afternoon duskiness. Careful not to get too close to the front windows, I again circled the kitchen but only rediscovered the trash, dirty dishes, and liquor bottles from Perry Stevens's stock. In the refrigerator were eggs, bacon, and meat from Perry Stevens Catering. No gun in the drawers or cabinets or tucked under the sink.

In the room where Conrad had died, the desk remained turned over, lamp broken, tools scattered. I circumvented the lingering image of the fallen man and searched under a small couch then around a tattered chair. Nothing.

Then lightning ripped the sky open, and the rain worked itself into a frenzy. Thick beads of water peppered the house, whipped against the windows, or in the case of the killer's escape route, struck against the yellow police tape and sprayed inside the room.

I deftly retraced my steps to the hall. Thunder raged as if crying out for all the dead like Conrad and Welles. Then I noticed the bathroom door that had been opened was now closed. My already high anxiety kicked up a level more. Gently, I turned the knob. I drew a short breath, but behind the door there was nothing.

I could barely hear the thunder or rain over the excitement that pounded in my ears. The bathroom window was also open and the ragged curtains struggled against the torrent like war-torn flags. I stole over to the window and closed it, drew the curtains shut, for the good it did. The small sink still contained the water but not the jeans.

I accidentally kicked a plastic jug on the floor. Bleach. A full unused bottle.

So the cops hauled the sneakers and pants away, I thought. A good sign. Even I saw they weren't thoroughly cleaned. Surely the police would match the blood remnant to Welles. But when had Conrad realized he'd gotten blood on himself? He wouldn't have waited this long to rid himself of incriminating evidence. And of course he wouldn't throw the clothes out; it would cost too much for him to replace them. He was in the process of cleaning his pants and shoes when—yes, that was it—when the killer arrived.

Which meant, my little voice confirmed earlier thoughts, Conrad knew the murderer. Quietly, I stepped into the hall and closed the door. So the murderer shows up, interrupts Conrad's procedure. Conrad sees who it is—relieved it wasn't the cops—and lets the person in. Then the confrontation. Finally, the murder.

I eased toward the bedroom. As hard as the rain was falling and the thunder crackling, though, I could probably have screamed as loud as a rabid Dallas Cowboy fan and not been heard from the street.

After the killer stabbed Conrad, I hypothesized, I showed up and scared the assailant off. Otherwise the murderer would have found the clothes and either finished the bleach job or carried them off. That way a suspect already in jail awaiting trial remained implicated.

So would the killer return? I asked myself, and felt clammy when the answer came back yes.

My pace quickened, though I remembered I hadn't found the gun yet. Then decided to get the hell out.

And had there been one more whip of lightning igniting the silver rain, I would've seen the figure framed in the open window before he saw me.

32

"What the hell are you doing?" The sharp, whispery voice might as well have been a gunshot for the fear that it lodged in me. For a split second I froze. As in a nightmare, my legs felt like cinder blocks out of my control.

Then recognition set in. A woman's voice. I willed myself to the window.

"Linda?" I asked.

"Get your ass out here, Neil."

"But I need to get—"

"Now!" she ordered.

The urgency in her tone ended my objections. I stepped on a pile of clothes then swung my legs out the window and jumped into the deluge.

"Close the window."

"But it was open."

"Do it."

I pulled it down. Linda grabbed my arm and yanked me into a run. Or rather, a sprint.

We dashed across the backyard, ducked and squeezed through the gap on the back fence and into the neighbor's yard. Glancing back, I saw the lights click on in Conrad's house.

"Shit, who's that?" I asked.

"The police, you big idiot." Linda wouldn't let me slow down. "Come on," she said, and tugged.

The next yard had a short Cyclone fence that Linda and I both semihurdled by planting a foot at the top and pushing off as we leaped. Linda slipped on the landing, but I caught her arm above the elbow and steadied her. We covered the yard in seconds. Instead of launching over another fence, though, Linda directed us around to the gate and back out to the street.

She pulled up under a huge pecan tree near the sidewalk. Rain careened off the brim of her Notre Dame baseball cap. Breathing heavy, crouched with her hands on her knees, Linda said, "Wait a minute."

"My VW's not too far."

"I know. I parked down the street from it."

I pulled out the small binoculars. The view of the back of Conrad's house was obstructed by rain, dilapidated fence, and the angle I had. Still, the lights were definitely on, and I thought I detected movement.

"What do you see?" she asked.

I told her, then added, "Not much."

No cop cars were patrolling the street. No officers were rushing after us. Linda straightened and tweaked my sleeve.

"Let's go. Walk normally. I don't think they saw us."

My clothes were plastered to me by the time we reached our vehicles. Linda, wearing a black denim jacket along with the cap, wasn't as bad off.

"I'm going to my apartment to change," I declared.

Linda shuddered.

Recognizing what seeing my driveway and the backyard would now conjure up in Linda's mind, I offered to meet her at C.J.'s office. "Give me ten, fifteen minutes," I added.

"No, I'm all right. I'll follow. Then we'll talk."

In a moment we were in the dry safety of my tiny flat,

having charged from car to door to upstairs without incident.

"I'm drenched," I commented. "How about you?"

Linda hung her jacket up by the door. "I'm all right."

"You need a dry shirt or anything?"

"Really, Neil, I'm fine."

"Want a drink?" I asked.

"Better stick to coffee for now."

"I have some ground Colombian in the freezer."

Linda stopped me. "You get out of those wet clothes, and I'll make a pot." When I didn't move she gave me a soft shove. "I do know how to make coffee."

"I'm sure you do."

"Then don't give that look."

"What look?" I asked.

"The one that says, 'This woman can't even boil water. I'm not going to let her near my fancy coffee.' "

I responded with a smile, a short laugh, and a thank-you as I walked off.

The coffee was finished brewing by the time I returned in dry jeans and a denim shirt. Linda poured me a mug and set it on the kitchen table while I finished toweling my hair. Thunder rumbled in the distance, having been led to the east on a leash of lightning. However, the rain continued, not quite as fiercely, but steadily. I drew up a seat.

"Okay, how the hell did you know I was in the house? And how did you know the cops were about to show?"

Linda sipped the coffee. "Luck on both points. I called your work on my mobile and reached Robbie."

"And the cops?"

"Robbie said I'd better go rescue 'that macho bone-head with the Marlowe complex.' " She curled a couple of fingers on each hand to indicate the quote.

"How nice." Forced smile. "And the cops?" I repeated.

"Vic Hernandez called me. He asked me out to dinner. I

said no. He kept telling me that it might be worth my while."

"And you asked why," I filled in while she tasted the coffee.

A nod. Linda put the mug down with care. "I did. And we went back and forth concerning dinner together until he got the message. Then Vic turned serious." She paused. "You knew you hired an ex-con for a dishwasher, right?"

"Of course. Conrad did time for stealing a car."

"That's what he told you?"

"Yeah. In fact, he explained that the car had actually been his brother-in-law's and he was borrowing it. His brother-in-law, though, got angry at him and reported the car stolen." I gazed at her over my coffee mug. Linda rolled her eyes. "I know," I added. "Classic *I-was-framed* story, but it soothed Perry, and he hired Conrad."

"And no one checked his background," she stated.

"Correct. Now that I feel sufficiently foolish, pitch me the real story."

"Conrad stole a car, all right, but after he assaulted and robbed the man who was driving it."

"Anyone we know?" I asked.

"No. The significance is that the police are beginning to rethink Conrad's role in the Welles murder."

A jolt of relief hit me. I imagined the police had checked out the pants and shoes. "About time."

"Instead of being merely a witness, they're coming to suspect he was also involved."

"Wise deduction," I said with no attempt to hide the self-congratulatory tone in my voice.

"As Perry's and your assistant," Linda added.

My mouth dropped open. "You're kidding."

"I wish."

"The man had walked off the job," I cried in exasperation. "We weren't even on speaking terms."

"Great alibi, isn't it?"

"Wait a minute," I said. "How do they justify Conrad testifying against Perry?"

"He got scared, didn't want to go back to prison. By coming forward he could save his own butt. But when you murdered him—"

"I didn't murder him!" I cut in immediately.

"Calm down. I'm talking from Vic's point of view."

"Warped as it is."

"When you allegedly murdered him," Linda continued, "it was revenge for selling Perry out as well as to quiet Conrad forever."

"If I was involved with the Welles murder, why didn't Conrad finger me along with Perry? How would old Vic answer that?"

"Good point. I didn't toss that hat into the ring. But I will. All I know is the cops are taking it one step at a time, and they're walking toward you."

"I don't believe this," I said.

"After talking with Vic a few minutes I knew the police were heading back to Conrad's house. I didn't know it'd be so soon, but the feeling was strong they were out to do a further in-depth scratch-and-sniff." Linda looked straight at me. "And you're damn lucky they didn't catch you there, or instead of drinking a nice cup of coffee with me you'd be sitting in a cell next to your boss," she added with a touch of scorn.

I swallowed hard, feeling pale. "Thanks."

"What were you doing there?"

"Guess I wanted to see if the police had found the pants and shoes. And I was looking for the .38." At Linda's quizzical expression, I filled her in on what Clay had told me.

"But you didn't locate the gun?" she asked when I'd finished.

"No."

She leaned back. "If you'd removed evidence from the crime scene, C.J. would've done the cops a favor and killed you."

"Somehow I'd convinced myself the key to this whole mess was inside that house." I went over to the counter and refilled my mug. Linda waved off my offer for more.

"A risky gamble, Marshall."

"It seemed worth it, considering."

"Considering what?"

I related my encounter with Earl and Esme.

"Good," she said. "Explains how the knife and blood could've gotten into Perry's car. A good bit of detective work. Going into the house was not."

"You've made that clear."

"Reinforcing the lesson, is all." Linda finished the coffee, stood, and thought aloud. "So after they finish searching Perry's house and your apartment—"

"My apartment?"

"Oh, forgot to tell you. I asked Vic outright if they were getting a warrant to search your place, and when he ducked the question by changing the subject, I knew they were." She picked up her purse. "We'd do well to go and leave it to your dippy landlord to let the cops in."

"This whole situation's getting crazier by the minute," I said, and turned off the coffeemaker. "How can we and the cops be so close concerning Conrad and yet so far on everything else. It's like we're on parallel planes of reality." I clicked off lights and grabbed a jean jacket and an Astros cap as we headed for the door.

"We are. The police perceive things one way, which, if you look objectively, can be fit to appear obvious and logical. We know better and hit it from another angle."

"The cops aren't taking one step at a time," I countered her earlier statement. "They're running. And it's turning into a race." I locked the door to my poor apartment. The idea of someone rifling, even legally, through my private life sickened me. Payback for me invading Conrad's house, I reasoned.

"Yes, Neil," Linda agreed. "I'm afraid it is turning into a race."

Something in her tone alarmed me. "And you think we're losing."

Linda didn't respond. It was the worst answer I could've received.

33

We took Linda's truck under the pretext that I'd be easier to find if I were driving around in my VW. It was a stab at buying all the time possible. The case the police were building against me—and Perry for that matter—was riddled with more holes than a fishnet, and smelled about the same, too. I was guilty of being at the wrong place at the wrong time, but that was the long and the short it. Such a full-court press without exploring all options first wasn't Lieutenant Gardner's style. The officer and I had our differences, but he was a fair man. What was going down had DA stamped all over it.

Which could explain why Hernandez, in his own way, let so much information slip out to Linda. The sergeant respected Ed Krieger almost as much as I did.

"What happened between you and Hernandez?" I asked, and broke the silence.

Linda tensed.

"I know it's none of my business, but—"

"But what?" she snapped.

"Nothing," I retreated. "Sorry. It's none of my business."

"Aren't you the least bit curious about my surveillance?" Linda sharply changed the conversation.

Water hissed beneath our tires, and rain drummed the roof, though it was slowing.

"I guess in all the excitement . . ." I weakly started to explain but didn't follow through.

Linda softened her tone. "Well, tracking you down was the most excitement I had all day. Until then the highlight had been watching Gideon York's muscle men polish the Jeep."

"Getting ready for another wild and crazy Sunday service."

"So I understand."

"You knock off shadowing him to help me?" I asked, feeling guilty.

"No. The storm blew in, and they closed the doors. It was deadsville there, anyway. After cleaning the Jeep, the two thugs played cards. York spent most of the day doing paperwork in his office."

"Working on his sermon, I bet. I wonder if he'll use any of the quotes I gave him."

"Yes, Neil, C.J. said you were impressive. Anyway, since it didn't look like they were going anywhere soon, I thought I'd pick up Nathaniel—especially after C.J. had tipped me off about the restraining order—and tail him awhile. Then the phone conversation with Robbie redirected my course."

Linda maneuvered her big truck to a stop at C.J.'s and her office. A few customers browsed the new-and-used record store on the ground floor. An old man behind the counter noticed Linda and flashed a two-fingered salute. She returned the salutation then followed through to the ignition and clicked off the big engine. There were no cops, no skinheads, and no C. J. McDaniels in sight. I was reaching to open the door when Linda touched my arm.

"Victor Hernandez is basically a nice guy. A good cop. Honest, you know."

"I agree, and I didn't mean to imply otherwise."

"No, dummy," she interrupted, "I'm answering your question."

I waited, knowing she wouldn't share her feelings had she not wanted to.

"Like a lot of Hispanic men, Vic's got this macho controlling attitude. The more he thinks you're his woman, the tighter he pulls on the reins.

"And you know me," Linda added with a half smile, "I have my own agenda, too. As soon as I felt someone rewriting it for me, I had to bail. I think you understand."

I responded with a nod and opened the door. Linda knew perfectly well I understood. Not so long ago I'd expressed similar feelings toward her and ended our affair when she'd begun to tamper with my agenda. The acknowledgment was her offer of apology. I'd accepted it, quietly. Linda smiled, and we let it go.

"What's the game plan?" I asked.

Linda beeped the truck alarm on.

"Hoping to catch up to C.J."

"Last I heard he was revisiting Agnes Berryman," I told her. "But I know he had a wait in store because when I went by to see Warren Clay, Berryman was coming out of the place. Or I should say, blasting out. God, were they steamed."

Linda hesitated at the outside door. I recapped what I'd seen, the sound bites I'd overheard, and my conversation with Clay.

"What do you think they were fighting about?" she asked.

"The television show, I bet."

"Did you ask Clay?"

"Indirectly," I replied. The rain had eased into a fine mist. I wondered why we didn't go inside. "Whatever the magnitude of the problem," I tagged on when I realized she was waiting for more of an explanation, "he said it was worse than not getting the show."

"Because Berryman was giving the spot to a particular someone else, or canceling?" she asked.

"Has to do with money. He indicated he needs a lot of money."

"Don't we all," Linda said, and swooped a backhand at the office. "C.J. could afford to upscale a tiny bit."

"C.J. likes the atmosphere," I responded immediately. But her gesture struck a chord. "You know, Clay waved his hand, too, when I asked him what he needed money for. I thought he was blowing me off. Now I wonder if he meant to imply something else."

"Like?"

"You waved toward the office meaning the building itself. Perhaps Clay was gesturing to the kitchen."

"Trouble with rent?"

"Or more," I said, and pulled my collar up. "For instance, keeping the business solvent."

"You think he wanted money from Berryman?" Linda asked, and frowned at me.

"I know, that does sound farfetched considering her attitude toward Clay."

"But her attitude toward Welles was much different," Linda thought aloud. "What if there was not only the television deal but she was an investor in the company? Or she owns the building Welles and Associates worked out of? Something along those lines."

"And if she pulled support for one—"

"She'd pull it for the other," she completed the thought.

"I guess we ought to find the connection," I said.

"C.J.'s digging in that spot right now," Linda said, talking more to herself than to me. "I'll leave a message with his service, alert him to a possible financial tie." She turned her back to the office and added, "On the car phone."

. "Except for putting Clay in a tight position, what's the importance?" I asked as we headed for the truck.

"I don't know, but it's a lead worth checking."

"When C.J. and I spoke with Berryman she didn't act like someone who was being blackmailed, if that's what you're pondering," I told her.

Linda deactivated the alarm. "Would you, if the blackmailer turned up dead?"

Duh, not hardly, I thought. "What are we doing?"

"There's no use twiddling our thumbs in the office."

"You want to see Warren Clay," I deduced.

"Why not? He seems to be a bundle of information."

"Once you get him past the anger," I made clear. "What about York and the skinheads?"

"I don't think they're going anywhere," she stated. "*Sabe?*"

"*Sí.*" And we finally got out of the damp afternoon.

34

I flew out of the truck like a wounded bear storming a hunter's camp. Linda used her car phone to call 911. Smoke billowed black as the devil's soul through the late Sherwood Welles's kitchen as flames consumed the structure with a gluttonous appetite. I kicked the front door open, stepped aside of the heat blast, and tentatively entered.

Crouched low, I yelled for Warren Clay. Bad move. I started to cough. My eyes burned and my skin stung. I drew the jacket up across my mouth and nose. It did little to help.

Flames tore up the stairwell. I couldn't get to the second floor.

"Clay, where the hell are you?" I took a cautious step.

"Neil, get out of there!" Linda ordered from the porch.

"He was in here."

Plots of fire seeded the interior along with broken glass and scattered utensils. I kicked my way farther in, leaning low and searching.

"Neil," Linda begged, edging up to the door.

I was about to retreat when I noticed the walk-in cooler was open. Deciding to give it a quick glance, I rushed over.

A figure lay sprawled on the floor. Not Warren Clay. I slipped my arms underneath her legs and back, held my breath as the jacket lowered away from my face, and staggered outside.

Linda caught me at the door, took one side of the woman, and helped me drag her down to the curb. A crowd gathered. Sirens roared louder. I fell to my knees and hacked and hacked. My head hurt.

"Wanda Sims," Linda muttered as she felt for a pulse, tried to determine if she was breathing. "What the hell is she doing here? Oh, God, there's a nasty bump on the back of her head."

I glanced at the woman. Wanda Sims. Linda was applying CPR. The rain had tapered off to a light tease. I closed my eyes and stood, hands on knees, fought a wave of nausea, and took deep, steady breaths.

Suddenly we were surrounded by paramedics, firefighters, and cops. Linda identified us, said some other things I didn't pay attention to, then guided me across the street to the bed of her truck.

"You want to lay down?"

"No." I propped myself against the gate and rubbed my head.

"Do you have any idea how close you came to passing out inside that inferno?"

"No."

"You were almost gone when you stumbled out the door."

I closed my eyes again and didn't say anything.

Linda pulled off my glasses and cleaned them. "You better let these guys check you out," she said.

"Why was Wanda Sims here?"

"Good question. Too bad she couldn't tell me. I tried talking to her."

"So she's alive."

"Yes," replied Linda, "but she's in a bad way. She was

mumbling something before they put the oxygen mask on then strapped her onto the stretcher."

"You able to catch what she said?"

"Something about not being married," Linda told me.

"Funny the things that surface in your mind." I made a mental note to relate Wanda Sims's earlier reaction when C.J. and I had followed up on the claims of Everett Baker.

Instead I asked, "Are the firemen aware someone else might be inside?"

"Yes. Take these." She returned the glasses to me.

I opened my eyes. "Let's get out of here."

"We ought to give the cops a statement."

"Fuck that. I've given enough statements for one day."

"What's your problem?" she asked with her share of irritation.

"Pulling Clay's charred body out of there is not going to help my cause," I told her. "Considering I was talking to him such a short time ago. Who knows who was watching. Or what's been said."

"You're paranoid."

I shook my head, not to disagree but to shake the dizziness.

"Running will only hurt," she added.

"But it's a race of time now, remember?" I reminded her.

"I gave our names."

"Then the arson division will track us down, too, when the time comes."

"Arson?"

"Come on, Linda, you know in your gut someone torched the place."

"You're getting way ahead of yourself. Acting emotionally instead of logically. We're not sure Clay was caught in the fire. For all we know, he may have started it, having left an unconscious Sims to burn."

"Why?" I walked around to the passenger door, opened it, and climbed in.

Linda took the driver's seat and turned the engine over. "I don't know. She's a dumb, weepy blonde, but she certainly doesn't deserve to be toasted."

We pulled away slowly. I leaned back and thought aloud, "What does Wanda Sims know?"

"Or what was she after? She was in that kitchen either to talk to Clay or to get something."

"What would she and Clay have to discuss?" I asked.

"A job? Maybe Clay promised she'd be his assistant if he landed the television show."

"Wanda's not Clay's type," I informed Linda. She caught my drift.

"Then perhaps it was a mistake. She was in the way when someone else paid a visit to Clay."

"Who? It wasn't the skinheads this time, though they are a tempting lot to pin the blame on."

"Why are you dismissing the skinheads?" she asked.

I cleared my throat, debated whether or not to say what was on my mind, then decided the point had to be brought up. "You think they'd have just knocked Wanda Sims upside the head?"

Linda swallowed hard. Her knuckles whitened as she clutched the steering wheel. "You're right," she choked out.

The windshield wipers lazily swept at the remnants of the storm. "So where's the common factor?" I asked aloud to break the tension. "How does this relate to Welles's murder? Or does it?"

Linda meandered through the area and remained silent.

"One of the girlfriends, the chef, and a burning building," I listed. "Whose building? Berryman's? Also known as the other girlfriend—whose friend, the food critic, slapped us with a bad review and then a restraining order.

Again, why? What is he afraid of? We know about his lifestyle. What else does he fear we'll discover?"

"Let's find out," Linda suddenly stated.

"But—"

"Hey, if we fuck giving official statements, we might as well fuck restraining orders, too." Linda whipped the truck around and pointed us toward downtown. She tried C.J. on the mobile, but his car phone was off and the office number turned over to the answering service. "Where is that old bastard?" she muttered before leaving the message.

C.J.'s going to need a full pad of paper in order to note everything that's been going on, I thought.

And most of it's not going to make him happy.

35

A few minutes later we were parked down the street from the old Rice Hotel. Linda phoned Nathaniel York's number and reached the maid. She didn't exactly impersonate a police officer, though she misled the poor woman on the other end of the line by identifying herself as Detective Garcia. At any rate, we learned what we wanted to know. York wasn't in.

"What if he doesn't show, or doesn't show alone?" I asked. "What if the lawyer's with him?"

"Guess you'll have to knock him on his ass," she replied matter-of-factly.

"Seriously."

"I don't know. Play it by ear."

People were evacuating downtown in droves as the workday came to an end. We loitered on a northbound street while the majority of the traffic headed south. I cracked a window. Linda glanced at me.

"I reek of smoke," I explained. "It's driving me crazy."

"I can't tell, the odor's on me, too." She smiled. "You were foolishly brave."

"Come on, Linda, you've already lit into me once."

"No, estúpido. No comprendes."

"Sí, pendejo. Comprendo."

"¿Qué comprendes?" Then she repeated, "What do you understand?"

"I charge headlong into situations without thinking first."

"Which is instinctive," she elaborated. "Courage can't be taught. Your actions are also selfless, and I find that admirable. But as for your *cojones*." She whistled. "You best learn to temper yourself or someday you're going to charge headlong into your last situation."

Thankfully, a yellow cab pulled up and our man climbed out, ending the conversation on my *cojones*. He sure was a chunky guy. The beige London Fog he wore for protection against the soft rain made him look like a cantaloupe with legs. Then I saw he wasn't alone. It wasn't the lawyer with him, though. It was Agnes Berryman.

I scoped out the area looking for C.J. Not in sight, which didn't mean he wasn't sneaking a cigarette and watching us like some sort of crusty guardian angel. Before I could ask Linda for her binoculars, she opened the door.

"You think a confrontation's wise?" I asked.

"You stay here."

"No way." And I swung out with her.

Nathaniel York was reaching back inside the cab for his briefcase when we approached. Agnes, waiting beneath a small umbrella, caught sight of us—me—first and tensed.

"What do you want?" she snapped.

"Only to ask you a couple of questions."

York paid the cab then whipped around. He tried the James Cagney look, but it came across more like Rodney Dangerfield. "You, you can't come around m-m-me," he sputtered. "There's a re-restraining order. I'm going to call the po-po—cops!"

"We don't have to answer any questions," Berryman assured him.

"Look, lady," I jumped in before Linda. "My boss is in jail for a murder he didn't commit. Someone whacked the eyewitness for the prosecution and I'm a suspect. And another man may be dead from the fire at Welles's kitchen. At the very least, a woman is in the hospital after she was clubbed on the head and left to burn."

As I spoke, Berryman's eyes widened. She steadied herself on York's shoulder.

"A fire?" Berryman asked.

"We just came from it," Linda informed her. "We'd gone to see Warren Clay. Instead, Neil pulled Wanda Sims out of the flames."

"What about Clay?"

"We don't know if he was in there or not," Linda replied.

"Oh, God," Berryman whispered. "He went through with it."

York braced himself as she leaned heavily on him. "This is outrageous!" he began.

"Can it, chubby," Linda told him. "We'll get to you."

A retort was cresting, but the glint in Linda's eyes had been honed to a fine edge. She was hankering for a fight.

Berryman wiped her forehead with the back of her gloved hand. "It's okay, Nate," she said to her companion, then turned to me. "Can we talk elsewhere?"

The Lancaster Hotel was only a couple of blocks away. I suggested we walk. Berryman agreed, but judging from the daze she was in, I think she'd have agreed to step out in front of a speeding bus. Nathaniel York, however, was a different story.

"I'm not going anywhere with them," he announced.

"What are you afraid of?" I asked. "What are you hiding? You're in a closet that's made of glass. You may never step out, but that doesn't mean everyone else doesn't see you for who you are. What more is there?"

York's face reddened and his fists balled. I knew he wasn't going to hit me, though, and he knew it, too. Bluster, bull, and connivance were his tools. Not physical force. It wasn't too difficult to see he was the type of man who liked to inflict pain, but went out of his way to avoid it.

"I don't have to listen to this bullshit," he muttered, and moved toward the building.

"You're coming with us," Berryman told him with surprising force.

He hesitated.

"Now, Nathaniel." She hooked her arm around his. Silently, he obeyed. I wondered if she could make him roll over and beg, too.

"What did you mean by 'he went through with it'?" Linda asked, her aggression receding.

"Who are you?" Berryman's heels ground against the pavement as we walked.

"Linda Garcia. I'm a private investigator."

"Really?" She sized Linda up. "You're much too pretty to be associating with lowlifes." Berryman eyed me.

I held my tongue, not wanting to trade barbs but to hear what she knew.

Linda forced a smile. Waited.

"I spoke to Warren Clay today," Berryman said. "It was painful, but I even met him at Sherwood's kitchen." There was a hitch in her breath. "You say it's on fire?"

"I don't imagine there'll be much of the structure left," I responded.

"What a shame." She shook her head. "You see, I'm executor of Sherwood's estate. He feared should anything ever happen to him that his stepbrother would make a claim, and that was the last thing he desired.

"I guess what I'm leading up to," she continued, "is that a business such as Sherwood's, as you know, is built on his name. His personality and public persona lured in the clients. Without him, there is really no such thing as Sherwood Welles and Associates."

"What about the associates?" I asked. "Are you one?"

Agnes Berryman looked up at me for the first time since we'd started walking. A weariness washed her features pale and she was depending strongly on York's physical support. Nathaniel propped her up with his bulk and remained in a silent rage.

"I have a considerable amount of money invested, yes," she finally said. "And that was why I had to weigh my decision carefully."

"You're closing the business," Linda anticipated.

"It will take more than I can give to keep it going," she said. "I've put out feelers, but few want to take over the company of a murdered man, and those willing won't do it without the television show as part of the package."

"That includes Warren Clay," I stated.

"Clay is a very good chef, and works well as part of the support staff, but as I told you before, he cannot lead. Of course he doesn't see it that way."

Cars sprayed by. We waited, among a small crowd, for a streetlight to change. When it did, and the people around us had thinned out, Berryman resumed speaking.

"Clay became very angry when I informed him of my decision," she said, "and, to a degree, I understand. He's paid his dues. Working for Sherwood was demanding. However, fate dealt Clay a nasty hand. I can liquidate, recover my money, pay off debts, or I can take a chance of losing that, and possibly more.

"Without going into detail, I pointed out to Clay that although he has his talent as a chef, it isn't enough to carry the operation. He went into hysterics, threatened to kill himself and burn the place down. I took that as more of his foolishness. I guess I was wrong."

Berryman fell quiet. She remained tucked beneath her umbrella as if it could protect her from more than just the rain.

I caught Linda's eye.

"I doubt we'll know whether or not he followed through on his threat until the fire's out and the building's cool enough to enter," she said. "But you'll need to tell this to the police," Linda urged Berryman.

"Yes, I suppose I do."

"Why do you think Wanda Sims was there?" I ventured.

Berryman scoffed. "Who knows?"

"To pick up something?" Linda offered. "A check?"

"There'd be nothing she needed there," Agnes stated. "She was paid through the show and worked at the station. I've never known her to go to the shop."

Shop, meaning, I supposed, Welles's kitchen.

"Have you?" she added to her silent companion.

York bristled.

"Well, have you?" Agnes demanded when she detected his hesitancy.

"Only when he fired her," he stated. "He did it at the shop."

Linda and I stopped. They paused and turned back to us.

"Fired her?" we said in unison.

Agnes Berryman let out a short, condescending laugh. "What's the big deal? I told you, Mr. Marshall, the day you and that detective barged into my office, that she was fired. In fact, if I recollect correctly, you brought it up."

"We knew you'd ordered Welles to fire her—" I started.

"But Wanda Sims denied knowing anything about it," Linda finished. "We were working on the assumption that Welles hadn't brought himself to can her before he died."

"Oh, no, he did," York interjected quickly. "I drove her there for the purpose of terminating her contract."

Amazement suddenly colored Berryman's pale weariness.

"I knew he'd put the deed off as long as possible," he

explained. "And you wanted the break made, dear. So I forced the issue."

"And knowing it'd get back to Agnes if he didn't cut the relationship off, Welles had no choice," I drew from what he was saying. Not waiting for a response, I asked, "Was this before or after he roughed you up on the television set? No, never mind, it had to be after. He threatened you again, though, didn't he?"

York didn't respond.

"You've been locked in a power struggle with Welles ever since he took up with Agnes," I speculated. "And fearing further retribution, you sicced the skinheads on him."

Linda's eyes darkened. *Vengeance is mine, sayeth the Lord.* Who no doubt was a scorned woman.

"And us," she added.

I felt the fear steam from York. So must've his boss.

Berryman jerked away from him.

"They're lying," he defended himself. "H-h-how would I know a bunch of gay-bashing sickos?"

Linda, in a league of her own, was on the verge of losing all sense and going after him. Fortunately for Nate, I was in the way and grabbed her by the shoulders.

"You have a restraining order," York reminded me. "You shouldn't be near me. I'll call—"

"Shut up!" I snapped, and met Linda's eyes. I spoke to York but didn't deviate from C.J.'s daughter. "Call whoever you want. The cops, your lawyer, your father, the skinheads. Actually, I'd prefer those neo-Nazi assholes. Because if we ever see them again, they're dead. And then we go after who sent them."

I released Linda, who'd relaxed, and faced York. "We will nail those thugs' asses to the barn door like a passel of raccoon hides. And whoever goes down with them, goes down."

York raised an arm against me, not to strike but to cower as if he'd had years of experience. "My father—" he began.

"Can go to hell," I cut him off.

Berryman collected herself, gained his arm back. "This is just talk, dear. Of course they're lying," she said, then turned to us. "Nate wouldn't betray me."

We were in front of the Lancaster Hotel now, with nothing left to say. Berryman broke the silence first.

"Why don't you and I have a drink, Nate."

"A marvelous idea, darling."

"If you'd excuse us," she told Linda and me.

Neither one of us objected.

36

My insides felt like a Jackson Pollock painting. Splayed emotion across canvas, trying to make chaos into order— or order out of chaos—I didn't know. I never understood Pollock, anyway. Nor was I sure of what I felt now.

Wanda Sims had lied to us about being fired.

I'd bet the ranch Nathaniel York was behind the skin-head attack on Sherwood Welles.

Agnes Berryman didn't buy into that. Why? And what was all this "dear" and "darling" crap? What was their relationship?

Finally, Warren Clay was willing to commit suicide and burn the place down? He seemed more determined to find his rightful place than self-destruct.

Or was that me projecting my own survival instincts on him? Clay was pretty volatile.

I churned. Linda was silent, hands shoved in her jacket pockets, digesting the events.

On returning to her truck, Linda and I discovered C. J. McDaniels, arms folded, half sitting on the hood, chomping away on his chewable Nicorette cigarette.

"I want to hear it all," he announced before we said a word.

Linda smiled wryly. "You didn't get to her."

"I didn't even catch up to Agnes Berryman until a short time ago," C.J. said. "She wasn't around, then I became preoccupied. When I eventually located her, she was with York, so I decided to just watch for a spell."

"If you'd come with me after lunch, you'd have picked her up at Clay's," I began, and then recapped my afternoon. Starting with the argument between Clay and Berryman, I jumped from Welles's missing .38 to Earl and Esme to the fire, the injured Wanda Sims, the missing Warren Clay, and finally, the downtown stroll with Berryman and Nathaniel York. I omitted the little break-in incident at Conrad's. Thankfully, Linda said nothing about it, either. When asked what she was doing with me, she brushed the question off by saying with the rain Gideon had locked himself in the church-fortress tighter than Noah on his ark, so she caught up with me at The Kitchen.

"The fire," C.J. stated, "was started by Clay?"

"According to Berryman, it was suicide," I responded. "A case of 'if I can't have the business, no one can.' "

"Why was Wanda Sims there?"

"Good question."

He stroked his chin. "You told anyone about the old couple witnessing Conrad in Perry's car?"

"No," Linda replied.

"Okay, that, along with the information about the shoes and pants, will be a couple of dandy presents for Alice. We'll see if she can work her magic and spring Perry."

"What about me?" I asked.

C.J.'s gum chewing slowed. "Always the problem child." He paused. "Come again why you think Nathaniel's tied to the skinheads."

"It makes sense," Linda answered. "Welles became physical with York once, who's to doubt he wouldn't again after York forced the issue with Wanda Sims."

"And he can put up a decent front," I added. "Remember how he bulled his way into your office? If he dealt with the skinheads the same way, they might never know he's gay."

"The facade doesn't last," C.J. pointed out. "Crumbles easily."

That was true.

"So why did Nathaniel send the skinheads after you?" the big investigator fished.

"He didn't like us stirring up the waters around his father," I replied, then recalled what the blue-eyed thug had told me during the second confrontation. *I vowed to kill you, and now I can.* "Or better yet," I returned to my earlier theory, "they weren't sent, they were released. And they came for me and not you because I interfered with their sadistic fun the night they were beating Robbie's poor friend half to death."

"Why restrain them in the first place?" he asked.

"The murder," I responded.

"The murder they didn't commit," C.J. reiterated. "I think we're all sure of that by now."

"Because Welles had a gun and chased them off," I said. "And whoever has the gun murdered him."

"Perhaps," C.J. said.

"Hold off on that," Linda cut in. "Backing up, it was a murder that could easily be charged against a gang of violent thugs, so they go into hiding."

"Until we hit a nerve," I said. "If Nathaniel York had let loose his dogs on Welles, then why couldn't he have gone along? He watches from outside as the thugs bust up the place, then becomes surprised when they're chased off. Or angry. He goes inside and, when Welles puts the gun down, knifes him. Nathaniel could get close enough."

"Nathaniel appears out of nowhere on a Friday night and Welles wouldn't be suspicious?" Linda asked. "Not that I believe York has the guts to show his face in such a situation. Hell, you saw him cower, Neil. If Welles chased off the skinheads, York would've hightailed his ass, too. Sorry. Your theory doesn't hold water. At the least, if Welles had faced Nathaniel after that attack, we'd be investigating someone else's murder."

It seemed like a good idea inside my head. Somewhere in the delivery, though, the scenario twisted into confusion.

"I figure we're halfway home," C.J. judged, "and this is how we're going to handle things. Linda, you keep an eye on Nathaniel. If I'm right, he's apt to go visiting after he and Berryman part company."

Linda smiled and nodded. "I follow you."

"Best move the truck to a new spot to be safe." C.J. directed his attention to me.

"I know, you want me to go home."

"Actually, yes, but I don't reckon you would. Instead of having you run off on some half-cocked scheme, I'm assigning a task. Check up on Wanda Sims. Make a courtesy call to see how the woman you pulled from the fire's doing. Find out what kind of condition she's in. Maybe we'll get lucky and she'll be conscious."

"Camp out at a hospital? That's worse than being sent home," I complained.

C.J. spat out his gum. "Just do as you're told."

"And what are you going to do?" I asked the omnipotent investigator.

He pushed himself from the hood of the truck and shifted his weight from foot to foot. "I'm going to do my damnedest to ensure you and Perry don't have adjoining cells on death row. Let's ride."

37

DEAD MAN'S BROTH

The cabbie dropped me off at my apartment, and I changed clothes yet one more time. At this rate I'd exhaust my wardrobe by midnight. After washing up I grabbed a copy of Donald Hall's new book of poems, *Without,* and headed for Ben Taub Hospital and Wanda Sims.

The clouds overhead hadn't quite broken, but on the horizon shafts of sunlight sliced through, creating a sort of tunnel effect. In part I was reminded of the times when I was a child hiding beneath a thick blue-gray blanket with the glow of a flashlight as I read beyond my allotted time. Only this was more surreal because the colors of the city, dampened by the rain, appeared darkly rich and vibrant, full of their own energy, like the sky in Van Gogh's *Starry Night.* I didn't know if this was a good sign or not. Or any sign. Most likely a strange vision made stranger by a tired mind.

Wanda Sims was out of intensive care and sleeping soundly. At the nurses' pod I did as C.J. suggested and informed them I was the man who carried her out of the burning building, and I was checking to see how she was.

Usually I didn't have much luck with nurses—I suspect they detected my phobia of hospitals and took it personally—but this time they were more than receptive. Words of praise, respect, and admiration were knitted together and placed on my head like a laurel wreath.

Blushing, I half dismissed the compliments, yet I also used them by playing up my need to visit Wanda Sims. It worked.

She was in a double room with no roommate. A bandage was wrapped around her head, her eyebrows and lashes were singed, and there was a bruise on one of her crimson cheeks. An IV was attached to her left hand, and her breathing was deep and steady.

"We wake her up every couple of hours on account of that bump on her head," the nurse beside me coarsely whispered. "A nasty knock that thank goodness was bleeding on the outside."

"When she comes around has she said anything about what happened?" I asked.

"The police wondered the same thing. They say someone hit her then left that poor child in the fire. It is so fortunate you came along." She stared at the fragile young woman. "Who would do such a thing?"

A number of people came to mind, but I only shook my head and waited for her to answer my question.

"Oh, no, she hasn't come around long enough to tell us anything. Best she can do is mutter."

"Anything you can understand?" I asked.

"Poor thing, someone must've quit on her recently," she continued to whisper. "Keeps repeating 'I wasn't married, wasn't married, wasn't married.' "

Same thing Linda had reported. Was Sims lamenting the fact Welles was dead and they'd never marry? Did she think she could've won him back? Or was it even Welles? Was it the fictitious husband? Since she'd lied once, I wouldn't have believed she wasn't a runaway wife had C.J. not checked the story out. So why, in her delirium, focus on something rather insignificant? You answered your own question, Neil, I told myself—in her delirium.

"I'm going to sit awhile and read," I told the nurse.

I smiled at her hesitation, which prompted a smile in return.

The nurse winked. "That'll be fine, dear. You can stay a little while." She patted my shoulder after I made myself as comfortable as possible in the chair at the base of the bed.

"By the way," I said as she was leaving, "I heard someone else might have been in the burning building."

"Not that I know of." She glanced at her watch. "Or let's say, if they did find someone else, that person didn't come here."

Implication—he went to the morgue. I thanked her and thumbed to the table of contents.

The Donald Hall book was an artist's voyage through sadness. Raw emotion, honest, and without melodrama, the work spoke of loss. The loss of his wife, Jane Kenyon, to leukemia. Of his aged mother's death. Of his mother-in-law's passing. Yet within the loss was evidence of all the love he'd received—and continued to give. I couldn't help but think of Keely Cohen, her leaving, and was grateful that her loss was a further commitment to living and not a permanent departure. The poignancy of the poems before me, and occasional glances at the woman in the hospital bed, placed life in perspective. I prayed for half the dignity Mr. Hall showed. And yet, in my plebeian mind, I heard an old Dolly Parton song: "I'll Always Love You."

I had read half the book when Wanda stirred. Careful not to startle her, I stood and edged over to the bed. Her injuries did nothing to diminish her beauty. And as she rose from the depths of sleep, muttering incoherently, the sensual vulnerability she exuded was even more pronounced.

"Wanda," I whispered. "Wanda, it's Neil Marshall. I met you this morning."

Her eyes popped open in fright.

"It's okay, Wanda. It's okay. I'm not going to hurt you. In fact, I toted you out of the fire this afternoon. You're safe now. You're at the hospital."

Fright turned to confusion.

"You went to Sherwood Welles's kitchen this afternoon. Why?"

"I was never married," she said weakly.

"I know."

"He made it look like I was."

"Who?"

"You've got to help her," Wanda cried, and leaned forward with a sudden burst of energy.

"What? Help who?"

"You've got to." She grabbed hold of my arm. "I don't like her, but he can't keep making up stories and hurting people."

"Relax," I told her. "Tell me who to help."

"He made it look like I was married." Wanda fiercely met my eyes, yet the fierceness was drawn from a deep void where she was so completely lost in her thoughts she was barely cognizant of me. Her nails dug into my skin.

"Who made it look like you were married?" I gently guided her hands from my arm and held them.

"Warren Clay."

"Why?"

"He hit me," she said.

"Clay did?" I rocked back a step. "Are you sure?"

"He's going to hit her, too." Her breathing grew heavy. I released her hands and nudged her back against the bed.

"Who, Wanda, who else is Clay going to hit?"

"I saw him do it."

"Do what? Hit someone?"

"It was horrible." Her voice squeaked, and she twisted into a fit of tears.

Wanda Sims was riding an emotional waterfall in a barrel of fragments. I hung with her.

"What was horrible?"

She squeezed her eyes, sobbed. "He picked up the knife when Sher put down the gun. The men were gone. I thought everything was all right."

I felt a prickling along my spine. The hackles on the back of my neck stiffened.

"What happened after Sherwood put the gun down?" I prodded.

Her words choked out in sobs. "When Sher turned around"—she drew a large breath—"the knife blade sank into his heart."

"Are you telling me that you witnessed Warren Clay murder Sherwood Welles?"

"Yes." Her head tossed back and forth. She placed an arm across her eyes.

"Yes, I saw it happen," she reiterated. "Because I didn't listen and snuck down from the office."

"You were at the office trying to get your job back and patch things up," I suggested.

Wanda responded with a sob.

"And someone broke in," I continued. "Welles called 911. That line about moving out of the way, he was talking to you so he could get his gun. Then he chases the men off. What did the men look like?" I stopped and asked, "Huge, dressed in fatigues, or skinheads?"

"Skinheads," she replied, barely audible.

So I was right about that, I thought. But way off with Warren Clay. And where did Conrad fit in?

"Why didn't you tell the police?" I asked.

"He was going to make me part of it, an accessory," she mumbled, "unless I went along with him. He was scared, and I was scared he was going to kill me. He said he would take care of it, and I wouldn't get hurt. He lied."

I stopped trying to sort out the information as something she'd said rose and booted me in the seat of my pants.

"You've got to help," she said. "He dumped something all over the kitchen and was lighting the stairs when I walked in. He chased me. Hit me. Because I told him I was never married and he was a coward trying to point blame . . ." Her voice trailed off.

I picked up the phone next to her bed. Clay had murdered Welles, set up Perry, and probably murdered Conrad, too. After things went from bad to worse, he torched the kitchen and almost added Wanda Sims to his list.

So what was to say he wouldn't bring closure by murdering the person who threw the last punch and sent him in a crazed fit to the canvas?

"Agnes Berryman," I said with dreaded realization.

But the very flow of the name chilled my lips as if I'd softly kissed a dead woman's cheek.

38

I tried both Lieutenant Gardner and Sergeant Hernandez but they were off duty. Talking to anyone else seemed more trouble than I needed, so I left no message. If Berryman was in danger, and it would be at her house, then that was Fort Bend County and the Sugar Land Police Department's jurisdiction, anyway. C.J.'s mobile was on, but he didn't answer. As Wanda Sims lay whimpering, I finally reached Linda.

"Neil, I got them," she announced upon hearing my voice.

"So do I."

"Snapped enough pictures of York meeting with the skinheads to make the paparazzi proud," she continued, not listening to me.

"Which York?"

"Nathaniel went to his father, just as C.J. predicted. Old Gideon then rode with his muscle men down to a sleazy part of Montrose. They met outside this biker bar. And I caught Gideon slipping them an envelope which the idiot opened right there and counted the money." She was giddy.

"Where's C.J.?"

"He called Vic Hernandez—unofficially, of course—and they've moved in for the kill."

What kill? How? I wondered, but played that off for now.

"Listen to me carefully, Linda," I said sternly.

"Neil, what is it?"

"Wanda Sims awoke. Well, sort of. She's kind of loopy—"

"Neil!"

"She claims she witnessed Warren Clay stabbing Sherwood Welles to death."

"Oh, God—"

"That's not the worst. I think he's gunning for Agnes Berryman now," I added. "Is she still with Nathaniel?"

"No, she left a couple of hours ago."

"I'll check out her Sugar Land home."

"No, Neil—"

"If I see anything, I'll call the cops out there," I tried to assure her.

"Neil, you're rushing into another fire," Linda told me.

"And what cop in Sugar Land do you know who'll discreetly check it out?" I asked. "If they blunder in, and Clay's there, he'll kill her."

"Don't do anything stupid," she ordered. "I do have contacts out there. I'll call and meet them. I'm a licensed investigator and carry some weight. You don't."

"Linda—"

"No, Neil. I'm the professional. This is my business. You stay with Wanda, find out what else she knows. I'll call you."

I gritted my teeth. Always the control thing. Through the silence she sensed my attitude.

"I have to see this through for myself. You can do your part by watching over the only person who can unequivocally set Perry Stevens free. And God only knows what other bits of evidence are floating around that bubbly mind of hers. ¿Comprendes?"

Her identity was at the crisis point after the attempted rape, and she was out to prove something. So would I help more by being there as backup or by backing off? I decided to back off, then decide whether to back up. *"Sí,"* I finally responded. "But I don't like sitting on the sidelines."

"I'll call soon as I learn something. Trust me." And she hung up.

I set down the receiver and returned to my seat. Wanda had drifted back off to sleep. I tried reading, but my mind was a windstorm of thoughts. Again, how did Conrad fit in? Say he was there looking for a job, why at that time? Sounds like a setup to me, I thought.

If that was the case, then had Clay planned to murder Welles and finger Conrad?

Or was he involved with the skinheads, too? After all, he was at the bar with Robbie and me the night we first became acquainted with the neo-Nazi violence. Something didn't make sense, but like the name of a character actor who was right on the tip of the tongue, I couldn't quite place it.

I tried the book again. Wanda's breathing eased into a steady rhythm. For a few minutes I was able to lose myself in someone else's world. Then the door swung open, the light of the hall sweeping across the dimness of the room, and out of the corner of my eye I noticed a man wearing a surgical gown and cap enter the room. He had his nose buried in a medical chart, and he closed the door behind himself.

"You don't need to wake her," I said, determined to finish one final stanza before closing the book. "She was alert and just drifted back asleep," I added.

"Has she talked?"

"Actually, yes—" Then the cold switch of fear flailed against my nerves. I recognized the voice.

Maintaining composure, I closed the book and looked up. My eyes paused first on the .38 pointed directly at me. I realized I was holding my breath. Slowly I emptied my lungs, then deliberately drew in deeply and released again slowly in an attempt to calm my thundering heart. I forced my gaze away from the gun until it fell on Warren Clay's crazed face.

"That's too bad, Marshall. Now I'll have to kill you, too, understand?" His grin passed into a sneer. "But maybe that's what you get for sticking your nose in."

"If you hadn't framed Perry—"

"I didn't frame Perry Stevens, you moron." Clay stepped in front of the chair, so he was now between Wanda and me. "Your idiot dishwasher did that all by himself, you know?"

"What?" I started to stand.

Clay waved the gun. "Stay where you are."

I obeyed.

"You see," he continued, "after it happened, I'd intended to frame Conrad. He'd called looking for work, so I arranged to meet him Friday evening. How'd I know he'd show higher than a crabmeat soufflé? The fool doesn't even know what he's doing. I catch him hiding in the bushes from Stevens, right? But after your boss huffs off, those pigs in leather storm the place. I'm no fool, I hide with Conrad."

As Clay replayed the night he jerked the gun around like it was a turkey leg he was ready to take a bite out of. That increased my anxiety level just a touch. I said nothing, though, to interrupt his train of thought. The longer he talked, the better chance I had of thinking what to do.

"Welles comes charging at them like Teddy Roosevelt," Clay told me. "So I know he's got the gun. The skinheads scatter, and I go inside. Almost got my head blown off, that son of a bitch. And the inside is a mess, you know?" Clay started to tremble. His breathing became labored. He ground his teeth to gain control, then continued, "Welles went into this rage. Somehow the attack was my fault. He accused me of not having any guts, of sending a bunch of thugs to shake him down instead of facing him myself.

"I tried to tell him I had nothing to do with that, but he wouldn't listen. He was convinced I was trying to ruin him because I was jealous. Not only jealous but disloyal for trying to leave and ungrateful for everything he taught me." A cackle escaped and his voice rose. " 'For everything Welles taught me,' you hear that? Finally, he called me a no-talent fry cook, and he fired me."

His breath seethed out between his teeth. Wanda Sims stirred in bed.

"So when he put the gun on the bench, I picked up a knife from the rack. When he turned around, I stabbed him." Clay refocused on me, though he nodded toward Wanda. "But you know that, because she saw. I didn't know she was there. I should've killed her then, but I was afraid there wasn't time."

"What about Conrad?" I was surprised at how calm I sounded, like I was asking him to identify a secret ingredient in a cherished recipe.

"I threaten the bimbo and get her out of the building," he said. "By this time Conrad's inside checking the body. He's so stoned he doesn't realize he tracked through the blood or got it on his clothes, and he's just staring. Until we hear the sirens. He gets real scared. Says he's an ex-con and can't be here and takes off. I grab Welles's gun, then take the knife and wrap it in some kitchen towels and leave with a plan."

"You planted the knife and towels at Conrad's house," I confirmed.

"It wasn't too difficult. Later that night he had passed out, and I stole in through an open window and left the evidence."

"So he got scared," I filled in. "Conrad had a history of blacking out. But the knife must've reminded him of staring at the body, and maybe he remembered hiding in the bushes from Perry and the thugs, though he could easily have been confused about what happened when. At any rate, he remembered the dead body, remembered Perry, and planted the bloody knife and towels in the Lexus."

Clay shrugged. "Didn't matter to me. One less competitor."

"If you went to all the trouble to implicate Conrad, why didn't you tip off the police before he could tamper with the evidence?" I asked. Seemed like a logical question to me, which was foolish when talking to the illogical and unbalanced.

"I—I tried," he snapped. "It was too late. Conrad had made his move. I heard Perry was arrested. The cops swallowed Conrad's line once they found the towel fibers and traces of blood in Perry's car."

"He sobered up awfully quickly for someone as wasted as you said he was."

"Wouldn't you if you woke up the next day with a bloody knife in your bed?" He seemed almost delighted at the thought. "An ex-con's got to have good survival instincts."

Well, they weren't that good, I thought.

"The problem with Conrad came in when he started to recall the events of the night in full," I prodded.

"He was angry. He wanted money to keep his mouth shut and to go ahead and testify against Perry."

"And not only did you not have any, you'd never run the risk of having a loose cannon such as Conrad holding anything over you." I thought a moment. "You called me that morning, early, to learn if I had any late-breaking news about Perry and Conrad. When I didn't, you figured this was your chance, and you whacked him."

"Yep. And I could've let you take the fall for the murder and not had to kill you if it hadn't been for her." Clay swung the gun in Wanda's direction then back. "Stupid woman got hysterical just because I set up a dummy history for her to throw the investigation off."

"You knew if the police brought her in for some heavy-duty interrogation, she'd crack," I stated.

"She bawled for two days like the perfect widow. I didn't think she'd crack until later. You know, I should have taken Welles's gun and shot her that night, wiped it clean, and put it in his dead hand. But I didn't think that fast. I didn't have enough time."

He stared hard at the resting woman. I felt his impatience grow. "Why'd you put us on Wanda's trail?" I asked to buy time.

"Marshall, you're stupid. I knew you'd find out about Sims through York or Berryman or someone. If I put you onto her, then it deflects from me, understand?" Clay backed up, switched the gun to his left hand, and steadily aimed it at me.

"There's no way you're not going to get caught," I said.

"No witnesses, no case." With his right hand he tugged the pillow out from under Wanda's head.

"Don't do it, Clay." I half rose before the nose of the .38 stopped me.

"I'll shoot you now."

"Everyone will hear," I pointed out.

"I'll shoot my way out of the hospital, if I have to."

"The police know."

"They'll have to find me." Clay placed the pillow down on the slumbering Wanda Sims's face and pushed.

Sims jolted, then began to thrash against the smothering. In a healthy state, she'd have a tough fight in that situation. Now she had no chance.

Eyes darted from me to the dying woman. Clay's face strained, but the blows and fits of clawing from Sims appeared to have no effect. The IV tore out. Her legs kicked off the sheet.

I had made up my mind to rush him the next time he glanced her way when the phone rang. The jarring sound automatically sprang me into action. It drew Clay's attention like a motorist hearing a police siren right behind him. I grabbed the gun with first my left then my right hand. We crashed into the small dresser that held the phone and turned the whole thing over. I heard a voice from the phone's mouthpiece. Linda's. Then felt a number of punches to the side of my head and knew that Clay had released the pillow.

I twisted to my left and, using my size to my advantage, shouldered him against the concrete wall. He gasped, stopped the hitting. The gun went off, a deafening sound that I was sure Linda recognized and the whole hospital heard. But he wouldn't let go.

I threw my weight and rammed him into the wall twice more before he grabbed my hair and almost ripped it out. I released his arm with my left hand and elbowed him in the ribs. A gasp. Again. Same result. I stomped on his foot, and finally he released my hair. I felt a blow to the back of my head and went with the force, carrying us through a curtain and against the neighboring bed. He hit me again. I spun to the left, keeping up the pressure on his gun hand, and we rolled down.

Then I had him. He was going to hit first, and I twisted my left forearm under his chin. The sound of his head popping against the floor seemed almost as loud as the gunshot. I was on top. The gun scooted from our hands. And Warren Clay went limp. Still breathing, but out for the count.

When I rolled free, breathing heavily, and looked up, I saw the angry eyes of one large security officer. And the barrel of yet another gun drawn against me.

This time, however, I welcomed the sight.

39

Two days later I was at The Kitchen boiling crawfish. Robbie, in his ever-present optimism—or it was a result of Trisha's influence and her cosmic sureness the show would go on—had never canceled the crawfish order. With two-hundred-plus pounds purging in the massive stainless-steel sinks, there was really no choice but to throw the party.

Jazz resonated from the stereo instead of Perry's usual classical music. Mostly old-style. Vaughan, Armstrong, Holiday, Bessie Smith, and such. Tunes I hadn't heard in a dog's day. It added to the marvelous spring day as we worked outside on the driveway. A slight breeze, temperature expected to hit the low eighties, plenty of sun. We'd expected a low-to-zero turnout, but once news broke of Perry's innocence, the phone rang off the hook and word got around the crawfish boil was still on. Even Lieutenant Gardner blessed us with his presence for a while, though partly in an official capacity.

"We picked up the skinheads yesterday," he told me. "With the slew of charges they face, ranging from breaking and entering to assault—possibly attempted murder, depending how the DA wants to steer this thing—to attempted rape, they're in for a rough road."

I glanced at Linda, who kept me company as I plunged basketsful of crawfish, corn on the cob, and new potatoes into a pot of highly spiced boiling water. She sipped a frozen margarita and nodded.

"Their brutality is not going to go unnoticed," she told me. "I want it on record against them what would have happened if you hadn't been there."

"Good," I replied, and sipped a Tecate. "What about the Yorks?"

Gardner, wearing a polo shirt and leisure pants rather than his usual gray or black suit, also drank one of the Mexican beers. Both a first for me to witness.

"I don't know," he responded honestly. "They've got a tough lawyer."

"Fischer."

He nodded. "We know Gideon, with all his 'America, love it or leave it' attitude, has been paying them off to disrupt primarily gay establishments. The reverend needed to keep up public appearances and had to live out his violent tendencies vicariously. Did you know he was planning a run at public office?"

Reminded me too much of Chip Gunn, another old adversary with visions of grandeur. And Robert Kennedy called politics an honest profession. What has happened?

Or has there always been corruption, and charismatic honesty only comes around once in a while? I was losing track of Gardner's conversation, so I dropped the train of thought before it really got rolling.

"It seems," Gardner was saying, "that Gideon knows his son's gay. It's an embarrassment that he doesn't want to be public knowledge, so he does anything to protect his son's image."

I thought of Agnes Berryman by his side for appearance sake, and of those magazine articles Linda copied for me. "Nathaniel, in turn, dishes out lousy reviews to gay establishments to appease his father and deflect rumors."

"Quite a team," Gardner quipped.

I pulled a basket from the water and let it drain. "Why go after Sherwood Welles?" I fished, though as C.J. and I had discussed, I was pretty sure I knew the answer. "He wasn't gay."

"It wasn't sexual orientation. It was the fisticuffs at the television studio," Gardner said. "Gideon was out to teach Welles a lesson that he couldn't toss his son around. So he sent them over to bust up the shop, and perhaps him some, too."

"But Welles got the jump," I added.

"On them, but not on Clay."

I carried the basket over to the newspaper-lined tables and drizzled the food down the twelve-foot stretch in the middle. Compliments rang out as people closed in after I retreated. Wearing plastic bibs, architects, bankers, lawyers, and businessmen and -women of all sorts began digging into the crawfish, twisting off the tails, splitting them open for the meat, and moving on to the next. You could tell the true Cajuns because they also sucked the heads.

I returned to the boiling pot and tossed more potatoes in the basket, then started them before going on to the corn and more crawfish. Gardner and Linda were sharing a joke.

"Yeah, those Sugar Land cops don't screw around," Linda said. "They had that place surrounded. When Berryman appeared in her bathrobe and a towel around her hair, mad as Susan B. Anthony at an English men's club, I thought they were going to string me up."

She raised her eyebrows. "And you were worried about being on the sidelines," she told me.

"Next time I won't be so—"

"Oh, shut up. You will, too," Linda interrupted.

Gardner's soft smile slid onto his lean face.

"So you're convinced now I didn't murder the former dishwasher-handyman at Perry Stevens Catering?" I asked.

"Pretty much," the officer responded.

"What do you mean, 'pretty much'? You never really believed I knifed the man, did you?"

"Oh, I believed it was quite possible," he told me. "And fortunately for you, Wanda Sims was awake enough to confirm Clay's confession, and didn't suffocate in the process."

I didn't know how awake she really had been, but I wasn't about to question the woman one iota.

Gardner finished his beer. "I must be going. Thank you for inviting me."

"My pleasure," I replied. "It's always nice to know the police are your friends."

"Ah, Neil." He laid a finger aside his cheek and paused. "I've been reading Ted Hughes recently."

"*Birthday Letters*," I said, "about his marriage to Sylvia Plath."

"Exactly. What did you think of it?"

"I liked the book, though I wanted to see more of his emotions, thoughts, feelings—instead of so much projection."

"Interesting," he commented. "I loved the book. Perhaps because he projects his emotions through others. Like I do."

I gave him a sideways glance.

"The police—me—is your friend. I'd talk poetry with you even if you were on death row."

"Thanks."

He smiled that gentle smile, nodded, and left.

Linda nudged up to me. "That man has a love-hate relationship with you, boy. He respects you, but you sure piss him off."

"I don't want to talk about it."

"I don't imagine you do." Linda finished her margarita and wandered off for another.

I upended my Tecate and Robbie was right there with another. "What, you trying to get me blitzed?" I asked.

"Figure you deserved it," he said.

"Where's Perry?"

He pointed over to a group of women that included Alice Tarkenton and several Houston Junior League members. Between Alice's sharp tongue and Perry's wit, the women were in stitches.

"Seems to be fine," I observed.

"He's a fish," said Robbie. "Put him in the right tank and he thrives."

"As opposed to the tank, as in jail, downtown?" I asked. "Clever."

"But surely not as clever as you," he replied.

"Keep the beer coming and we'll see." Beyond Perry, down at the corner, I noticed a limo pull up. Before I could speculate which highfalutin client this was, out popped Tommy from the backseat. He ran around the car and, with the chauffeur's help, guided a gingerly moving Charles out.

"Well, I'll be," Robbie said through a large smile. "I didn't know he'd been released from the hospital."

"They both look like they could use a drink," I commented.

"I believe you're right, Neil." He winked and trotted off to greet them.

The potatoes had enough of a head start, I decided, and added another round of crawfish and corn. While deep in concentration, I felt someone touch my arm.

"You saved my life twice," Wanda Sims said. Her voice had gone husky. I drew a deep breath.

"You're welcome, but it's no—"

"To me it is, Neil."

"You're welcome," I could only repeat, and checked the crawfish.

"With your testimony, I'll probably only get a hand slap for withholding evidence," she told me.

I popped open my new beer. Wouldn't want it to get too warm. Wanda's eyes were all over me.

"Yeah, well, with you saying you heard Clay admit to murdering Conrad, you got me out of a tight spot."

"Maybe we make a good team?"

Physically, tempting. Intellectually, I shuddered. "As friends." I took the safe route.

Linda returned with C.J. in tow.

"Well, I owe you, Neil," Wanda said, and kissed me on the cheek. She flashed a wave to C.J. and Linda before mingling with the other guests.

"What was that all about?" Linda demanded.

"I saved her life twice. What can I say?"

"You arrogant bastard."

"Don't hit the chef," C.J. said, and restrained his daughter.

"I'm not going to hit him," she announced. "I'm going to ignore him." And she marched off.

"Wonder where she gets her temper?" I asked.

"Wonder why she cares?" C.J. shot back.

Me, too, I thought, and watched her slim figure file into The Kitchen for shade and margaritas.

"Gardner clue you in to the threatening recipes you received?" he asked.

I checked the food, worked on clearing my head. That was a good example of Linda being a pain in the ass. Jealous—and what on earth for?—and, so, well—

"Neil," C.J. called. "Are you listening to me?"

"Yeah, the threats, recipe, whatever. Yeah, earlier Gardner said they found the original on Clay's computer. He theorizes Clay wanted to scare us away from Perry to join him. Kind of weak, but that's all we have right now."

"I buy it," C.J. said. "Make Perry a target and he figured you'd abandon him like he did Welles. Then when Welles died, he cut sending them, thinking it was more ammunition against Perry, as in a motive that somehow he connected Welles to the threats and did something about it. Stepbrothers, competitors at each other's throat."

"Clay is a disturbed puppy," I said.

"There's quite a few of them." C.J. spat a piece of Nicorette gum into Perry's begonias. Those poor flowers took so much abuse. "By the way," he added, "we've got a score to settle."

"And how long have you not had a cigarette?" I asked.

"Long enough."

"If I cut my hair and you smoke again—" I began to threaten.

"What?" he cut me off.

"Then I'll chase after your daughter, marry her, and make your life miserable," I blurted.

He opened his mouth, closed it, then tried it again. "Son, I reckon that would be my best nightmare." And he ambled into the festive afternoon.

I couldn't believe I'd said that. I thought so fondly of Keely, who wasn't here. But she was making her own, new life. I'd let go at Christmas. So I believed.

I refused to spend a lifetime of letting go.

In the morning, long hair was history.

NEIL MARSHALL'S TEXAS PESTO

A Southwestern twist on a traditional recipe. Byron Edwin Franklin originally came up with the idea. It became an immediate success. This is my version, but kudos to you, Ed.

1 to 2 full bunches of fresh cilantro—about 2 cups
1 teaspoon salt
½ teaspoon of ground black pepper
½ teaspoon of cayenne pepper
2 cloves of garlic
1 seeded jalapeño, sliced
¼ cup pecans
1 to 1½ cups olive oil
½ cup Parmesan cheese

Using a food processor, combine the cilantro with the salt, pepper, cayenne, garlic, and jalapeño. Mix until coarse, scraping the sides of the bowl as needed. Add the pecans and one cup of olive oil. Mix. Add the Parmesan and blend until the pesto is the thickness of a good gravy. If necessary, add more olive oil.

This makes about 1½ to 2 cups.

This is especially good with angel-hair pasta, diced Roma tomatoes, and your choice of fresh shrimp, crawfish, or grilled chicken. Actually, this is a great sauce for any grilled meat. In fact, sometimes all you'll need is your finger to appreciate this mixture.

ON WRITING MYSTERIES
by
Tim Hemlin

In recent years, I've heard talk about the rise of standards in the mystery genre. I find this curious, to say the least.

Granted, there is plenty of good writing stocking bookshelves today, but there has always been good writing. (All one has to do is turn to the masters who toiled in crime fiction when crime fiction wasn't cool.)

Well, I've done the trip down academic lane and smelled the roses of a well-respected creative writing program, and I am a mystery writer. If, at the end of my career, I'm judged half the writer Dashiell Hammett, Raymond Chandler, John D. MacDonald, and Ross Macdonald were, I'll figure myself a success.

When beginning a new project, I often reread the first chapters of Hammett's *The Thin Man*. It is all of two and a half pages, sparsely written, but it characterizes Nick and Nora Charles with deft humor. Consider the following exchange:

> We found a table. Nora said, "She's pretty."
> "If you like them like that."
> She grinned at me. "You got types?"
> "Only you, darling—lanky brunettes with wicked jaws."

Playful, minimalist, setting the tone of a wonderful novel. Great repartee like that could have been written expressly in their heyday for William Powell and Myrna Loy, who were, in fact, the screen incarnations of Nick and Nora.

Good writing is often enhanced by creative metaphors. Ross Macdonald, with his Lew Archer series, was a supreme metaphor maker. In *The Underground Man*, a character is described in the following way: "His hairy head seemed enormous and grotesque on his boy's body, like a papier-mache saint's head on a stick."

The prolific John D. MacDonald showed repeatedly how to weave a great plot, often beginning with a killer first line, as in *Darker Than Amber*: "We were about to give up and call it a night when somebody dropped the girl off the bridge."

Rebel hero Travis McGee goes on to relate how he and his friend Meyer save a woman who has been bound, weighted, and dropped to face a watery death.

There is never a dull moment with MacDonald, including diatribes that range from the state of the automobile industry to race relations. It is perhaps MacDonald's social commentary that places him as a heavyweight in the literary ring. For example, in *Darker Than Amber*, an African-American housemaid states:

> We're after our share of the power structure of this civilization, Mr. McGee, because, when we get it, a crime will merit the same punishment whether the victim is black or white, and hoods will get the same share of municipal services, based on zoning, not color. And a good man will be thought a credit to the human race.

Not a strikingly new sentiment, but written by MacDonald in 1965 as civil rights legislation was in its infancy.

Raymond Chandler, my literary grandfather, once said, "The story of our time . . . is the marriage of an idealist to a gangster and how their home life and children turned out." And he spent his writer's life exploring the harsher side of human existence. In *The Lady in the Lake*, private investigator Philip Marlowe searches for the missing wife of a prominent executive. Chris Lavery has apparently been having an affair with her. However, Marlowe discovers . . .

No police cars stood in front of Lavery's house, nobody hung on the sidewalk and when I pushed the front door open there was no smell of cigar or cigarette smoke inside. The sun had gone away from the windows and a fly buzzed softly over one of the liquor glasses. I went down to the end and hung over the railing that led downstairs. Nothing made sound except very faintly down below in the bathroom the quiet trickle of water dripping on a dead man's shoulder.

The detail in this excerpt passes the jealousy test—i.e., I wish I'd written it. No smell of cigars or cigarettes; the buzz of a fly and the quiet trickle of water; the sight of a dead man's shoulder—Chandler tapped three of the five senses. Furthermore, equally important is what *isn't* in the scene: no police cars, no one on the sidewalk, no tobacco odor. It's a seemingly simple passage leading into Chapter Twenty of an exceptional novel.

This is merely a collage of writers who have influenced me—a brief appreciation, if you will, of the leading practitioners of the hardboiled school. To my mind, you don't get any better than Chandler, Hammett, MacDonald, and Macdonald. They attacked the darker side of life, turning it into light, and they entertained as they made cogent observations on the human condition. Today their work is reborn and reimagined by such writers as Robert B. Parker, Earl

Emerson, and Sue Grafton. My own work is not as dark, not as hardboiled; but my pursuit for literary excellence is just as strong.